D0090556

BY CHANCE

RANDOM HOUSE | NEW YORK

BY CHANCE

A Novel

Martin Corrick

By Chance is a work of fiction. Names, characters, places,
and incidents are the products of the author's imagination or
are used fictitiously. Any resemblance to actual events, locales,
or persons, living or dead, is entirely coincidental.

Published in the United States by Random House,
an imprint of The Random House Publishing Group,
a division of Random House, Inc., New York.

RANDOM HOUSE and colophon are registered
trademarks of Random House, Inc.

Grateful acknowledgment is made to Farrar, Straus and Giroux,
LLC, and Faber and Faber Limited for permission to reprint
an excerpt from "Wodwo" from *Collected Poems* by Ted Hughes,
copyright © 2003 by the Estate of Ted Hughes. Rights outside of
the U.S. are controlled by Faber and Faber Limited. Reprinted by
permission of Farrar, Straus and Giroux, LLC, and Faber and Faber Limited.

LIBRARY OF CONGRESS CATALOGING-IN-PUBLICATION DATA

Corrick, Martin.
By chance / Martin Corrick.
p. cm.
ISBN 978-0-375-50813-4
1. Working class men—Fiction.   2. Life change events—Fiction.
3. England—Fiction.   I. Title.
PR6103.O77B9 2008
823'.92—dc22   2008009710

Printed in the United States of America on acid-free paper

www.atrandom.com

9 8 7 6 5 4 3 2 1

FIRST EDITION

Book design by Dana Leigh Blanchette

But what shall I be called am I the first
have I an owner what shape am I what
shape am I am I huge if I go
to the end on this way past these trees and past these trees
till I get tired that's touching one wall of me
for the moment if I sit still how everything
stops to watch me I suppose I am the exact centre
but there's all this what is it roots
roots roots roots and here's the water
again very queer but I'll go on looking

—*From "Wodwo,"* TED HUGHES, 1967

BY CHANCE

1

Very well: here's a brisk afternoon in winter, evening coming on, the last of the light falling on a seaside town of white-painted houses with blue doors. A solitary man is lodged on a bench on the quayside, a man in late middle age, a square-looking man with two large suitcases, his overcoat tugged closely about him, a man going by the name of James Watson Bolsover.

He's looking this way and that—what's his problem? Anxious, is he? Something bothering him? But wait—surely that's a smile on his lips? Whatever his troubles, at heart he's a happy man, this Bolsover, waiting for a ferry, eager to depart, eager to begin. Oh yes, I'm happy. I'm perfectly happy! He looks this way and that and it occurs to him that this pretty harbor, lodged between the ocean and the dark hills behind, is the very threshold of fable, from which the hopeful migrant, escaping from persecution real or imagined, departs for a new world—at which Bolsover laughs aloud. Oh yes, these are different times, modern times, and no doubt this pretty little town rents itself to the makers of sentimental films, the heroine's dress fluttering prettily as she waves from the pier head, the departing ship leaning to the wind, rising to the ocean swell—

He turns suddenly and stares along the length of the quay, but there is nobody in sight. Teatime, no doubt, in this innocent little place—the chink of cups, harmless chatter, polite laughter. A herring gull slides across his field of view and he is reminded of the elegant and not impossibly difficult mathematics that allow flight to be understood. In the formula $\frac{1}{2}\rho V^2$, for example, the Greek letter *rho* relates to the density of air and V stands for its velocity: the expression is a universal of aerodynamics, essential to the calculation of lift and drag and hence to the achievement of flight. Isn't that formula just as elegant, just as magical, as the herring gull? Certainly it is. The more you understand—so Bolsover thinks, in his simple way—the more beautiful things become. Here's a fragment of mathematical language based on Newton's fundamental laws, and the gull in flight—he allows himself this fancy—is an expression of that truth: the gull is truth written in space, written in free air, written with the bird's white wings on the dark gray of the sky! Oh, certainly it is!

One must not be harsh in judgment. This man knows that he is not the inheritor of a considerable mind. Fine consciousness cannot come naturally to a working man born in Swindon. However, he has tried to improve himself, and to a degree has succeeded. He is thoughtful—we might say, rather too thoughtful. He needs to understand, and to that end has read a great many books—fiction, poetry, history, science. Oh yes, his reading lacks discrimination: he's aware of that, too, and knows that, in consequence, his mind is a junk room. But the attempt to understand is worthy, even honorable, and has expanded both his knowledge and his imagination. He is willing to contemplate possibilities, can envisage himself writing the script for a romantic film, a film of love and adventure in which a tall ship makes ready for sea, the gulls raise their clamor, a lovely girl waves her handkerchief from the quay, and so forth. Bolsover has written many things in his time, mostly of a technical nature, to be sure, but it's all words, after all, and surely a film wouldn't be beyond him—EXT., DAY, WINTER, the camera panning across the harbor to discover the captain in close focus, a man alone, gnarled cheeks, strong hands clasped behind him, eyes gazing out toward the empty horizon in a way one must presume to be meaningful—but no, I'm Bolsover. I'm just an ordinary man sitting on a bench, waiting for a ferry, doodling, riffing, just an ordinary man—

Movement catches his eye and Bolsover stands up suddenly—who's this? Along the quay glides a girl in roller-boots, perhaps ten years old. She's wearing a fluffy pink jacket, a pink skirt, pink tights, and pink boots. Her legs are long and thin, reminding Bolsover of the flamingos he's seen in the pages of *National Geographic,* tall birds stalking African shallows—ah, yes, that same angularity, that awkward grace!

Aware of him, keeping her distance, the girl describes a sequence of easy circles, her boots clicking across the joints between the stones, her knees a little bent, her body riding poised and steady. She's very good. She's practiced all right, this girl, and she's putting on a show, elaborately casual, for him and for herself.

It's just a girl in roller-boots—Roller*blades,* perhaps; one must be precise. Bolsover sits down. She circles and he leans back, spreading his arms along the back of the bench, watching her. All right, then. Just a girl who wants an audience. He looks up at the hurrying clouds; it's a brisk day, sure enough. Early that morning, from the window of the train, he had spotted the warning wisps of cirrus and predicted exactly this ragged sky—he knows his stratus from his cumulus, having developed, in a recent period of spare time, a working knowledge of meteorology. He's interested in all sorts of things, this fellow. A brisk day! Oh, yes, it's a fitting day on which to depart one's former life, begin another. Begin again? A silly notion, since life's all one. Can people change? Could my old ma be imagined in a long summer dress and a straw hat, clipping deadheads into a basket and giving visitors, from time to time, the benefit of a trilling laugh? Ridiculous! And as for Dad—you awkward old sod!—Dad could never have dozed in a deck chair in a Surrey garden, rustling his newspaper and whistling through his mustache. Ah, yes, Mum's red hands, Dad's awkward deference, his humble walk, his ancient trousers bagged and polished by a foreman's life on the railway— no disgrace there, but no grace either, and the pair of them long dead, long years mourned. Bolsover abruptly sees them plain and clear, the two that bore him all those years ago, and feels a powerful but quickly passing sorrow. Only his sister, Sylvia—yes, Sylvia lying on her stomach, endlessly reading some girls' comic and kicking her buttoned shoes in the air—only Sylvia aspired to grace, and in consequence sought out and married an unspeakable fellow she called Frederick, in whom she had mistaken silence for depth, vulgarity for strength, idleness for grace. My sister, Sylvia . . . Yes, he had a sister once, and now she has entirely forgotten her brother.

Bolsover looks again at the ragged clouds. It is not true that Sylvia has forgotten him; she has discarded him, as being unworthy of her. That is the truth.

In such a fashion, while the girl in pink circles about him, Bolsover freewheels through the past, from time to time glancing—perhaps a little anxiously—along the length of the quay; but they remain alone, the solitary man and the wheeling girl.

He had been a square boy, young Bolsover, neither handsome nor witty, and had possessed an air of simplicity. In the usual English way he was poorly educated and, in his early life, not well read; but he was always curious. He wanted to know how things worked, where they came from, what their purpose was, what they were made of. He was not a systematic thinker: he was simply curious, and maintained his curiosity despite his parents, who were not the sort to see purpose in idle curiosity. Idle curiosity? Is it wrong to want to know why things are as they are?

According to his first notebook, the boy was ten years old when what he later called "the first big question" came to him. It was the summer of 1954 and he was strolling home from school when the words "How did I get here?" sailed into his mind from the clear blue sky, stopping him on the corner of Bywater Street. In those days there was a bomb site on that corner, dating back to the first winter of the war. Brambles and wild growth had colonized the cellars of a collapsed house and created a secret garden, something every child should have. The boy slipped through the fence and went straight to his hideaway. The remains of a chimney still stood; if he lay on his back, he could look up through a funnel of sooty bricks that somehow made even a common scrap of blue sky look remote and strange. The boy lay down on the tiles of the hearth, put his hands behind his head, and asked himself the question again. "How did I get here?"

The obvious answer—that he was simply a consequence of his parents' meeting—was the kind of answer that didn't explain anything. It wasn't the beginning. Something made them meet, something made them marry, something made them have a child, and the child wasn't just anybody, the child was *himself*. Everything must have a cause: so much was clear. The boy knew that the late running of the twelve-thirty on a Wednesday in August 1940 had caused his father to encounter a pretty lady on the down platform; that was the story his father often told, especially on Friday evenings when he was at his most jovial.

A late train: was that why he existed? No, there was more. Dad and Ma had met and had fallen in love. Love! Now, there's a funny thing. Was it love or the late running of a train that had made him? And if it was love—well, the same thing must have been true of his grandparents and his great-grandparents and so on, back for years and years into the past. Was he here because of all that loving? Was he the consequence of love that stretched back into the past, right back to—back to where, exactly? Where and when had he started?

The boy opened his satchel, took out a notebook. *How did I get here? What caused me? Where did I come from? Where did I begin? Why am I myself, and nobody else?*

That notebook is a dog-eared thing, dark red, with "Saint Bartholomew's School" in black letters on the cover. Bolsover is left-handed. Reporting on his physical skills, schoolteachers always ticked the box marked "below average," and his handwriting remains horribly jagged.

So here's a boy of ten, knowing nothing of philosophy or metaphysics, the son of a railway foreman and a part-time hotel maid, curled up in a secret nook with a notebook and a pencil. He's thought of a hard question and decided to keep track of his thinking by writing notes. It's a new and intriguing game—and of course it's a perfectly sensible way to approach a problem, though unusual in a boy of his age and class. In truth he was an odd little boy. He had a distinctive way of walking, bouncing slightly on his toes and holding his chin up as if he were trying to look over a high wall; his oddity caused him often to be followed, on his way home, by a gaggle of children imitating his walk, giggling, and calling insults. A group of boys once set upon him, pulled him to the ground, removed his trousers, and threw them into the canal; it became an amusing game, and more than once the contents of his satchel were scattered about the street.

Of course the boy learned to ignore casual abuse of that sort. He learned to slip by on the other side of the road and, instead of friends, to occupy himself with his own thoughts.

Bolsover's first notebook reports his strong feeling, formed very early in his life, that he was *unlikely*. Looking back, he saw that there were many moments in the past when the causal chain that produced him might have broken. It wasn't just a matter of a late train and two people who met and took a liking to each other; that encounter was merely one of many events that had played a part in his existence. Every event must be the consequence of events preceding it—surely that was the case? Way back, an unknown couple had born a son who had become an engine driver. One day the driver had overslept, and his train was late. That was one of the strands, but it wasn't the beginning, because the engine driver's parents had been someone's children, and they in turn must have had parents. *When had he begun?*

However far back you looked—or so it seemed to this boy—there was always another layer to be uncovered. Perhaps there were a million late trains, a billion decisive moments, far more than could ever be counted; and that must mean that everything had to have gone exactly right or he wouldn't be here.

Unlikely? It appeared to the boy that his existence was not so much unlikely as *impossible*.

Another notebook entry, made much later in his life, wonders whether his own existence—indeed, everybody's existence—isn't "peculiarly sensitive to initial conditions." He had picked that phrase up somewhere, no doubt in connection with butterfly wings. But if that is the case, doesn't it also follow that everything following some initial event must be predetermined? And life simply doesn't feel like that. It feels as though one has choices, and has control over one's own destiny; it really does.

These questions constantly chased about in Bolsover's mind, refusing to be resolved. Even as an adult he often joked about his own unlikeliness. "You couldn't make me up," he'd say. "I'm quite impossible, you know. But then, so are you," and he'd tap the arm of his listener—like as not, a somewhat puzzled listener—to emphasize his point. "Here we bloody well are, don't you see, both of us quite impossible, and all the world's impossible, too!"

At school only a single teacher made an impression on young Bolsover. He was a tall man called Wootton, equable enough though a little distant in manner. He had a slight stoop, a mop of dark hair, and a face considerably more hawkish than his nature, a useful attribute in a teacher. During a discussion of family photographs lost in a fire, one of the class called the incident "a tragedy," and the schoolmaster became suddenly and strangely passionate.

"The word 'tragedy,' " Mr. Wootton said, "is grossly misused in many accounts of illness and everyday accident. Suppose a friend of yours were to die—a pretty girl, perhaps. The papers would very likely say it's a tragedy. You yourselves might be tempted to call it that. Now, let us be quite clear about this."

Mr. Wootton drew himself up to his full height. "The death of a single inconsequential person is not a tragedy," he said, banging his fist on his desk. *"It is not a tragedy!"*

There was a long silence while the class tried to work out what their teacher's unusual fervor might signify.

"To apply the word 'tragedy' to an ordinary death," Mr. Wootton said in a calmer tone, "is a misuse of language. The prettiness of the dead girl makes not the slightest difference, nor does her sex. Oh, yes, it's an event that generates sorrow and lasting pain, but *it isn't a tragedy.* Do you understand? Death is a fact of ordinary life, and *tragedy isn't ordinary.*"

There was another silence. Few thought Mr. Wootton had provided sufficient reason for his outburst. Was it worth making such a fuss about a single word?

Bolsover was intrigued. "But, sir," he said, "surely it's a tragedy if *anybody* dies, and if it's a young girl—"

"It's just an accident," Mr. Wootton said. "It's just another sad accident. We all die, some die earlier than others, and that's how things are."

Bolsover thought for a moment, and then asked, "Has anything like that ever happened to you, sir?"

"It has not, Bolsover," said Mr. Wootton, "and if it had, it would be none of your business."

That was a firm answer, but it was still difficult to see how the man could really mean what he was saying.

Mr. Wootton tried again. "A tragedy is one of two things," he said. "In classical tragedy, a man of talent and power is seen to destroy himself and his world as a consequence of *hubris*. The word is Greek. We may translate it as 'pride.' The hero gets above himself, and that failure of character causes him to attempt something that is both morally wrong and beyond his powers. In consequence he fails and dies. That's the whole point of the tragic drama," said Mr. Wootton. "A play in which the hero is a great man, and dies because he abuses his talents and his position is called a tragedy."

After a pause, Mr. Wootton continued. "There is a second meaning of the word 'tragedy.' It describes an event in which a considerable number of people are killed, perhaps by accident, as in a train crash, or by design, as in a war. It should not be confused with the classical sense of the word."

Bolsover immediately asked, "How many deaths make a tragedy, sir?"

"That's a good question, Bolsover," Mr. Wootton said, "to which I cannot give you a precise answer. It's a moderately large number. Let's say, in excess of twenty."

"So if nineteen people die, it's not a tragedy," said Bolsover, fired by the debate, "and if another person dies a bit later, it suddenly becomes a tragedy, does it?"

"Exactly," said Mr. Wootton, who had plenty of experience in dealing with provocative boys. "The point I'm making," he continued, tapping his desk with his ruler, "is not only a detailed point relating to the meaning of a single word, but a general one in regard to language, which is precious, and must be used with care. If language is used carelessly, if its fine edge is blunted, something will be lost from the world, perhaps forever. *Something will be lost.* Do you understand? A particular and perhaps vital distinction may no longer be made."

After a pause Mr. Wootton repeated, with slow taps of his ruler, "Use language carelessly and much will be lost."

The class remained silent but unconvinced. Afterward, the majority agreed that Mr. Wootton's passion couldn't just be about *words*. It must be something to do with a girl, otherwise why mention a girl in the first place?

Young Bolsover saw Mr. Wootton's argument as marvelously illuminating. He wrote an excited account of the debate in his notebook, including the two definitions of the word "tragedy" and the phrase "Something will be lost."

In his notebook the boy continued the line of questioning that he had begun in the classroom. If the word "tragedy" doesn't describe a single death, what *does* describe it? Is it possible that a word has gone missing from the English language? When something awful happens to a completely innocent person—no matter whether a child or an adult—isn't that *just as bad* as the death of an important fellow in a play who has lived most of his life already? The fact that the victim isn't guilty, and doesn't contribute to his own downfall, surely makes it *worse* than a classical tragedy, in which someone who ought to know better gets their due comeuppance. Isn't that so?

What is the missing word? If an innocent dies, is it perhaps a *calamity*? That word might have served, if its meaning hadn't been degraded by a recent musical. Catastrophe? Much too grand. *Why can't an ordinary death be called a tragedy?*

Young Bolsover found Mr. Wootton sitting in the staff room at the end of school that day, and put the matter to him.

"You raise an interesting question," said Mr. Wootton, stubbing out his cigarette and removing his feet from the table. "English being broad and various, a solution to your dilemma must surely exist. Let's take a stroll along the corridor and see what comes to mind."

They strolled in silence for a time. Then Mr. Wootton said, "There seem to be two distinct issues here: the nature of the event itself and the state of mind it induces. You're suggesting that the death of a single innocent person may generate more anguish than the death of a great person, or indeed the deaths of many people. I can't disagree with you. But I'd say that such a death, while painful, is rarely significant in the wider world. Classical tragedy *is* significant in that wider sense, and its special name indicates that fact. And most people would agree that the death, say, of some thousands is also significant. What you're looking for, I think, is a different kind of term, one relating to the amount of pain an event causes to those closely involved with it."

"Surely there ought to be a word for something so *unfair*, sir."

"I understand what you're getting at, and I can see that there's a problem here. A term people often use is 'personal tragedy,' though I don't care to use a modifier in that clumsy fashion. There's also something called *tragicomedy*, of course, a combination of tragic and comic events. One has to say that tragicomedy, if anything, is the best general descriptor of the human condition."

Tragicomedy! The boy stopped his strolling and noted the word immediately, and if he had looked up, he would have found Mr. Wootton looking at him with amusement and affection.

Not for a moment did young Bolsover believe that Mr. Wootton's sudden passion had a romantic origin; it was perfectly obvious that the issue of words and their meanings *required* passion. In a subsequent note, one of many on the subject, the boy wrote: *If you don't care what words mean, you can't SAY anything, you can't LEARN anything, and you can't KNOW anything. THE MEANING OF WORDS IS THE MOST IMPORTANT THING IN THE WHOLE WORLD!*

If the notebooks are a true record, intellectual excitement of this kind was rare during the boy's eleven years of compulsory education. That's quite normal, of course, since English schools make a virtue of dullness, and schooling is mostly a matter of endurance. But just occasionally a child encounters a teacher who is prepared to stub out his cigarette, remove his feet from the table, and take a companionable stroll in pursuit of knowledge. Mr. Wootton, a grown-up person with a university degree, didn't immediately ask, "Why do you want to know?" as most adults did; he simply assumed that a question required an answer. He showed the boy that it was a good thing to have an inquiring disposition; indeed, it is not too much to say that Mr. Wootton encouraged young Bolsover to be himself.

If you're going to work things out you'll need to know a lot of words, and it's no good waiting for them to come along. You must hunt them down. Very well: young Bolsover would read everything he could find, and soon he'd know all the words there are. Then he'd be able to work *everything* out.

But where to begin? Prowling the shelves of the school library, he'd just decided there were far too many books in the world, when the title *100 Great Writers* caught his eye. Of course! Such a book would save him a lot of trouble. He immediately began to copy names into his notebook: *Austen, Blake, Browning, Anne Brontë, Charlotte Brontë, Emily Brontë—* so many Brontës! *Brooke, Byron, Conrad.* It was going to take a while to read them all. *Darwin, Dickens, Donne.* How many books are there in the world? Thousands and thousands. *Hemingway, Hopkins, James.* More than that—tens of thousands. *Lawrence, Melville, Milton, Orwell.* Millions, even. *Shakespeare, Shaw, Shelley.* So many! But wait a minute—if I read one book a week, in two years I could read every one of these writers! *Waugh, Wells, Woolf, Wordsworth, Yeats.* One day, when I've read everything, thought young Bolsover, I'll find a way to make my living from words.

He wasn't yet sure how he'd do that. When he was a little boy he had written a story called "The Diary of a Penny." His friends had liked that story, but now he was older, and he knew that the main thing in life is to find out what's true and what isn't. Writing stories—inventing things that never really happened—well, that just confuses matters.

2

Time has passed, darkness come. Bolsover's head has fallen to one side, eyes shut, gray hair stirred by the wind, one arm stretched along the back of the bench, legs crossed, coat fallen open. A clock chimes in the little town at his back—not entirely musically—and Bolsover opens one eye, remembers the ferry, sits up sharply. Nobody in sight save a man coiling ropes. No, not ropes: *warps*, that is the proper word for them, *mooring warps*, and the man would once have been called a *longshoreman*. Would he? A *stevedore*, perhaps. Bolsover turns his head and checks his suitcases: all present, of course. Ah, the anxiety of possession! We are all owners now, and our significance is our property. Ridiculous times! In my lack I have discovered lightness of being: I am fleet of foot, I am nimble, I may go where I please!

Bolsover frowns abruptly, wondering how often a man may begin again, and whether he will know the last time when it comes. It's a fine thing to start afresh, to be on the move, yet there is also a need to remain, to settle, to dwell, to belong. A solitary traveler is an object of suspicion, potentially a vagabond. Come on, Bolsover, tell us about yourself. Bolsover—now that's a curious name—from the north, are you? And what do you do for a living, Mr. Bolsover? Hobbies? Children? Are you a professional man? What's your favorite color? On your own, are you? Enjoy being alone, do you? Divorced? No woman in your life, Mr. Bolsover? Perhaps you've never met the right person? Bit of an eccentric, are you? Introverted sort of chap? Women think you a bit—well—you know what I mean. Unusual. No offense, of course.

He looks about him. The girl on wheels has gone. There is nobody in sight save the fellow coiling warps, that longshoreman, that stevedore.

When Bolsover left school in 1960, there was not the slightest chance of a poorly qualified sixteen-year-old finding any sort of employment that related to words.

"What do you mean, words? Don't give me that bloody nonsense," said his father when Bolsover mentioned the possibility of trying for a job on the *Swindon Weekly News.* "You get yourself a job with a future, my lad, and never mind fads and fancies. Words! What's wrong with the railway?" A lot of fathers talked in that manner in those days; no doubt some still do, though one hopes that civilization, in general, is advancing.

In the event, the young man became apprenticed as a mechanical engineer at F. R. Butler Ltd., a manufacturer of pipe work, pumps, couplings, tanks, cocks, and useful things of that sort. Since he could afford nothing else, he continued to live with his parents, and from his weekly wage of two pounds ten shillings he gave his mother one pound, which seemed pretty generous to him.

It was Bolsover's good fortune to start as an assistant to a man called

Robbins, a toolmaker and shop steward who read *The Manchester Guardian* and stood ready to deliver an assertive commentary on any and all issues. Young Bolsover had never heard talk of that kind, and was delighted by it. In a sort of way, Mr. Robbins sounded like Mr. Wootton, but with an extra something—yes, *panache*, a recently discovered word for which the young man was pleased to find an opportunity.

Between his social and political lectures Mr. Robbins taught the boy to use hacksaw, file, pillar drill, lathe, micrometer, and surface plate with proper care and accuracy. Bolsover discovered, again to his surprise and delight, that he had the eye and touch needed for such work, and that he derived great satisfaction from a completed piece of tooling. Some of it, viewed with a bit of imagination and one eye shut, had a resemblance to postmodern sculpture; so much for his alleged lack of physical skills.

In his first week he said to Mr. Robbins, who had frowned on his working through a tea break and thereby missing a significant lecture on the day's headlines, "You know, I do like to get on and finish things, once I've started."

"Do you, indeed," said Mr. Robbins. "Your attitude will make the heart of capitalism sing, dear boy."

The man had a distinctive style of speech that Bolsover was able to categorize, thanks to the teaching of Mr. Wootton, as *ironic* and *skeptical*.

"It's human nature, dear boy, to want to tell a good story, or listen to one. But you've got to be careful. When somebody tells you a dramatic story, you've got to ask, *How do you know it's true?* If he can't give you facts, the evidence, you've got to assume it's bullshit. People say that facts are dull. Facts aren't dull, boy. Facts are how you know the truth."

That was one for the notebook: *Facts are how you know the truth.*

Mr. Robbins seemed to know everything but believe in nothing. "I don't believe in belief," he frequently said. Bolsover was doubtful at first. Surely *everything* doesn't have to be proved, does it? Surely there are things one *just knows to be true?* In due course he asked Mr. Robbins about God.

"What did I tell you last week? What are the facts? Where's the evidence for God? Answer: there ain't any. None. Miracles? Self-delusion. Would it be nice if there were a cozy God to look after us? Of course it would. Is that why we invented him? Yes. What does that mean? It means that God is nonsense, dangerous nonsense, the sort that kills people. God, dear boy, is a fiction, and it is quite extraordinary that anyone can take the idea seriously."

Such talk made Bolsover shiver, but no harm came to Mr. Robbins as a consequence of his blasphemy; indeed, his vigorous condemnations of churches, ministers, sacred texts, miracles, and divine intervention always put him in a cheerful mood. Rather than offering succor, was religion no more than a gloomy burden? When Bolsover put this idea to Mr. Robbins, he received an approving clout on the shoulder: "Well said, my lad! At last you're starting to see things straight!"

For the next several years Bolsover worked his way round Butler's factory, visiting in turn the tool room, the press room, the machine room, the drawing office, the welding shop, the inspection department, the paint shop, the accounts department, the test lab, and the dispatch room. After that, there was little he did not know about the design, manufacture, and testing of pipes, pumps, tanks, and cocks.

It was also necessary to learn something of the physics of gases and liquids, a difficult but intriguing subject. Thereafter, when he had an idle moment, he might consider the flow of air round a door as he opened it, and in winter he would lean from his bedroom window to watch the vortices produced by the wind swirling round the house, their helical form so nicely displayed by the falling snow.

During his four years of apprenticeship at Butler's the young man was content. He liked learning, and learned a good deal. He did not make many friends. He was still inclined to solitariness, still kept up his inquiring notebook, and still maintained, in his secret heart, an ambition to work with words.

Shortly before his twentieth birthday, Bolsover's parents, disabled by heavy smoking, died of bronchitis within three weeks of each other. It was mid-March. The wind battered at the house, rattling the sashes as the young man wandered from room to room, opening and shutting drawers and cupboards. No, it couldn't be called a tragedy, although that exhausted word was used by every relative and friend. Principally, the event was an ending, to some degree painful but to a greater degree peculiar: sudden death somehow gave a tweak to the world, making the familiar strange and the future—which on the previous day had seemed as easy and familiar as an old overcoat—fresh and uncertain.

How do I know what I should feel? If I don't feel what others do, is that wrong? How do others really feel, anyway? Could they be lying? Do people sometimes enjoy sorrow? Why should I feel guilty when it's not my fault? Why should I feel excited? The young man was still scribbling in his notebooks, of course, and the death of his parents generated several pages of unanswerable questions.

Since his sister, Sylvia, was not mentioned in their father's will—presumably because she was a girl and married, and it was Frederick's business to provide for her—young Bolsover was the sole legatee, and his principal legacy the family house. It was a small, plain Victorian end-of-terrace house, not a bad little house. Conveniently close to Butler's, it had a number of features Bolsover particularly liked: a wrought-iron gate that clanged when the postman called; a stained-glass transom above the front door; a brass door knocker in the form of a lion; and, in the wooden garage that leaned against the side of the house, an ancient car, his father's prewar Vauxhall, supported on bricks, as it had been since before he was born.

"One day," his father used to say, "I'm going to fix that car. It's a collector's item, that is, worth a mint of money. You'll see."

Now his father was dead and the car remained, mighty and ponderous, something of the past that could not easily be shaken off. Dad's Vauxhall! More powerfully even than the house, the old car signified the young man's new status as an owner, a person with history and responsibility. Many times in those first weeks young Bolsover creaked open the garage door to gaze at the tall radiator and the enormous headlamps, eased himself behind the great steering wheel—and once or twice, sitting there, he was sure he heard his father calling his name.

Property made young Bolsover if not a natural with the girls, at least a possible. Susan, the girl next door, spoke to him over the fence: "Oh, you've inherited the house, have you? Lucky you! Does it need lots of work? Can I have a look?"

"Of course," said Bolsover, and she brought two friends with her: Jane, who was tall and had strong opinions, and tiny Katherine, who was quieter than the other two and had big dark eyes. Oh, yes, Katherine was altogether lovely.

The girls clicked round the house in their heels, ignoring the young man and chattering and arguing among themselves—they'd have to rip out those rusty old fireplaces, install central heating, and redecorate the whole place in pastel shades of blue and cream. As for the tiles in the hall, well, they were actually rather nice, though they needed a good clean—but, oh dear, the poky kitchen, the larder smelling of mice, the ancient stove, the sagging sofa, and all those gloomy Scottish landscapes!

Bolsover was certainly no extrovert, but he was a reliable worker, an honest and sensible young man, and he owned his own house. For those reasons it's not entirely surprising to find, little more than three months later, that he has acquired a wife. Here she is, sitting neatly on a brand-new sofa and reading *Amateur Gardening*. Her name is Katherine, of course, a small, pretty, brown-eyed girl of nineteen whose long dark hair, in a certain light, has an auburn sheen. She wears it plaited and rolled into a neat bun at the back of her head, sometimes pinned up with a wooden pin and a blue ribbon, sometimes with a silver comb, sometimes with a white flower she has made from a scrap of silk, sewn with the smallest, neatest stitches that can be imagined.

The delicious flutter of the three girls through his house, and the depth of the silence after they had gone, astonished Bolsover. They were vivacious, amusing, colorful; and what was he? He looked in the hall mirror and saw a poor apprentice, shabby, inward, solitary, a man still young but deeply immersed in work, a dullard. The girls had thrown up the sashes to let in the sharp spring air, swept the floors, cleared the cupboards, and thrown masses of things away—"Oh, no, you can't possibly want *that*!" And then, by some miracle, one of them—the most beautiful of them all!—had taken a liking to him! Yes, she wouldn't mind a walk in the park. Yes, she'd quite like to see a film. Could they go to the shops and choose him a new jacket?

Katherine: her long, narrow fingers, the way she inclined her head when talking to him, her shy glance from beneath dark lashes, her secret smile, her tiny feet, the hollows at her ankles, the soft gleam of her eyes, and the way in which, when she was embarrassed, she would hide her face behind her hand. Ah, her lovely face! It was the narrow oval of her face that immediately captured Bolsover's heart—a fine nose with the slightest curve, high cheekbones and slightly hollowed cheeks, neat little ears, a slim, vulnerable neck. Oh, yes, having seen her once, he was ever afterward able to recall her face.

"Bones like a bird," her friend Susan said.

"Oh, yes, a lovely girl," the neighbors said at the modest reception. "So pretty. But you wouldn't have said he was her type." And afterward, back in their own kitchens, they shook their heads over pretty little Katherine, murmuring the words "delicate" and "nervous."

He knew Katherine was delicate, of course. Bolsover had eyes in his head. It was because she was delicate that she needed him. Young Bolsover was not delicate: he was a strong young man who had sensitive hands despite being left-handed. He could make and mend. He was a man who knew pipes and valves, a man who already owned a house and was responsive (so he believed) to mood and feeling. He even had a certain skill with words, except when overcome with love: *Darling Katherine, you're such an absolute sweetie, and I think of you every minute.* In truth, Bolsover's love, as expressed in his notebooks, is so naïve and personal that one wonders whether it should be revealed; but it is manifestly simple and honest, and to omit such evidence would be untrue to the man. *I thought of you all night, and all morning, too. On Sunday I want to go walking in the park again, and perhaps we'll hold hands.*

Their first conversations were full of false starts and silences, but in a week it was clear that Katherine was developing an increasing interest in young Bolsover. In some ways she was not unlike him: another only child, she urgently wanted to leave her parents' house. "We just don't get on. We're not the same sort of people." She liked being alone, she liked reading, she disliked large groups, noise, muddle. She wanted to organize her own life in her own way and was astonishingly methodical: within three days of their meeting, the majority of Bolsover's possessions— those that she had not advised him to discard because they were worn out or unnecessary—had been allocated their proper places, in which, she quietly insisted, each item should now remain.

He dared not talk immediately of marrying, although the idea had flown into his mind when he'd first set eyes upon her. There was a practical difficulty: although he was now twenty, he was still an apprentice, with three years yet to serve, and in those days an apprentice did not earn enough to marry. However, his years of training meant that he knew the business, and there was a possibility that he could convert his apprenticeship into a permanent post.

F. R. Butler was entering the decline that was typical of British manufacturing in those years. The personnel manager leafed through his files, shaking his head.

"Nothing suitable at the moment, I'm afraid. Anyway, you'd be ill-advised to abandon your apprenticeship until it's complete."

He hesitated, looking at the last sheet in his file. "Of course, there's old Arnott. He's due to retire in four months."

"Arnott? Who's he?"

The personnel manager was surprised. "You must know old Arnott—he's been here most of his life."

"I've never met him. What does he do?"

"He's got an office at the back of the machine room. He's our technical writer. Are you interested in writing and that sort of thing?"

"I might be," said young Bolsover. "I might be."

A technical writer? What were the duties of such a person? The answer was that Butler's products required specifications, instruction books, information sheets, codes of practice, handbooks, safety manuals, and training schemes, all of which had to be written, checked, distributed, archived, and regularly updated. For thirty-five years Arnott had undertaken all those tasks, and when it was offered, he was happy to take his retirement a little earlier than planned.

There you are: here's one of those moments when things collide, and go off at a tangent, and everything is different afterward. What if Arnott hadn't wanted to retire?

When he told her about the possibility of becoming a technical writer, Katherine wrinkled her nose in the most delightful way.

"Is it the sort of thing you'd really like to do?"

"I think it is. I really think it is."

"And it would be easier than working in the factory, would it? Not so smelly, not so dirty?"

"Yes."

"It's a permanent post with a pension, I suppose."

"It is."

"Then I think you should try it."

"In that case, I will," he said, and kissed her—rather awkwardly, in fact, because she turned her head away at just the wrong moment, but no matter, for that sort of thing often happens when people are new to each other.

Bolsover was offered a trial for a month, liked the job, and proved a capable fellow when it came to writing. His post was soon made permanent, and the young man worked in the same room at Butler's, surrounded by tall filing cabinets and the din of the machine room, for the subsequent sixteen years.

———

The majority of technical writing is produced for the record rather than for immediate use. It's necessary work, of course, and must be accurate, but it's worthy rather than creative; its writer is a clerk of a slightly superior kind who scratches away in a solitary fashion, having little connection with the urgent business of manufacture.

Occasionally someone would knock on the green door marked TECH/W, look in, and say, "Oh! Where's old Arnott?"

"He's retired."

"Arnott retired? Good lord! Arnott gone! Are you the new man?"

"I am."

"I wanted a copy of AN/223/0142."

"Certainly. If you'll wait a moment, I'll get one."

The limited social opportunities of his job did not bother young Bolsover, who, as soon as he sat down in old Arnott's chair, was immediately engaged in the common struggle to ensure that words mean what their writer intends. Willful, elusive, and perverse by turns, the words would multiply themselves at the least excuse, import unwanted meanings, and wander off the point. He saw that he must assert himself immediately. At the end of his first week, he defined his aims as Accuracy, Brevity, and Clarity, pinning a notice to that effect above his desk.

ABC was easy to remember but difficult to achieve. If one attempts fine definition, he discovered, even the simplest subjects become complex; an accurate document is rarely brief, a brief document will certainly not be clear, and a clear one won't be precisely accurate. Having made careful notes during a discussion with technical experts, he would insert information into a draft only to be told that it wasn't true, that it wasn't what had been said. Since Bolsover believed his notes of the meeting to be accurate, he was puzzled; but he soon saw that truth depends upon who picks the facts, who writes them down, and who reads them. Putting something into writing changed it; there was usually more than one truth, and truths often conflicted; the best writing, he decided, identified the most useful truths rather than the purest.

In time he learned to read his work aloud, finding that his ear could often detect errors that his eye had missed. This practice enabled him to observe the curious tendency of some of his words to linger in the air, perhaps because they possessed the almost indefinable quality that people call elegance.

Elegance? Among those cocks and pumps, pipes and flanges? He knew, of course, that his use of that term in such a context ran absurdity close; but he found it the only term that described his *best* words, those that were not only perfectly true but perfectly chosen and perfectly placed. He told nobody of this elegant discovery, of course, since the concern of all technical writers is science, not art. *Words must not get out of hand. If they do, meaning will get out of hand, and something will be lost.*

Alas, poor Bolsover, one might think, chanting those plain words about pipes and valves, day after day in his solitary room! But he need not be pitied, for he had found his niche. His was a craft and he a craftsman serving other craftsmen. His own work complemented theirs, every word, sentence, dot, and comma working to the common purpose, a valid, honorable purpose—the making of things that did as their designers intended. To be one with the makers—was that not a noble duty? One evening, in the local library, he was astonished to find Joseph Conrad—a very great man indeed—writing that "to take a liberty with technical language is a crime against the clearness, precision, and beauty of perfected speech."

Well! Fancy that! He immediately copied this remark—certainly it was elegant, as well as true—into his notebook, followed by another gem that gleamed a little farther down the page: "An anchor is a forged piece of iron, admirably adapted to its end, and technical language is an instrument wrought into perfection by ages of experience, a flawless thing for its purpose."

A flawless thing for its purpose. Extraordinary! If that wasn't ABC— or as near as dammit. How astonishing to discover that someone—and a great writer, at that!—had been down this road before him!

————

One might assume, given all this hard thinking, that Bolsover's off-duty habit of inquiry might have diminished, but such was not the case. He often told his dear Katherine and her friends Susan and Jane that the discovery and definition of truth—and its converse, the avoidance of self-deception—is the behavior that distinguishes humanity. It's programmed into us; we must seek problems and solve them. Isn't that why so many people occupy their spare moments with gardening and tennis, painting and crossword puzzles? A proper human being, the young man explained, doesn't just sit and gawp at the world but tries to work it out, define it, understand it, and is relentless in so doing; and at the word "relentless," the girls nodded cautiously, glancing at one another.

His inquiring habit turned up far more questions than he could resolve, and many of his investigations became hopelessly entangled. Bolsover, maturing now, was forced to recognize that his progress in any particular field might be limited to discovering which questions had the best prospect of answers. He doubted that anyone could know the truth in an absolute sense; *true* and *untrue* were the unachievable poles of the possible. Here was the most significant change in the man: while the child wanted certainty, the adult settled for somewhat less doubt.

The adult also discovered that the unknowable included his own self. Despite being the only person who stood any chance of doing so—except, of course, someone spying on him, someone peeping into his thoughts by some trick or other—he could not answer simple questions like *Who am I?* and *Where did I begin?* He often *thought* he had answered such questions; but the following morning, to his annoyance, he would discover that the answer was obviously invalid, perhaps even absurd. Could it be the case that the answers to questions of that kind possess a temporal dimension? At the moment of formulation, does an answer begin to expire, so the question must be asked again tomorrow, and a new answer found, time and again? *What has truth to do with time?* That was indeed a serious puzzle, the sort that can last a whole lifetime.

From his habitual nosing about, his marvelous and quite unexpected marriage, and the unpromising matter of technical writing, Bolsover constructed for himself a various and stimulating life. He liked the solitariness of his occupation, its regular and unhurried nature. He liked the crowded, smoky bus that he caught up the Fernley Road at six-thirty every weekday morning. He liked walking through the factory gates, through the din of the machine shop, and into the familiar room with TECH/W stenciled on the door, his books and files lying ready on his desk, their pages marked with folded spills of paper. He liked writing all day in his wire-bound notebooks, his awkward, angular hand traveling steadily downward, paragraph by paragraph, until every part was complete, and the document impossible to improve. And when the factory bells rang at the close of the day, he very much liked going home to discover Katherine in their quiet, calm home. She made a patchwork cushion for his office chair, its hexagons arranged as a large red flower, and gave him a little Swiss alarm clock in a wooden case that he placed on the corner of his desk. Every weekday morning for the sixteen years between the summer of 1964 and the autumn of 1980, save for two weeks at Walton-on-the-Naze every August, Bolsover sat down, removed the cap from his pen, opened his notebook, and began where he had left off, taking great care with his work and having not the slightest desire for change—or, as some would say, having a complete lack of ambition.

It is possible, thinks Bolsover, still sitting on the bench, still waiting for the ferry, that the biggest questions are simply unanswerable. Consciousness, for example: the curious bat, Mary in her room, the disconnected brain kept alive in a vat—all these ingenious philosophical constructions have shed little more light on human consciousness than the scribbling of novelists. Though it's now a question, he thinks with sudden irritation, whether fiction is any longer a significant player, since it has become addicted to superficial fads and fashions, so much tosh that is forgotten tomorrow. And he takes out his notebook, uncaps his pen, and writes himself another note: *If fiction is not concerned to understand, what is its subject? Is its purpose merely to pass the time?* For a moment he pauses, and then continues: *Indeed, what is fiction's object, and are subject and object the same?*

After that little burst of creativity he caps his pen with some satisfaction, puts it and the notebook into his pocket, and looks about him.

Wait—what's that? Something glimmers out at sea—a row of lighted windows, the sound of a distant engine—at last, the ferry!

"Hey, mister!" The girl is back. Seeing that she is about to lose him, she whirls into action, swerving again close to the edge of the quay and then dashing toward the ticket office, showing him the way. The gray-haired man stands up, buttons his coat, and turns to collect the suitcases that stand beside the bench. Horrible suitcases! He is nearing sixty years old, yet he still makes stupid, commonplace mistakes. For the life of me, Bolsover thinks, staring at them, I don't know why I picked a pair of suitcases so large, so bulky, so repulsive a shade of green. Oh, my suitcases! Extending handles! Little plastic wheels! Sovereign Diamond Journeyman Trolley Cases! By their name alone I should have known them! Not, of course, that such an error is harmful to anything but my own self-image as a man of taste, a man who knows—and he laughs so loudly that the beady-eyed gull, patrolling on its shadowy wings, swerves in alarm. A man of taste, shamed by a pair of green suitcases! Oh, Bolsover! How extraordinary that life should combine so carelessly the significant and the trivial, the absurd and the sublime!

Hearing the whiz of wheels, he looks up—that clever girl! She has fixed little lights on her arms, lights on her whirling boots! Bolsover tries to wave as he grapples with his cases. Yes! She's become a pattern of whirling lights in the dusk, whirling silver lights! She comes whirling at him out of the dark, and as she goes by, she's laughing at the joy of it, for she knows what she's doing, she knows she's magical—and here she is again, come to say goodbye, to swirl about him, bid him farewell, farewell to old Bolsover! What a girl she is, that girl on wheels! In and out of the yellow lamps she goes, wheeling her arms, her lights glinting silver. "Hey, mister!" she calls to him. "Hey, mister. Waddya think, mister?" She is grace and youth and freedom, but there's something else—urgency, knowingness, pain?—something that makes her unforgettable.

"Wonderful!" he calls out, and "Oh, be careful!" as she flies again toward the edge.

"See you, mister!" she calls, flying for a last time so close that he might have touched her, Bolsover calling after her, "Go carefully! Oh, please go carefully, young lady!"

And he watches the silver lights as they whirl away along the quayside, the flickering lights of the girl on wheels, and gazes after her until she is entirely gone from sight.

3

Revenons *à nos moutons.* Towing his cases, Bolsover steps into the departure lounge and finds himself among—who are they? Can they be soldiers? Camouflage jackets, boots, rucksacks, some sort of weaponry? But no: their weapons are cameras and telescopes, tripods and binoculars—they're bird-watchers, twitchers, birders. "Twitchers"! "Birders"! Why not simply "bird-watchers"? All right, the only law of language is usage, but "birders"! Why? For God's sake, why? To save a syllable? A birder ought to be "one who birds," and what, pray, is the meaning of the verb "to bird"? Bird-twitchers! Twitch-birders!

Enough of that. There are many of these birders, surely a hundred or more, jamming the doorways, occupying all the seats, overwhelming the ticket desk. Bolsover edges forward with his cases, excusing himself, hopelessly urban among the camouflage, and is forced to a halt, ten yards from the departure gate.

A tall man with a tripod and an astronomical pair of binoculars gazes sadly at him and says, "Bit of a crush, old chap."

"Too right," says Bolsover, choosing, he hopes, an appropriate demotic.

"Not a birder, then," says the man, eyeing him. He has an aquiline look, this man; perhaps birders, like dog owners, come to resemble the objects of their affection.

"No," says Bolsover.

"Thought not," says the man. "Got your ticket, have you?"

"Yes," says Bolsover.

"Just a sec," the tall man says. "I'll get you through the bloody mob."

He takes off his tweed cap, raises both arms in the air, claps his hands, and shouts, "I say, folks! Chap here wants to get through! Chap with a couple of green cases! He's got a ticket. Let him through, you chaps, would you!"

It's an order, and the chaps obey. They are indeed all chaps, these birders, and the tall man evidently a chief among them. Bolsover is taken through the throng, it seems to him, somewhat in the manner of a victorious sportsman, and in a moment the birders also get the joke, laughing, applauding, clapping him on the back and heaving him forward, their long lenses waving over his head.

"Thank you so much! Thank you! So kind!" Tugging his wretched cases, he can only grin and yell at his sudden fans—"Thank you! Awfully kind! Thank you so much! Frightfully kind! Oh, thank you, thank you!"—and in such a manner, hand to hand, Bolsover is passed up a steep gangway by the willing birders, surrenders his ticket at arm's length to the sailor guarding the steel door, and is at last projected unharmed, Bolsover and his cases, into the belly of the ship.

His ticket includes a Luxury Lie-back Recliner—ridiculous name! It's only a blessed *seat,* for God's sake! But it's already occupied by two

young people, a boy and a girl, side by side and fast asleep. How charmingly innocent, to sleep so entangled in a public place! They might be
taken for siblings—but they cannot be, nor merely friends. Though the
boundaries between love and friendship, male and female, are now so
blurred that it's possible to be either, both, or neither. Is there a spare
seat anywhere on this wretched ship?

He tows his cases up and down the aisles without result and returns
to the sleeping couple. The occupant of the next seat, a narrow-faced
man in a baseball cap, is watching his dilemma with interest. Will he
evict these innocents and send them stumbling sleepily away to seek
their fortune among the birders' army? Or will he simply lift his hands
and leave them in peace?

Enough, Bolsover! He sets off for the passenger lounge, wondering
whether it's logical to complain about one's own indecision, and whether
such a notion doesn't imply a multitude of Bolsovers stacked within himself like Russian dolls—generous, self-righteous, stingy, fussy, sentimental, all complaining one to another about their master. And long ago,
seeing him wandering in this increasingly lost fashion, his mother would
have said, "Come here, lovey-dovey. Come here, little fellow. Come up
on Ma's knee," and he'd climb up and be enveloped. But surely there is
space for me and my cases somewhere in this blessed ship.

The passenger lounge is solidly packed with birders and their gear,
but his new friend the tall birder is waving his tweed cap from a corner.
"Share my floor, old chap," he says, patting the carpet beside him.

"You've no idea," says Bolsover, arranging himself and his cases and
sinking to the floor, "how delightful it is to sit down."

"I'm terribly sorry," says the tall birder. "It's all our fault—or,
rather, the fault of a North African rarity."

"A rarity? That's the cause of the crowd, is it? A rare bird?" Here's
a curious thing: a fragment of avian life, a congregation of feathers and
fluff weighing only a few grams, has alighted on a tussock and set this
army on the march.

"Absolutely," says the tall man. "An extreme rarity. The cream-colored courser. Not a native of these parts—comes from the Sahara, the Middle East, North Africa, that sort of thing. Lovely little creature. Delicate. They put it on their stamps in that part of the world, you know. *Cursorius cursor.*"

Bolsover nods. "A courser? Wasn't that a kind of horse? A horse bred for speed? And *Cursorius cursor* would be—"

"A champion runner," says the tall birder. "The legs of a wader, but uses them for running." He extends his hand. "Wilson's the name. Jack Wilson."

"Bolsover," says Bolsover, "James Bolsover. People usually call me Bolsover, for some reason."

Long ago he had read an essay concerning the manner in which polite people explore conversation with a stranger, mutually adjusting tone and level and aiming at a nice balance between assertion and accommodation: *transactional grammar*—that's what it's called. Since reading that essay Bolsover has been unable to avoid an awareness of his own performance.

"Bolsover? Place in Yorkshire, isn't it?"

"Derbyshire, in fact."

"Sorry. Wretched southerner knows damn-all. You don't sound like a northerner."

"Oh, I've never lived there. Nowadays there are Bolsovers all over the place, I dare say."

"No doubt," Wilson says. "The little courser runs all over the place, too, but he's a damn good flyer as well. Intriguing little bird."

Intriguing? Possibly. Bolsover, conscious of his debt to this man, accepts the change of topic. "What does the bird look like? Apart from being cream-colored, I mean."

"The cream-colored courser," Wilson says, slowly and precisely, "averages twenty centimeters in height. Its plumage is a pale sandy buff or sandy rufous above, with a black stripe from behind the eye to the nape of the neck and a white stripe above that. The hindcrown is blue-gray, the underside pale sand, the lower belly white. Primaries and primary coverts are black, the secondaries sandy, the underwing black with a narrow white trailing edge to the secondaries. Bill black, legs long, feet yellowish. That's him. The cream-colored courser."

"Right," says Bolsover. "Good."

The tall man laughs. "Bit of a thing of mine, birds."

"And the courser's presence is unusual, I take it." One says such lumbering things in an effort to row the talk along.

"Never been seen on the island before. Not a single sighting. At this time of year, it's most unusual for a little chap of that kind to be so far north."

"Just the one?"

"Just the one. Of course, the bird might have been wrongly identified, and we'll all look silly. But if it's truly a cream-colored courser, it's two thousand miles from home, and in winter, too."

A proper pause follows this statement. Then Wilson asks, "Business on the island, have you?"

"In this company, my plumage betrays me," says Bolsover.

"Quite so," says Wilson, giving a polite laugh.

"I'm on my way to a new job, in fact."

"I say! Exciting stuff," the tall man says, at which point their conversation is interrupted by an announcement—"The ship is about to depart. Please take heed of the following safety message. In the unlikely event . . ."

"Take heed"? Such odd language—but never mind that, for a ship's departure must be witnessed even if it's a mere ferry and in the habit of coming and going. Asking Wilson to guard his cases, Bolsover makes his way up the crowded stairways to the boat deck.

The rail is icy under his hands, the night air carries a trace of rain, and the harbor's yellow lights illuminate an acre of wet, empty tarmac. He leans over the rail, peering fore and aft, but there's no sign of the girl on wheels. Below, on the quayside, shadowy men stand ready to free the warps. The ship's whistle sounds huskily, as if clearing its throat, and

there follows the kind of pause that occurs on the first upswing of a con-
ductor's baton, a lingering moment at which it seems that nothing is
going to happen, but then the whistle toots again, an officer leans from
the wing of the bridge and signals to the men below, warps are lifted
from bollards and hauled aboard, the ship trembles beneath Bolsover's
feet, and his eye is drawn down to the gap between quay and ship, a
widening gap filling with a strong swirl of water, at which moment there
should surely be a blessing of a solemn kind: *Lord, now lettest thy servant
depart in peace, according to thy word.*

Of his mother—the pretty girl on the down platform, as opposed to the
prematurely aged woman who died some forty years later—Bolsover
usually recalls little more than the warmth of her body, the scent of pow-
der, and a pair of strong red hands; but now, leaning on the ship's rail, a
sudden and quite different sense of her comes upon him. Wasn't there a
time, in the beginning, when he did not know where he ended and she
began? Did they live near a river? Family history had never mentioned
such a thing, but now the memory of water steals upon him with increasing power: yes, she took him alone, more than once, to a place beside a
river, and walked there beside the water. His mind is suddenly infused
with images of light glinting from slow-moving water and something
quick and sleek—a water rat or an otter, is it? Someone else is there, a
shadowy figure who might be male, and there is an edge of anxiety in the
memory, as if Bolsover had known even then that one day she would
leave him. How could that be? What can a baby know? He takes out his
notebook and rests it on the rail.

*What can a baby know? Can it somehow perceive without comprehension,
know without thought? What is the nature of such experience? And what is lost
when, the child growing up, experience is organized into meaning?*

Bolsover remains at the rail, watching the harbor lights fading into a
blur of rain. The ship, meeting the first long swells of the open sea, settles into a steady and regular motion; I have done this before, the ship

implies, and I know what I'm about. Out comes the notebook: *it's easy to understand why mariners conceive of a ship's being alive, for trust cannot be felt between men and a mere artifact, a thing of steel.*

Of course old Arnott's retirement wasn't essential to Bolsover's marriage to Katherine; had it not happened, he would have found another job that would support the two of them, since their marriage was now a shared assumption. Yes. But Arnott's retirement, considered as an event, was oddly similar to the late train that carried his mother to meet his father: it seemed to be a necessary link in a particular chain. In a sense, Arnott had enabled their future. That man, a complete stranger, now belonged, with the late-running train, to Bolsover's intimate history. Evidently some events were of that sort—they were linked together in chains—and others were not. Was that true? At a given moment, many possibilities existed; a moment later, one had been chosen and the others rejected. Most of the time those possibilities—the links, pathways, turnings—weren't perceived; indeed, they must be so many and so complex that they could never be perceived. What kind of thing was this extraordinary network? Could it be that everything was connected to everything else by an infinity of tenuous and invisible strands? *I look back, and think I know by what route I came. But history must be false, since it is partial; how many connections are there?*

At eleven o'clock on the morning of 29th July 1964, at the Swindon Registry Office, Katherine promised, in a voice almost inaudible, to take this man to be her husband, to love, honor, and obey him, and he took her to be his wife, and in his turn promised to love and honor her.

Young Bolsover was twenty years old, his wife nineteen. They had met for the first time in April. By the end of June, they had learned to talk to each other with relative ease, walked in the park, held hands, and fleetingly kissed. In July they kissed at greater length and with more intensity, watched *A Hard Day's Night*, *Dr. Strangelove*, and *Mary Poppins* at the Regal, got married, bought a new sofa, and started to discuss what should be done about the old Vauxhall in the rotting garage. These things are not negligible; but there was one thing that they had not yet done, and it constituted a considerable difficulty.

Everything about Katherine was miraculous, but her willingness to marry him was most miraculous of all. She was obviously remarkable, a person of distinction, and he was not: that difference defined his behavior. She was a gift for which he must somehow pay, and how else but with love? By which he most likely meant worship, for there is a biblical ring to the notes he made at the time.

I shall love her forever, and shall never be found wanting. So have I promised her and myself.

It did not occur to him to wonder what might be the particular needs of this young and anxious girl, and whether they could be met by simple adoration, but thoughts of such sophistication can hardly be expected from a young man when he marries.

She was astonishingly small and light—so light that he could sweep her up into his arms with one quick movement, at which she would squeal and giggle and pretend to be frightened, throwing one arm round his neck and crying out, "Don't drop me, don't drop me!"

Wasn't this a tremendous thing, to carry one's darling little wife about the house in this manly fashion, to hold her close and press his face into the marvelous freshness of her hair? Her limbs were so finely drawn that he could circle her upper arm with finger and thumb; her skin was the thinnest of coverings; and the details of her bones, muscles, and sinews were immediately displayed when she bent her head, or moved an arm, or stretched out an ankle. Often he studied her as she worked at some task—she was constantly busy, tidying the house, sewing, reading, planning her garden or working in it—and, watching her, he felt astonishment at her presence. For no reason that he could perceive, fortune had allowed this fine and rare creature to alight upon his life— and not only to alight, but to stay. To stay! She wanted to stay with him forever, stay with Bolsover forever!

From time to time, when he was admiring her, she looked up, caught his eye, blushed, and looked away. It was strange that she seemed not to care for being adored, but he saw that too much affection made her anxious and silent, and that he must ration himself. Was that because they were not the same sort, he being large and awkward, she light and delicate? She was, in comparison with him, such a very tiny girl, with the same darting nerves as the quick, inquiring robin that flickered about her when she worked in the garden. *She's afraid I'll hurt her.* He moved clumsily and could not dance, whereas she, in his opinion, danced whenever she moved—the idea of a dance, of the two of them dancing together, appears frequently in the notebooks of that period. *We might take up dancing. I could learn to dance, couldn't I? But no matter; we'll wait and see. One day I must dance with her. Should I take dancing lessons, secretly, and surprise her? No, because she doesn't like surprises.*

In the meantime, as he waited for her to be ready for him, he worked at his writing, fixed dripping taps and squeaky hinges, and remarked, several times each day, how lovely she was—to which she began to reply, after a week or two, with a little giggle, "Oh, don't be silly."

I'm not being silly, my darling. I love you, dearest Katherine.

Rather than making love, people now have sex, presumably a far simpler business, yet it's still not uncommon that couples fail to consummate their marriages immediately. In the 1960s—which were not as liberated as they are now portrayed—the problem was much greater. The English tradition required that love should be made secretly, in the dark, silently, and as a matrimonial duty; sex was not something one talked about, except in smutty and jocular terms. Hence it was quite possible, in 1964, to know almost nothing about the act, and certainly to be ignorant of the fine points of technique that are now discussed on the front pages. For a significant number of people, the opposite sex was almost as great a shock as it had been for poor Ruskin a hundred years before.

The case of Bolsover and Katherine was therefore a perfectly ordinary one. Here was a young and unsophisticated man with no sexual experience, and a girl of such extreme nervous sensitivity that she flinched if—while she was washing up, say—he lightly kissed the back of her head. Neither came from a social class with a custom of speaking openly about sexual behavior, and neither had received any instruction on interpersonal matters; they had simply picked up a confusion of gossip and folklore in what was then the usual way.

"We needn't hurry into—well, you know," Katherine said before they were married. "We've got plenty of time to get used to each other, haven't we? You won't mind waiting a little while, will you? Until we get used to each other?"

"My darling, of course I won't mind! I'd never do a single thing to harm you, or go against your wishes."

For several days after the wedding he waited for a word from her, but she said nothing. He was not unduly concerned, since they were delightfully affectionate—holding hands, kissing quite often, and playing the lovely game in which he picked her up and whirled her round while she laughed and cried out, pretending that she wanted him to stop.

What she thought about this he did not know, since he did not ask. It would surely be unfair to subject her to pressure, and probably counterproductive. One day soon she would surely tell him what she felt, and what steps they were going to take to resolve the issue. In the meantime, every night, she changed into her nightdress in the bathroom, skipped quickly into bed, put out the light, said good night, curled herself into a ball, and immediately slept, or seemed to. During the night, whenever he woke, she was lying absolutely still, her breathing so light as to be inaudible. He did not attempt to disturb her, lest she should be frightened. In the morning, by some magic, she was always up and dressed first, and cheerfully calling up the stairs that his breakfast was ready.

Bolsover grew more concerned, of course, as the days went by, not only because Katherine said nothing but also because his own desire for her had become urgent.

Should I be feeling like this? Is it normal? Tonight I cannot think of anything but wanting her. When he thought of her, his penis—often at the most awkward times, such as in a meeting at work, or while he waited at a bus stop—sprang urgently upward. Such a thing was surely wrong. *I should not be lusting after her.* Considering his wife's lightness and beauty and his own clumsy weight, his feelings appeared monstrous and brutal, not the feelings of a man but of an animal. Alas, it's a great pity that Bolsover had no close friend to tell him that the desire of a man for his wife is a fine thing, and should be a matter of mutual delight.

Katherine, he called her at first, but that soon appeared too formal. He quickly progressed to Kathy, then Kate, and finally Kitty. "My little Kitty," he would murmur as he lay beside her in the dark, saying her dear name very quietly, so as not to wake her. When the sun was up, what with his work at Butler's and the routines of home, the anxieties of love and desire diminished a little, and he could convince himself of their simple delight in being together.

This was the summer of 1964, a most exciting year in which everything appeared quite new, and Kitty, that extremely well organized young person, wanted everything to be just so. It was much easier that way, she told Bolsover, and he quite understood that domestic disorder, though he did not particularly notice it himself, wasted time that could be used for all manner of useful and creative tasks.

Every Sunday afternoon they sat together at the kitchen table reviewing the past week and making plans of a serious and thoughtful kind. Again Bolsover understood the need for such care, since their mutual aim was to secure strong foundations for their life together. Kitty proposed that they should open a post office savings account into which they would pay, to begin with, a pound a week; admittedly it was a lot of money to find, but it would help to insure against accident or illness. Bolsover trusted his wife's good sense, but he found it difficult to share her concern for the future while he was sitting close beside her in the kitchen, feeling the warmth of her body, and stealing from time to time a glance at her lovely neck, or the curves of her breasts. Perhaps when she talked about the future, she was referring to the possibility of children; at present that did not seem very likely, but it could be interpreted as a positive sign, if he put his mind to it.

Many of their conversations concerned Kitty's plans for the house. She had made a list, in priority order, of the improvements that had to be made. It began with the complete refurbishment and re-equipping of the kitchen.

"The kitchen's the heart of a house," Kitty said, "and it hasn't had a penny spent on it for years and years."

That was perfectly true. She also proposed that the old Vauxhall must be got rid of immediately. It was another sensible suggestion, of course, since it was only taking up space. Once it was out of the way, she said, they might replace it with a small secondhand car. In this context they discussed whether Kitty should try to find a job—just a few hours, part-time. It was Bolsover's suggestion; as well as improving their financial position, he thought (but did not say) that it would give her another interest, allow her to get out of the house more often, let her meet people other than her husband, perhaps make her more relaxed. She frequently seemed tired, and needed to go to bed early. However, Kitty thought it best to wait, since there was so much work for her in the house, and of course he agreed.

Bolsover pumped up the old Vauxhall's tires, removed the bricks from beneath its chassis, and placed an advertisement in the *Daily Echo* with an asking price of twenty-five pounds. Only a single response was received, a cheery enthusiast assuring them that the Vauxhall was a common model, and being thirty years old, it wasn't worth a bean. However, he would give them a fiver to take it off their hands.

It wasn't much, but as Kitty said, a fiver is a fiver, and with its help they obtained a large white GEC refrigerator on hire-purchase. It was the first substantial improvement they had made, and it pleased Kitty greatly; the marble slab was removed from the old pantry and the refrigerator inserted in its place.

Thanks to Kitty's careful household accounting, a cylinder Hoover and a Philips electric polisher for the hall tiles were soon acquired. An

HMV record player and a Roberts portable radio (both secondhand) replaced the ancient radiogram, and a pair of wrought-iron table lamps
and a Persian rug improved the sitting room still further.

"It looks really lovely now," Kitty said.

Indeed, it was surprising how much you could do on a single wage if
you put your mind to it. A local garage offered terms that enabled them
to buy a 1958 Austin A40 in Damask Blue, with imitation leather uphol-
stery. A gas stove with eye-level grill, a television set, a set of Wedg-
wood china (six servings was all they needed, Kitty said), a secondhand
gent's Raleigh bicycle with Sturmey-Archer three-speed to save on bus
fares, an extending-leaf dining table in genuine beechwood with a set of
six matching chairs, four aluminum saucepans with double-thickness
bases (better heat dispersion without burning)—all these things arrived
in the next few weeks, making Bolsover aware of the deprived life that
he had previously endured.

Kitty decided that, except for the heaviest work, she would take full
responsibility for the garden, a plan that Bolsover strongly approved.
He knew nothing about gardens. His mother, he told Kitty, had known
little more, but she had been fond of a rose that used to grow beside the
front door.

"What color was it?"

"A creamy, pinky color, I think."

"It's still there," said Kitty.

She took him by the hand and showed him some brown sticks projecting from the earth.

"But it hasn't any flowers," he said, which she thought very amusing.

"It's been over for months, you silly man," she said. "I've already
pruned it. Don't you know when roses bloom?"

"I'm not sure I do."

"I shall teach you all about gardens and gardening," Kitty said; she
was in a very happy mood that day. "Now, can you remember the name
of your mother's favorite rose?"

"I don't think so."

"It's called 'Peace.' It's a hybrid."

"Peace," Bolsover repeated. "A hybrid."

Kitty clapped her hands. "That's the first name you've learned, and soon you'll know every single one of the flowers and shrubs in my garden!"

All this was very satisfactory. If they could build their affection and mutual trust through such activities as gardening, buying things, planning the future—well, things would soon change. Surely they would. It was a good sign that Kitty had reached out and taken his hand in a most natural and easy manner. That showed her underlying easiness with him, despite—well, despite other things. Surely it did.

It was many years before Bolsover heard of the term "displacement activity" and suddenly saw how all these routines, plans, purchases, and practical activities had assisted Kitty and himself in avoiding for so long the only issue that really mattered.

Bolsover was a poor student of gardening. Kitty did not seem to mind—indeed, it became another of their lighthearted games; she would point inquiringly at a plant and he would attempt to bring its name to mind.

"It begins with *P*," Kitty would say, and he might say, hesitantly, "Potentilla?," causing her to laugh very gaily and tell him how silly he was, since she had told him its name was pieris only half an hour previously.

It puzzled Bolsover very much that she could be so joyful and free with him at one moment, so fearful and reserved at another, but in time their garden games would surely play a part in bringing them together, and help to reduce her fear of him, if fear it was.

"Kitty's the gardener," he would say to visitors, and she would show off the latest developments. He was proud of her, of course, and pleased that she found happiness in her garden, and in organizing the house so neatly, but the days and weeks kept going by, and there was no change in their circumstances.

Sitting at his desk one day, twirling a pencil this way and that between his fingers, Bolsover found himself wondering about the official definitions of the terms "wife" and "marriage," and the part played by consummation in the legality of a marriage contract. Kitty was not yet a woman he could say he had taken to wife, in the ancient sense of that term—but such thoughts were quite wrong, not to say treacherous, and he forcibly turned his mind to the operating parameters of the 409B High Temperature Valve.

He learned to be careful. In their daily relations he tried to read Kitty's mood, to respond to her in ways that pleased her, and to disturb her as little as possible. But he knew that the central difficulty must be tackled sometime, and that Kitty would not initiate the discussion; he would have to do so himself.

During August of that year, having made careful preparations to ensure that the circumstances were right, Bolsover twice attempted a discussion of the issue. The first occasion was at the end of a concert broadcast from the Royal Albert Hall; she loved to listen to music, and it seemed to help her relax. After the closing bars of the concert, he waited for a few moments, switched off the radio, turned to her, took her hands in his, and said, "Dearest Kitty, my dear wife, we must talk about why we are not yet together as one."

He realized, as soon as he had spoken, how ridiculously formal the question sounded. That surprised him, since he had written down various alternatives, had picked what had seemed to be the best, and had practiced it a number of times in front of the bathroom mirror.

Kitty became still and dipped her head low, which was not a good sign. She whispered something inaudible, and he asked her, "What did you say, my dear?"

She said, a little louder, "You promised. You promised to give me time. You said you didn't mind."

"I know, Kitty, but we have been together quite a long time now, and I think something must be done. Either we must talk about it ourselves or ask someone else for help."

At which she abruptly took her hands from his, ran upstairs, and hid herself in the bedroom.

The effects of that encounter took some days to settle. His second tactic was to write her a letter, marked on the envelope with a dozen kisses, which he placed on her dressing table as he left for work. It was, in his opinion, an affectionate and gentle letter, making useful suggestions. When he returned that evening, the letter had gone, but she said nothing about it. Eventually, having had no response for two days, he asked if she had read it. She nodded silently, avoiding his eyes.

"Would you like to say anything about it?"

She shook her head.

"If you prefer, you might like to speak to someone else about this—the doctor, or someone in your family. Dear Kitty, I know this is troubling you, and you must speak to somebody. If we can't speak about it together, perhaps you can speak to someone else. A minister, maybe."

She shook her head again.

"What about your mother?"

She shook her head even more vehemently.

He was silent for a moment, and then said, "Darling Kitty, something has to be done."

"Not yet," she whispered, folding and unfolding her hands. "Please not yet."

Which appeal he found impossible to ignore, so he knelt down beside her, took her hands, and told her not to worry: "Darling Kitty, in the end it will be all right. You'll see."

During the summer and into the autumn the couple conducted their social lives in a manner that was manifestly close and affectionate. To the outside world, Bolsover was certain, they gave no hint of difficulty. In company Kitty was charming, smiling frequently at him, allowing him to hold her hand and to hug and kiss her. She talked eagerly to her friends Susan and Jane about their homemaking and their gardening, giving a strong impression of complete content; and of course he could do nothing but support her account, which was, in its details, perfectly correct, except that it omitted the most significant matter of all.

Bolsover was not the sort of man to think of the problem in terms of a husband's conjugal rights. He knew the matter to be a shared agony, and could see that Kitty's difficulty was real. She wasn't pretending; she was afraid. It was a question of her state of mind, and he must find a way in which it might be altered. For many weeks he could think of no solution other than continuing his warm and gentle behavior toward her; if he loved her enough, might she not, in time, come round, and lose her fear of him?

She would not. Weeks went by, and nothing changed. Night after night Bolsover lay awake—his penis tenting the bedclothes—trying to solve the problem in the only way that appeared possible: by thinking, by working it out, by turning over every stone and leaf until he found the answer.

Until, on a particular night, Kitty came in from the bathroom, said, "Good night, dear," as she always did, and he replied, "Good night, darling," as he always did, and she turned out the bedside light, curled up on her side of the bed, and was silent. And he lay awake, and calculated that it was the hundredth night of their marriage.

Now it must be solved, this difficulty, now, or else—but he could not contemplate the alternative.

She had washed, undressed, and come to bed in *exactly* the way that she always did. That's how she is, that's her nature. Can a person's nature be altered? Only, perhaps, a fragment at a time. He must draw her into new habits bit by bit, somehow *beguile* her, *tempt* her, *enchant* her. Ah! That was an interesting idea, but he was no pied piper. He couldn't even dance. He could fix things when they were broken, and he could write in a very accurate, brief, and clear way, but he was no enchanter.

He laughed silently at himself. Here, surely, was the crux of the problem: whatever she needed was something that he could not provide. He had come at the problem in his usual mechanical way, trying to fix a broken marriage as he would a broken clock, but a marriage is not like a clock, and to fix it requires not only logic but—was this perhaps another advance?—imagination. Yes, imagination.

Go back a step. In some sense a marriage surely *is* like a clock: it has components that must work together. If a clock doesn't go, there's a reason that lies within its own mechanism and can be discovered by a competent mechanic. *There's a reason for everything.* I believe that to be the case, thought Bolsover.

What are the components of a marriage? Why, a man and his wife, who must mesh—yes, that was a useful word—must mesh precisely, or the marriage will not run. He had unconsciously assumed that the problem was Kitty's, when it was mutual. He himself must change a little, and Kitty must change a little, he thought, until we match, until we mesh.

How might this be done? *Don't try to change everything at once.* Surely that was sensible. *Choose something, and change it just a little bit. Make small adjustments.* This was promising. *Make interesting changes. Make them fun. Make them enjoyable. Make them safe. Make them happy.*

There are things she is interested in—gardens, flowers. And what do I know about gardens and flowers? Very little. What else is she interested in? Reading. Stories. Could I write something for her? A story? Apart from "The Diary of a Penny" he had never written a line of fiction. *My business is facts.* Well, hadn't he just said that he, Bolsover, would have to change? Perhaps he could learn how to write stories. *I could charm Kitty with a story.*

It seemed to Bolsover that this notion had brought the faintest of light into the darkness. Carefully he got up from the bed and went to the window, finding indeed that there was a trace of gray light in the eastern sky, and that the outlines of Kitty's garden were becoming visible.

What a thin idea this is, thought Bolsover, what a fragile and transparent notion. *But what else can I do? I don't know. I can't think of anything else. I shall try this idea, and if it doesn't work, I shall think of another idea, and then another, and in the end, my darling Kitty, I shall find a way to mend the clock.*

———

At his desk that morning Bolsover put aside his technical writing and placed his own notebook squarely before him. Save for half an hour when sleep overtook him at lunchtime, he worked at his story all day, finding it the most arduous task that he had ever attempted. How does one construct a story—something that must seem real, and must at all costs move the reader—without a clear set of facts to draw upon, without anything but a handful of tentative, fragile notions? It was, he found, much easier to reject an idea than to accept it, and a great many pages were torn out and thrown away; but by the evening he had completed a few pages of *something*—far from satisfactory, of course, but nevertheless a completed installment. This frail opening would be the start of his campaign to change the way they lived, he and Kitty, by telling her a story—yes, by *romancing* her. That was it. It was a romance.

The following night Kitty came quickly out of the bathroom, across the landing, and into the bedroom as usual. She turned out the light, hopped quickly into bed, said "Good night, dear," and curled up on her own side of the bed. Bolsover lay for a few moments in silence, staring up into the dark, and then he began to speak in a measured tone.

"Dearest Kitty," he said, "I've been working on a story for you. It's a story about a place called Ravensdale, a valley that lies beyond the ocean, beyond the desert, beyond the farthest mountains. Through the valley runs the river Raven, bringing fresh water to the rich, dark soil of the valley, in which every seed flourishes."

For a moment Bolsover paused. Kitty said nothing, but in her stillness he detected surprise and attention. When he'd begun to speak, there had been the smallest movement; perhaps she had turned her head toward him in the darkness.

"The journey through the mountains to Ravensdale," continued Bolsover, "is so long and arduous that few travelers find their way there. The people of Ravensdale live in peace. The years have passed in Ravensdale, the seasons come and gone in Ravensdale, and nothing seems to have changed in Ravensdale, that secret valley, which its people know to be a land of perfect harmony.

" 'We shall never leave the valley,' say the people of Ravensdale, 'because we want for nothing.' Along both sides of the river are fields of wheat and barley, while the higher slopes contain orchards and orange groves, fine pastures, and forests of pine and birch. 'Ravensdale is a place of perfect harmony,' say the people of that secret valley.

"Even when the winter snows come and life is not so easy, the people of Ravensdale do not mind, because they know that spring will come and the alpine flowers bloom again. Have they not lived in this way for as long as anyone can remember?

"No, they have not. For many years there was conflict between those who lived on the north bank of the Raven and those who lived on the south. In truth, nobody can remember how the conflict began, but whatever its origin the people of the valley became divided along the line of their lovely river, the Raven. The people of the north never crossed to the south, and those of the south never crossed to the north. Despite their living in the same valley, the people of Ravensdale feared each other, and the more they were afraid, the less they wanted to mend their quarrel with those on the other bank.

"Now it came to pass that a girl called Anna, the daughter of a miller who lived on the south bank, was blackberrying in the woods when she heard the voices of men shouting orders, the neighing of horses, and the jingle of harness. Through the trees she glimpsed color and movement on the far side of the river. Anna was an intelligent and curious girl, but she was impulsive and had not the least idea of danger. When she saw men wearing blue uniforms with white sashes, and helmets with high plumes of orange feathers, she thought how delightful it was to see strangers, how charming were their costumes. She ran forward to the riverbank, intending to welcome these people to Ravensdale, that secret place of perfect harmony.

"But the strangers, when they saw her across the water, began to shout insults and wave their swords. Anna was at first astonished, but then recalled what she had been told many times: that she was not to speak to the folk across the river, that they were enemies, that they intended harm to the peaceful friends who lived on her side of the river.

"So Anna retreated from the bank of the Raven until she was hidden among the trees and watched as the men on the far bank saddled their horses and made ready to depart. The last to leave was a young soldier with a plume of orange feathers on his helmet. As he reached the edge of the trees, she saw him turn for a moment and look back toward her, and then he spurred his horse and disappeared into the forest."

At this point Bolsover paused. "Darling Kitty," he said, "the story of the secret valley of Ravensdale is a long story, and I don't know how it will end. All I know is that Ravensdale was once in conflict, and that the girl Anna, the miller's daughter, became involved in that conflict. I'm going to continue the story every night and discover where Anna's adventures may lead us. Tonight I shall tell no more of the story, except to say that Anna rushed home to her father's house, the house of the miller, to tell him about the soldiers she saw on the far bank of the river Raven, soldiers in blue uniforms with white sashes and tall orange plumes."

When he had finished, there was silence for what seemed a long time. He turned his head and saw that Kitty was looking at him steadily, her face resting on her open hand, her eyes gleaming in the darkness.

"That was lovely," she said. "I liked the orange plumes particularly."

"Good," Bolsover said.

"I think your story is charming, and I am greatly touched by it." And Kitty reached out her hand toward him. He took it and held it but made no further move, and after a while they fell asleep.

On the first night of Bolsover's storytelling that's all that happened, but it filled him with content. Kitty had listened, she had liked the story, and she had even reached for his hand, which was a considerable change in her behavior. Perhaps his idea would work. He seemed to have found a way of talking that was fit for his purpose. His story was simple and derivative, but that didn't matter; nothing mattered, except that Kitty had reached for his hand.

The more he thought about it, the more Bolsover considered the first installment of his story to be a triumph. It had immediately touched her, and a change in her behavior had been achieved. Now the trick must be repeated every night, so that he and she might inch a little further along the road to happiness.

For a second day pipes and valves were postponed while Bolsover wrote and rewrote the next part of Ravensdale. His story was to be a love affair, of course. The plot was simple enough; the difficulty was to sustain a convincing magic.

"The secret valley of Ravensdale, that land of perfect harmony, lies beyond the great ocean, beyond the desert, beyond the farthest mountains."

He intended them to be seductive, those rolling, repetitive words and the characters from half-remembered folktales: the miller, the mayor, the colonel, the strong-minded girl, the handsome soldier, stereotypes, all of them, placed in a simple world of light and dark. Scenes came sharply into his mind: the colonel's gray standing at the miller's gate, flicking its tail and shifting its hooves in the gravel, for it was bred for the chase and did not care for waiting. In another scene, astride the same animal, the colonel himself, a man of importance, is guarded by a sergeant and a file of soldiers, their orange plumes moving to the rhythm of their trotting horses. The miller's house is a fine one, built with the miller's own hands from pine logs, each log cut and trimmed and dragged down the mountainside by him alone, for the miller was a proud man who wanted no help from anyone. And here is the mayor in person, a bumptious fellow, never without the gold-trimmed tricorn that is his badge and privilege. The mayor steps to his gate and greets the colonel not with a bow, for the mayor bows to nobody, but with the offer of his hand, which is coolly accepted by the man on the gray horse.

Soon, but not too soon, Bolsover would write of the first meeting, a clandestine, proscribed, and urgent meeting, between the young soldier and the miller's daughter, Anna. They would meet in the forest. Bars of sunlight, falling between the trees, would draw from the girl's dark hair unsuspected tones of red and gold, making the young soldier's heart turn over—yes, that's how it would be.

The second installment came quickly into Bolsover's mind, and he was even able to devote a little of that day to his tubes and valves. During the remainder of the week the story began, it seemed to him, to tell itself— which Bolsover thought highly satisfactory, being new to the artistic life, and unaware of the dangers that the phrase may signify.

When Kitty heard the second installment, she several times interrupted him with comments. He had written a particularly good scene, he felt, between the colonel of Horse and the mayor of Ravensdale in which they exchanged formal insults. The scene ended with the colonel laughing cruelly, making his high-tempered horse skitter sideways a step or two, at which Kitty cried, "Oh, yes! What an awful man is that colonel!" That was exactly the sort of engagement that Bolsover sought; and at the end of that episode, Kitty again took his hand in hers, and not only that, but moved herself a few inches nearer.

In such a manner, with a sense of high excitement, did Bolsover begin the romance that was to have such an extraordinary and—as far as he was concerned—astonishing outcome.

4

"Did you hear the announcement?" asks Wilson.

"No. What was it?"

"Bad weather on the way. Batten down the hatches, old chap."

"Seems all right to me," says Bolsover. He has had enough of waiting and thinking and is unhappy to be sitting on a hard floor as a consequence of his own indecision.

"Don't you sometimes think," he says to Wilson, "that birding is a bit of an obsessional activity?"

"Good Lord, yes," says Wilson. "Making lists, ticking things off, attention to the tiniest detail—of course birding is obsessional. Whoever said it wasn't? Birding never makes us money, never raises our status, never attracts a woman, yet we carry on doing it. It's a neurosis. All I'd say in its defense is that it's more fun than trainspotting."

"Surely it's a competition," says Bolsover, conscious that his attempt at generating an argument is failing.

"Some birders treat it that way. Some keep trying to achieve new personal targets and beat records. The big day—do you know about that? It's when a birder—a twitcher, the most obsessive kind—tries to beat the record for individual species in a single day. The world record is close to five hundred."

"Five hundred! And how many have you spotted in a day?"

"Me? Oh, forty or fifty, I suppose. I don't keep count. Most of us don't bother too much about that sort of thing. I know we're mostly men, of course, and I'm told Freud would say that repressed sexual urges lead to our compulsive behavior. It's certainly the case that the great majority of birders are male, but I've never noticed anything odd about us. Rather the opposite, if anything. A dull lot, on the whole."

"Type S brains," suggests Bolsover. "List makers."

"Oh, you've heard that, have you? Seems dubious to me."

"Something makes you do it."

"Too much money, not enough to do," Wilson says. "Simple as that. Got to do something, haven't you? Gets you out and about. Fresh air and exercise, all that."

Bolsover hugs his irritability to himself. Everywhere about the ship the birders are attempting to sleep, those camouflaged men, their weapons to hand, the troop, army, host, multitude, throng—no, a *flock* of birders, telescopes and cameras, rucksacks, balaclavas, boots, notebooks, all of them in pursuit of that pale runner, a bird entirely unaware of them, the little *Cursorius cursor*. Birders! On such and such a day, at such and such a place, I saw such and such, I saw it myself, and a great rarity it was, too, and exactly like the pictures I studied in readiness for that day. Ah, birders! Men on the loose, an army of stalkers. The little courser, all un-aware, caught in the lenses of a hundred telescopes, stilled in a thousand photographs, and some of those birders must surely think of pulling the trigger, bagging it—just like the racks of feathery corpses he'd once seen, come to think of it, at the old queen's country palace, Osborne House, the birds brought down by Prince Albert's gun. Bolsover squirms on his patch of carpet, the tough, bristling carpet of the saloon, to which some godforsaken designer has given a pattern of blue and gray slashes quite unlike anything seen in nature—and yet, I never heard of a birder doing the slightest harm to a living soul.

At which, having somewhat recovered his temper, Bolsover sleeps, dreaming uneasily of his mother carrying him beside water and walking with that stranger, oh so many years ago; and it is quite possible that these are not memories at all but scenes of his own mind's making, wrought by the anxieties of travel and the restless working of his own imagination.

Two hours later Bolsover wakes. The ship's motion has become a rolling lurch, and the deck thrums beneath him with the urgent work of the propellers. The birders' army lies abandoned about the decks as if defeated on a battlefield, pale-faced, one or two moaning quietly. Bolsover looks at his watch, finds it is midnight, and is suddenly gleeful. I've never been seasick in my life! I'm fit as a fiddle! Doesn't that prove I'm a man whose heritage is water? Blow wind and crack your cheeks! I'll go on the prowl and see what there is to see.

Working his way through the bodies, he climbs the stairs to the boat deck, but finds the doors have been secured. "A bit choppy now, sir," a sailor tells him. "Best stay below."

"But what am I to do?" asks Bolsover, denied.

"Well, sir," says the sailor, "you might care for a glass of something. I don't suppose the bar is busy." A drink, when he might have communed with the storm!

Indeed, the bar isn't busy. Melancholy birders lie about its floor while the barman, his hair stylishly glued into rows of small spikes, sways easily with the movement of the ship, polishes glasses, and whistles along with the music that falls from somewhere in the ceiling—no, it's not the ceiling. The word is "deckhead": that's the proper nautical term. Some of the birders are asleep, most are pale-faced; poor fellows, they lack the instinct for the seaborne life.

"Whiskey," says Bolsover, leaning an elbow on the bar. "And yourself?"

The barman is glad to have company. He and Bolsover sip their whiskey and discuss storms at sea, seasickness, birders, and the curious life of the ferryman, to and fro, to and fro.

"So, what do you do, then?" asks the barman.

"I write stuff," says Bolsover.

"Stuff? Books, you mean?"

"Sometimes. But not the sort of book you can buy in a bookshop. Technical stuff. Engineering, electronics, that sort of thing."

"Ah," says the barman. "Not famous, then."

"No. Not famous in the least."

"I can't say I read a lot, myself, but the skipper's one for the books. I reckon he's read every book there is. You should see the shelves in his cabin! He was on the Far East run—the China Sea, Pacific, the Timor Sea, all that. Weeks on passage, nothing in sight. He used to get through a book a day, so he says. Hundreds, he must have read."

"There's a story by Conrad about a typhoon in the China Sea—"

"Conrad?"

"Joseph Conrad. Have you read him?"

"Me? Blimey, no! But he's the skipper's main man! Give me the name of a book."

"*Lord Jim*?"

"That's one of them! *Lord Jim*! Give me another."

"*Nostromo.*"

"*Nostromo*! That's another! *Nostromo*! Hey, you really know the man! Is he a big name in the book world, this Conrad?"

"He sure is. He was a skipper, too, in the days of sail."

"Well! And he's the old man's favorite! Joseph Conrad!"

Another whiskey, a toast to Conrad, and the barman leans close to

Bolsover. "You ought to talk to the skipper," he says. "He'd like to meet you, since you're a fan of that Conrad. It'll make his day, you can be sure of that."

"Really? He'll be busy, won't he? In this rough weather?"

"Oh, there's not so much to do, and the old man's always good for a chat. You'll see. I'll give him a call."

The barman reaches for his phone and it occurs to Bolsover that relations between ships' captains and their barmen are surprisingly intimate; but no doubt that's the way of things in the modern merchant service.

"Anderson, sir. Got a writer fellow in the bar. Thought you might like to talk to him. He knows your man, sir, that Conrad. Read 'em all, I reckon he has."

The barman listens, looking at Bolsover.

"Oh, no, sir. He's pretty steady on his feet. The bar's dead tonight. A few asleep, that's all. Aye, aye, sir. I'll bring him up."

Bolsover follows the barman along corridors and up steel stairways of increasing steepness. *Aye, aye, sir.*

"Make sure you hold tight, sir," says the barman. "You go careful now."

"I'm all right," says Bolsover. "I'm perfectly fine."

The captain of the ferry is a short, spherical man with small feet. Although the ship is pitching heavily, he stands in the center of the darkened bridge as if bolted to the deck.

"Well, sir," he says, shaking Bolsover's hand, "you're a reader of Conrad, I hear."

"Conrad and a good many other sea writers," says Bolsover, gripping the edge of what must be a chart table. "Melville, Jules Verne, Marryat, Mark Twain—"

"Marryat!" The captain laughs. "I was brought up on Marryat. Marryat and Conrad, those two. My father was an enthusiast for Marryat. He saw himself as Mr. Easy, organizing Jack's going to sea. In a way he was exactly that, since you see me here. But in the end Marryat's jollity palls, don't you think? I prefer Conrad as more suited to my profession and a good deal deeper. Now, Mark Twain—he's a comic genius, but essentially a riverboat man. Shallow water. And Melville—well, to my mind he's a man who twists and turns, and takes some following."

"Ah, *Moby-Dick*," says Bolsover.

The captain nods. "Jules Verne, now—I enjoyed him as a lad, but later found him too simple for my taste. I like a novel to last, and I don't think Verne lasts. Do you know what I mean? A book that stays in the mind—that's what I want. Conrad stays in the mind. I'm sure you'll understand, Mr—?"

"Bolsover."

"You'll understand, Mr. Bolsover, that when I walk out on the wing of the bridge, look astern, and see my ship's wake already fading away, leaving not the slightest impression on the face of the waters—well, when I see that endless making and unmaking, I'm humbled, Mr. Bolsover, every damn time. That's why Conrad is so congenial to my taste. Conrad lasts, Mr. Bolsover, and Conrad is true to the sea and true to humanity."

"Certainly," says Bolsover, hoping that he may sustain his part in this grand conversation. "Surely Conrad is one of the greatest of novelists."

"Writers of nautical fiction," says the captain, "prefer extremes of weather to the interminable regularity of ordinary seas, which is the majority of a sailor's experience. Too many storms, Mr. Bolsover, too many storms! Yet they must find their drama somewhere, I dare say, and nothing's easier to summon up than a gale. Conrad, of course, is a seaman, and he knows that a calm sea can be as dangerous as a rough one."

"*Nostromo*—now there's a book of calms," says Bolsover. "Conrad has a liking for grandeur, and he draws many an immense calm. Not that he can't do a pretty good typhoon when he tries."

"I see you've read Conrad closely, Mr. Bolsover."

"I have, though I'm no sailor. My experience of the sea was got from a deck chair at Walton, gazing at the North Sea as if it were the far Pacific."

The captain gives his little bark of a laugh. "We're in a declining minority, I suppose, those of us who still enjoy the old man. I don't say he's always on his best form, but when he is—well, look at *Youth*, for example. Come to think of it, that's another calm one."

"The burning ship," says Bolsover. "He took that story from his own experience, I think."

"I believe he did." The captain studies one of the glowing screens and then turns back to Bolsover, raises a hand, and declaims: " 'A high, clear flame, an immense and lonely flame, ascended from the ocean, and from its summit the black smoke poured continuously at the sky.' "

"Marvelous," says Bolsover.

" 'A magnificent death had come like a grace, like a gift, like a reward to that old ship at the end of her laborious days.' "

"Marlow," says Bolsover.

"Marlow!" The captain is delighted with his fellow enthusiast. "That's where Marlow says that being young at sea, having nothing except hard knocks, that's the best time of one's life. Oh, yes."

The captain steps forward to a control panel, makes a small adjustment, and returns to his position.

"And speaking of calm," says Bolsover, "that takes us to the French man-of-war."

"It takes us into the heart of darkness," says the captain. "I believe I know that passage too—'In the empty immensity of earth, sky, and water, there she was, incomprehensible, firing into a continent.' " He is silent for a moment, nodding his head. "We are such stupid creatures, Mr. Bolsover."

At this weighty moment there is a silence between the two men. Nothing is visible through the dark windows. Bolsover looks at the glowing screens, listens to the whir and hum of equipment, and tries to learn the movement of the ship, that he may stand as steadily as the captain. High on the bridge her motion is exaggerated, sometimes violent:

the ship moves smoothly through several of the great seas and then, catching one wrongly, shudders as if punched. A second later, spray rattles at the bridge windows.

"One might say," says the captain, "since I'm a committed mariner with a wife, two daughters, and three granddaughters, that my ferryman's duties are convenient. I leave home when they've had enough of me and I come back when they've begun to miss me. On the other hand, it's a considerable frustration, after many years in command of a fine ship upon great waters, to drive this little tiddler and go home every few days to fix a dripping tap."

How astonishing life is, thinks Bolsover, and how delightful, that it should suddenly construct a moment such as this, a moment that seems a privilege, a reward, a gift. A reward for what? For being here, that's all. And its cause? Ah, who's to say, but who cares about that, when such a thing happens? He watches the captain's face, which displays a suitably pugnacious strength, and listens to his even voice while the ship lurches on its way.

"I went to sea as a cadet of sixteen," the captain continues, reaching forward to make another adjustment on the panel before him. "I went to sea because my father gave me *The Observer's Book of Ships*. I was five years old. Soon I was dreaming the sea, day and night. At the age of ten I took a train to London Bridge and wandered along the wharves. Shaw Savill, Blue Star, Brocklebank, Ben Line—I knew the ships, knew their routes, knew their house flags. I even got to know the names of their skippers, cheeky lad that I was. I didn't notice, of course, but the place was dying. Those were the last of the great days of the Port of London. Along the wharves, cranes working, sacks and pallets coming ashore— coconuts, bales of silk, coal, fruit, spices, iron ore—every product under the sun. I signed up the moment I was sixteen. It was a Tuesday, and on the Thursday I set sail for Bombay, Rangoon, Singapore, and Hong Kong. Four years I was away on that trip. Four years."

"The South China Sea," says Bolsover.

"I did what I'd dreamed. When Conrad talks of scenting the land after weeks at sea—oh, yes, I know exactly what he means. When I first smelt spice on the wind, I had to ask the third mate what it was. 'India,' he told me. 'That's the smell of India, my lad. India!' I thought I was the luckiest man in the world, and maybe I was. Now that I'm near retiring, I wonder how people can live if they have no great memories."

There is little that Bolsover can say in response to such talk; indeed, the captain may have forgotten that he's there.

"The sea gives a man time to think, and I've made the most of it. At sea we're free and we're captive, Mr. Bolsover. The ship's our home and she's a prison, too. Her natural condition is sinking, and that's what she'll do if we leave her to herself. The crew's a chain, with the strength of a chain and the weakness of a chain, so the smallest link can take us down. We make rules to keep out the sea, rules made by experience, centuries of it. It took me years to see that the law of the sea is morality disguised as practice. The right thing is the good thing. Transparent morality. Conrad said it: 'The exacting life of the sea has this advantage over the life of the earth, that its claims are simple and cannot be evaded.' "

"What's right on land is surely the same," says Bolsover, "but we see it less clearly. The ship's too large and the crew too many. When we act, we can't see the consequences."

The captain nods. "That's very good, Mr. Bolsover, very true. As for life on land, I'm afraid I'm one of those who see us well set on the road to our own destruction, one way or another. Something of humanity is rotting away, don't you think? Such a tide of aggression, greed, self-regard, and plain stupidity has risen that we look to lose everything."

The captain's remark makes for silence on the bridge. "Dear me," he says at last. "Forgive me, Mr. Bolsover, for importing such gloom into the proceedings. I store these things up in the long watches of the night and pour them on the head of an unsuspecting visitor. I'm sorry."

"No need to apologize," says Bolsover. "No need at all. I don't doubt what you say. I've thought the same myself."

"Come the dawn, things will look better, no doubt. They usually do."

"The trouble is," says Bolsover, "if we ran life ashore as you run life afloat, people would call it fascism."

The captain turns to look at him and says, "So you don't think I'm a great loss to the political life of the nation?"

"I'm afraid I don't, sir," says Bolsover.

"You're right," says the captain. "You're damn well right. So be it! I'll stick to sailoring!" He thumps Bolsover on the shoulder and peers out into the darkness. "If you look ahead and a point to starboard," he says, "you might catch the loom of Handsome Point, though it's thirty miles off."

Bolsover looks into the black window and sees nothing but his own dim reflection.

"Tell you what, Mr. Bolsover," says the captain, "button your coat and get out on the wing of the bridge. You'll see the light from there all right. There's a fishing boat close by—you'll see her lights passing down the port side. Make sure you hang on tight."

Outside, the gale tears and flogs at Bolsover's coat and handfuls of spray dash into his face. Gripping a handrail, he edges outward until abruptly he catches the glimmer of the fishing boat's lights, red and green and yellow lights, mere specks that fall and leap among the gray-backed seas. Good God, can there be men aboard her? How can they endure such motion? He looks to the horizon—yes, there's a difference in the darkness far ahead, no more than a suggestion of light—and there it is, a slow pulse, one, two, three, and a pause; again, one, two, three, and a pause. He hangs on with both hands, joyful to be at the heart of this tussle, marveling at the power of nature and the skill of the men who made this ship and set her against these blind forces. From time to time the huge face of the moon gleams out through racing, ragged clouds and turns the sea a sudden silver, the sea marked and streaked with foam, great dark waves humped and moving like gigantic creatures of the deep, and man so trivial among them. Now he sees what the ship is about, as she lifts to three waves, sometimes four, and hits the next mightily, so the spray flies over. Oh, whom can I tell of this, whom can I tell of the waves, the spray, the tossing lights of that frail boat, the loom of the distant light—on this great day of my life, whom can I tell?

Inside again, screens glow, machines securely hum, and the gale merely taps at the windows. The captain, standing steady in his place, hands Bolsover a towel and declaims: " 'And God said, Let us make man in our image, after our likeness, and let them have dominion over the fish of the sea, and over the fowl of the air, and over the cattle, and over all the earth and over every creeping thing that creepeth upon the earth.' " He nods his head several times. "That's our difficulty, Mr. Bolsover. We think we're in charge. And what shall we make of our charge, Mr. Bolsover? What shall we make of it?"

"Oh, that's a question," says Bolsover, wiping salt water from his face and staggering as the ship gives a particularly awkward lurch. "It's one I can't answer, that's for sure." The captain is one for grand talk, all right.

"I think we might take a couple of knots off her," the captain says, and adjusts a small knob. "You'll have noticed the seas are steeper now the flood tide's running."

Bolsover has noticed no such thing, but is flattered by the captain's pretense.

"As for being a sailor," says the captain, waving his hand to encompass himself, the bridge, the instruments and controls, the glowing screens, the dark windows, and the storm that whirls around them, "I still can't get enough of it. Even in this tiddler I proceed in the grandest manner, with an unmatched point of vantage. The sea lies before me, the ship steams on toward the unreachable horizon, ships pass, the evening comes, the dawn—it would be curious if forty years of sailoring hadn't made me a little odd, Mr. Bolsover. When I'm talking to my neighbor across the fence, I can see the look in his eye. Did you catch the loom of Handsome Point?"

"I think I saw it," says Bolsover. "Very faint, it was. Three slow flashes."

"That's it," says the captain. "It's a fine tall light on a ridge of rocks off the southwest corner of the island. We've got all these gadgets to tell us where we are"—he waves his hand again at the dials and screens—"and yet, when you raise the glim of Handsome Point, it says more than any of them. That little spark shines through and shows us the way home. I'm a sentimental man, Mr. Bolsover, as you've noticed. The sea has that effect, and reminds us what matters. Make sure you take a stroll to Handsome Point one evening, and remember the time you saw the light from the bridge of this little ship."

"I will," says Bolsover. "I will indeed."

"Myself, I think it's time for a sandwich. Would you care for one? I believe they're corned beef. They usually are."

Bolsover eats his sandwich and peers into the darkness while the ship lurches on through the night. He knows his conversation with the captain to be a game, evanescent and absurd, the sort that men play for their own romantic purposes, and yet, in some curious sense, it is valid. They have been able to speak of fundamental truths, for which talk, on land, there are few occasions. His mind is easier now than it has been for many weeks.

As Bolsover leaves the bridge—he does so with great reluctance—the captain says, "I'm pleased to have met you, sir. If you're aboard again, make yourself known to the ship."

Make yourself known to the ship. Bolsover repeats the remark to himself as he clambers down the stairways to the passenger lounge. The captain had spoken in a grand manner and was fully entitled to, for he is a ship's master, the holder of a most ancient and responsible office. And Bolsover, by their talk, by the captain's respect for him, has been honored; yes, something of the dignity of a captain's office has attached itself, at least for a moment or two, to Bolsover, a man who is of no account whatsoever.

———

The sea is certainly calmer now. The birders are sitting up, stretching, rubbing their eyes. Bolsover returns to his uncomfortable berth beside Wilson, hugging to himself an inner gleefulness: he has been up all night when most were incapacitated, he has conversed with the ship's master, talked of Conrad, known the storm, eaten a corned beef sandwich on the bridge, and seen, at least dimly, the loom of Handsome Light. He's been on watch (he allows himself the phrase) on the bridge of a ship at night, in a gale of wind!

He's more than a little tired now, and glad that the ship will soon be secured alongside, but before he sleeps, he must record the events of the night—the enormous and primitive force of the gale; the foam-streaked waves; the tiny, bobbing lights of the fishing boat; the astonishing brilliance of the moon; the captain so calmly driving his ship into the dark. Bolsover scribbles as fast as he can, attempting to capture those moments before they slip away, which is a fine purpose for writing—*and each wave, its white crest curled like the mane of a brave horse, threw itself at the ship, yet in vain, for the ship each time rose again, and went on, steady on its course, the master steady at the helm.*

Oh, yes, his writing takes more chances these days, and is not as concerned with precision as it once was; it's the Ravensdale effect, one might say.

5

K*itty, my darling Kitty.* For the sixteen years of his marriage, his wife's name came first into Bolsover's mind when he woke, and was the last word he spoke at night. Certainly theirs was an enclosed life, and one that many would call limited, but it was intensely meaningful to them both. To sustain their love at such intensity was a considerable achievement, and possibly a rare one; it seems possible that it was actually assisted by the need to overcome, in the beginning, a difficult hurdle. Bolsover's romancing of his wife by means of storytelling—that preposterous idea, that elaborate and outrageous gamble!—was entirely successful. Which is to say, it achieved the result he intended; but the *nature* of that result, when it eventually occurred, was completely unexpected.

What had he expected? Why, something mystical, affectionate, romantic—to be enfolded at last within his wife's loving arms, to become one with her in sacred union—something of that sort. He had imagined something like that, but was aware of his own ignorance. D. H. Lawrence, he had noticed, used the term "cleave together" to describe lovemaking, a phrase that seemed oddly ambiguous. Didn't it imply a contradiction, joining together *and* splitting asunder? How could that be? Perhaps it was just another peculiarity of a writer whose picture of sex and love often seemed to veer toward the absurd.

But Bolsover had not experienced the act of love, and hence could not know the truth of it. Similarly his wife—so transparently virginal—was desperately afraid of the act, afraid of penetration. Bolsover used those cold terms to himself with no awareness of anachronism, although he knew, in some dim way, from the things that people sometimes said and wrote, that the act itself—despite its seeming, in an engineering sense, straightforward enough—must generate feelings of an extraordinary kind.

But before he could know the truth, the Ravensdale story had to reach an appropriate climax. It was clear that his story must intrigue Kitty, involve her, draw her in and steadily increase in intensity until—well, until it worked. Or didn't work. But he wasn't going to think about that yet.

He had no hesitation in calling the miller's daughter Anna: it was a simple, honest name. The young soldier from the north he called—more ambiguously, we might judge—Ralph. These two young people, having fallen in love at first glance, were determined to meet and eventually to marry, despite the mutual hostility of their families; that was the device that drove the story. It was a familiar scenario, of course, but since (so Bolsover had read) there are no more than seven plots, he could forgive himself that fault.

In the course of the first few episodes, by means of various deceptions, evasions, and narrow escapes, Anna and Ralph were enabled to exchange a few fleeting kisses, but each time were quickly interrupted. Hasty encounters between the lovers, secret letters delivered by go-betweens, scenes of violent family disapproval, breathless chases through the forest (in one of which Ralph narrowly escaped with his life by casting off his clothes and swimming the river)—all these ancient storyteller's strategies, Bolsover discovered, were useful to his purpose. And what was his purpose? Why, to draw out the story, to heat it up, and to delay the end as seductively as possible, which is the simple purpose of all storytelling. This discovery was something of a revelation; the purpose of action and event in a story was not, as he had assumed, to take the story forward, but to *delay* it, to keep it alive and above all to postpone its ending. As he worked on the story, it became clear to him that a story lives in its telling, and its end is a kind of death. Now he understood why so many writers had expressed a hatred of resolution and all that goes with it—the telltale compression of the pages, the tidying-up, the awkward twisting and knotting of plots, and the eventual submission to the petty convention that stories must have an end. *My story will grow as naturally as a tree. Why shouldn't it? It can do whatever it likes. Why should a story go in any particular direction? Why should it be forced to end?*

Bolsover's increasing literary fervor should not be entirely attributed to sexual frustration. There is risk in fiction, and risk is intoxicating; on occasions he found himself working with an intensity that he had never before experienced. He discovered it necessary to split himself in two, first proposing an idea and then testing it fiercely to ensure that it wasn't just a foolish fancy. How does one know whether something works? He couldn't *know*, he decided, because it wasn't a question of knowledge but of *instinct*—that and the passing of time. When first he wrote a line he could not know that it would work as he intended; some lines would wither, others thrive, and only when sufficient time had passed could he decide which was which.

Working in this increasingly intense manner, Bolsover thought up a great many excellent ideas which the story consumed as if it were a ravenous fire. That idea made him pause; perhaps there *is* a natural way in which a story can end. *A story may end when everything's burned up. When the log pile is empty, when every log and branch is consumed and there is nothing left but ashes, only then is it proper for a story to end.*

Happily, since he had no shortage of imaginative ideas and a powerful drive behind his story, Bolsover was in no danger of burning himself out. As he worked, he grew more and more impatient with the conventions of fiction and the limits that it placed on his creative freedom. *What can be improbable when everything—everything!—is invented? What's wrong with coincidence? Why attack old Thomas Hardy because his plots are unlikely? Don't people know the difference between real life and a story? I'm making this up. None of it happened. I shall do what is right for the story, and if you think it's unlikely, that's your problem. As for coincidence, it's no more than things happening together, which happens in real life all the time. CO + INCIDENCE equals TOGETHER + HAPPENING.*

At this time, Bolsover's notes on his developing artistic philosophy are noticeably more assertive than usual.

Two episodes, four, six, eight, ten. After so much creative intensity, Bolsover began to feel that his powers of invention were becoming strained and that the lovers' consummation could hardly be postponed much longer. Kitty was now thoroughly immersed in the story, urgent each night for the next episode. She still undressed in the bathroom and hopped quickly into bed, but now she reached for his hand at once, pulled herself close beside him, and had taken to leaving the bedside lamp alight: "Darling, I want to see your face while you're talking."

With particular care he established a suitable location for the lovers' climactic tryst, a wooded glade beside a lake, and provided them with a conveniently warm summer's evening. He made sure that Anna and Ralph would not be interrupted: nobody could know their whereabouts, nobody had guessed their plan. And finally, on a bank of moss and wildflowers, toward the end of the twelfth night of the story, the author brought his lovers together at last.

"Anna lay back among the mosses and wildflowers," Bolsover wrote that morning in his room at Butler's, machinery clattering around him, "and saw that the spark of the evening star had emerged against the growing darkness of the summer sky. She turned to Ralph, and he reached out and touched her cheek—" And as he said those words— now it's evening, and he is reciting his story aloud to his wife—Bolsover felt the slightest movement, Kitty's wonderfully soft lips descended upon his own as gently as a moth alighting, and the remainder of his romantic episode was swept from his mind.

Days of intense creative effort had made Bolsover a little hysterical. The requirements of his plan went far beyond the writing of a simple romance, for he intended his fiction to be dovetailed into reality. The intended outcome of his story would take place in the real world. He must let it go. Its final sentences could not be written, but must follow inevitably from those that went before. He and Kitty must become Ralph and Anna, his story escape from the page and come alive.

As an imaginative task, one may say that Bolsover's objective was daunting. The writing of an ordinary fiction, one without particular connection to outside reality, contains, like any artistic task, the strong possibility, even the likelihood, of failure. Throughout its making, fiction must dance with failure, for that is the process that generates the tension necessary for success. That's bad enough, but almost all fiction is only a story, its pain the routine anguish of art; imagine then the level of anxiety generated by a story that must become real, whose readers must become its characters!

Up to this point it had all been Bolsover's doing, but now it was Kitty who took the lead. No doubt she was infected by her husband's tension and the increasingly heated events of the story; perhaps she did indeed come to see herself as Anna, and Bolsover as Ralph. All this is possible, but whatever the reason, at its climax Kitty took the story from Bolsover's hands and made it into something quite different, something unplanned and unwritten.

After so much reluctance, so many indications of anxiety, shyness, and fear, Bolsover had never imagined that his wife would show passion, let alone violence. He had thought he understood her inmost nature, and knew it to be essentially delicate and gentle. But the woman who lay with him that night was quite new, and driven by something close to fury. She uttered noises that he had never before heard from a human being, cries that were purely animal, and obviously outside her conscious control. Sometimes these sounds were not unlike the baying of a wolf. At other moments she made a lower sound, a kind of growling. She tore at his skin, her nails drawing blood from his arms and chest, and toward the end she began to sob and laugh at once, her body racked with enormous shudders. Finally she lay exhausted, gasping and crying, tears pouring down her cheeks, her body so hot that she might have had a deadly fever.

Bolsover's astonishment at his wife's behavior caused him some difficulty. In the first moment, feeling her nails on his skin and hearing the strange sounds she made, he thought she had gone mad and was attempting to do him harm; but as she threw aside the bedclothes and climbed upon him, he knew her intention without doubt.

There had been no passion in his childhood, and he had come to think of it as dangerous and absurd; wasn't control of one's emotions the first essential of civilized life? But Kitty's fury had been generated by his own massive and deliberate effort to upset her mental state, and he knew he must accept the consequences. He did accept, though he did not understand. That first time, she shocked him, no doubt of that. It was only later, as he contemplated the transformed relations between himself and his wife, that he began slowly to feel the greatest delight about the whole thing.

He had thought—no, he had *assumed,* for there had been very little thought about it—that Kitty possessed the character she displayed to others, that her inmost nature was inherently reserved, nervous, ordered, and delicate. As far as he was concerned, that was Kitty, and that was everything she was. But now she had thoroughly exploded his assumption, and his attitude to her was revealed as foolish and superior. A quite different Kitty, a woman of physical strength and ferocious passion, had been hidden within her all along, and by some miracle, for those few minutes, she was released from captivity, and showed him an utterly new and astonishing persona.

His fussing around her, he now knew, had been harmful. He had encouraged her to see herself as a fragile doll, even as a kind of simpleton, a person to be protected. What a fool he was! His role, he now knew, was to *enable* her passion, to assist its release. From that moment onward Bolsover felt a new respect for his wife, and a desire to understand her complexity more fully. She had access to things absolutely unknown to him: raw feeling and transforming emotion. He must disregard the past few months and everything he thought he knew; he must begin again, and learn to love her in quite a different way. Yes, that's what he would do.

It was an hour before Kitty calmed down. She fell asleep enfolded in his arms, thereby creating in him highly agreeable feelings of love, which went a good way toward calming the confusion that still whirled about in his mind.

The following morning Bolsover discovered that his successful strategy was to have another unforeseen outcome. Having achieved its purpose, he had assumed his storytelling would end; but when he spoke casually to Kitty in those terms, she was dismayed. "Darling! Ravensdale can't possibly end! It must continue! A story can't just stop in the middle like that! What about all those people—Anna and Ralph, the mayor, the miller, the colonel? Oh, I must know what happens to them! The story must continue *forever*!"

Of course it must! Again Bolsover was forced to recognize his own stupidity. Now that she had said it, it was obvious that Kitty would want the story to continue. She drew confidence and well-being from regular patterns. He had now established, with much thought and effort, a new pattern of behavior that delighted her. *Of course* she would want it to continue! Had he not told her himself that the story need not end?

But the thought was daunting. It had gone well, it was true, but writing Ravensdale had been a demanding task. He had got behind with his duties at Butler's; one or two people had already expressed surprise that certain important documents were not yet available. Could he, an ordinary man and no artist, continue writing that story at such intensity *forever*? I cannot do it, he said to himself. Then he had an idea.

"Darling Kitty," he said, "I would like to continue the story, but it's a considerable piece of work, and I can't do it on my own. I simply cannot. But I think we could do it *together*. We could talk about it together, and share new ideas, and make it up as we went along. Ravensdale would be our special place, a kind of garden that we can make just the way we want it, just as you do with your own garden."

For a moment Bolsover thought Kitty would reject the proposal. She looked at him with her head on one side and her eyes narrowed, but then she said, clapping her hands as she often did when excited, "Yes! Let's do it! We'll write it together!"

The key word, Bolsover afterward knew, had been "garden." Kitty was strongly attracted to the creation of an imaginary world in which anything could happen—anything at all—and she immediately began to contribute excellent ideas to the story. Ravensdale became a joint production, each installment no longer planned and written but talked into being, emerging on the spur of the moment, in the manner of a game of Consequences.

Kitty might say, "At first, Ralph could see no way out of his prison. The door was secured, and bars covered the window."

To this Bolsover might respond, after a moment's thought, by saying, "But Ralph, never daunted, had searched the cell and found a file that had been hidden in the mattress by a previous occupant. He was only waiting for a quiet moment before filing through the bars and running off like the wind."

"But wait," says Kitty. "Who's this at the window? Whose delicate hands are those that grasp the bars?"

"It's Anna," says Bolsover. "And at the sight of her, Ralph begins to saw at the bars like a man possessed, in order to reach his beloved—"

"In a moment the bars are cut clean through—"

"He leaps through and grasps her in his arms——"

"She kisses him——"

"His clothes fall from his body——"

And so forth. A great many of their joint episodes ended in such a manner, and their storytelling—which some will regard as a mighty childish activity for a pair of grown-up people—became a great source of passion and amusement to them, and utterly transformed their relationship. The Ravensdale story grew many new branches during the subsequent sixteen years, some of them following the conventions of romantic fantasy, others diverting in directions that were often comic, erotic, or simply bizarre. No longer was Ravensdale a burden to Bolsover; no longer did he worry about the conventions of fiction, the efficacy of the story's language, the appropriateness of plot, or how the story should end, since that question would never arise. And meantime, lying beside him was his delicious and remarkable wife, who had been liberated by the magic of his words.

6

Silence. The ship still as a house. Someone tugging his arm. Bolsover wakes—it's the tall birder, what's his name, Wilson—and the lounge is otherwise empty. He is folded, stiffened, his right arm surely never to move again—but no—with an effort, a sharp pain, Bolsover stands.

"I'm sorry. I must have—"

"My dear fellow," says Wilson, steadying him. "What a night, eh?"

"Yes, indeed," says Bolsover. "My notebook, my cases—"

"Right here, old chap."

"Thank you so much." Bolsover slots out the natty handles, takes a step—yes, he can walk—and follows Wilson from the saloon, his cases trundling at his heels. There's a sailor at the door, a cheery fellow, and the two men clatter up a ramp and at last reach steady, immobile land. For a moment Bolsover's legs are insecure, but on they go, up another ramp, along a corridor, through a ticket office with photographs of ships on seas of brilliant blue, and out into a calm and sunny morning. Bolsover looks this way and that. Nobody about. They stop and look back.

"Well," says Wilson, "there we are."

The little ship is securely moored, silent and empty. Her name is printed in bold white letters on her bow: PROVIDENCE. Bolsover laughs, and Wilson looks inquiringly at him.

"Oh," says Bolsover, "it's just the ship's name. It's funny."

There's no sign of movement behind the windows of her bridge, but he waves just in case, for he owes the captain a salute.

A taxi waits. Bolsover turns to Wilson, thanks him for his help and his company. "I'm at the Alpha Hotel, if you'd care for a drink sometime."

"Jolly good," says Wilson. "I'm for the bus." He sets off toward a line of coaches and the winding queue of birders, telescopes at the port.

"Cheer up, mate," says the taxi driver. People say that to Bolsover from time to time, mistaking his introspection for gloom. "Today is the first day of the rest of your life."

"I just want to go to the Alpha Hotel," says Bolsover, who occasionally wishes he had the capacity for violence.

"No worries, mate," says the taxi driver.

The green cases having been slung in and the lid slammed down, the taxi is away up a steep, narrow street, away from the din of gulls, the fishing boats and their clutter, all those ropes and nets, floats and pots— which are not pots at all, but traps, wicker traps for catching slow, primitive creatures who never learn but just keep crawling in. Up the High Street goes the taxi, shops passing close on each side; a window draped in maroon silk; a display of straw hats and beach balls; home-baked pies;

fresh fruit; special offer on skate today; Murdoch's, the estate agent you can trust. Under a pretty archway with a clock, then left and right to a square of large houses in gray stone, solid houses built a hundred years ago by people with money. The taxi turns into a gravel forecourt and stops beside the large green and gold signboard of the Alpha Hotel, to the lower edge of which is hooked a small panel: NO VACANCIES.

Bolsover pays off the taxi and drags his cases up five stone steps and through a pair of double doors. Nobody at the reception desk. Ring the bell. It's early yet.

A minute passes, and then a plump dark-haired woman bustles out of an office behind the counter and looks him up and down. "Mr. Bolsover," she says. She's middle-aged, a woman with a black suit, white blouse, high heels, and the look of being in charge.

"Quite right," says Bolsover. "Good morning."

"Welcome to the Alpha Hotel. I'm Mrs. Konstantinopoulos."

"Good morning, Mrs.—"

"Konstantinopoulos."

"Konstantinopoulos. Yes. Good morning."

She consults a file and begins to fill in a form. "I heard the wind in the night," she says, not looking up. "A lively crossing you had of it, I expect." Several large rings on plump fingers, turquoise and agate, semi-precious.

"We did indeed. A marvelous crossing."

Mrs. Konstantinopoulos looks up. "Marvelous?"

"The captain invited me to the bridge. I saw the storm from there."

Mrs. Konstantinopoulos raises her eyebrows. "Fair enough, Mr. Bolsover, if that's your sort of thing." She passes him the form. "I've filled in your details. If you'd just sign."

She has the rustling voice of a smoker and the trace of an accent that might have originated in the east end of London. She knows who I am, thinks Bolsover as he signs the form, but of course she'd have to know something, wouldn't she, since she's running the show. *Mrs. Kon-stan-*

tin-op-ou-los. Wasn't there a Greek politician by that name? I believe there was. *Kon-stan-tin-op-ou-los.* There's a flavor of something in the air. Someone's frying bacon. *Konstantinopoulos.* Got it.

"Here's your key. Room thirty-one. When you're ready, would you care for some breakfast, Mr. Bolsover?"

"Thank you, Mrs. Konstantinopoulos. I would indeed." Perfect.

"People find it easier to call me Mrs. K," she says, giving Bolsover a smile of a brisk, professional sort.

"Mrs. K," he says, with a tiny bow. Some you lose, but it's important to make the effort.

She finishes her paperwork, shuts the file, places her hands upon it and looks at him directly. "Now, Mr. Bolsover, your friends in London will have told you that we're accustomed to people in your situation. We keep ourselves to ourselves. We aim to be sociable without asking any more questions than we have to. Our guests just tell us whatever they want to tell us, and if anyone gets too inquisitive, Mr. Bolsover, I'm sure you'll tip me the wink."

"Thank you," says Bolsover, nodding. "That's fine with me."

"Live and let live is our motto," she says.

"I know exactly what you mean, Mrs. K," says Bolsover.

"Good! I'm sure you'll be happy here for as long as you need to stay. We'll have a little get-together in the residents' sitting room at six this evening—a glass of wine, a chance to meet our other guests, nothing formal. Does that suit you?"

"That's fine. Thank you."

"I'm afraid there's no lift, but Ronnie will take your bags." She steps to the door at the rear of the reception area and calls sharply, *"Ronnie!"*

Ronnie, a young man with a sultry look, strolls into the foyer and tests the weight of one of Bolsover's cases. "Heavy, these are," he says.

"Books," Bolsover says. "Books tend to be heavy."

"Must be a lot of them."

"You're right."

"Ronnie," says Mrs. K, "you just get on and take Mr. Bolsover's cases up to thirty-one."

"Have to be one at a time," says Ronnie.

"I'm so sorry, Mr. Bolsover," says Mrs. K. *"Get on with it, Ronnie."*

"I tell you what," Bolsover says, "if I'm going to call you Mrs. K, you ought to call me Mr. B."

Mrs. K is momentarily disconcerted, then delighted. "Mr. B!" she says, clapping her hands. "Mrs. K and Mr. B! What a good idea!"

Bolsover follows Ronnie up three flights of stairs and along a crooked corridor. The hotel smells of ancient dust, and its floors creak.

"Here you are," Ronnie says, stopping and leaning against the wall. "Do you want the other case?"

"If it wouldn't be too much trouble, Ronnie," says Bolsover. "That would be very kind."

A hotel room is unfamiliar, unlike most of the rooms in one's life, thinks Bolsover, looking at the blank door of room thirty-one. One enters with a little caution, wondering if something unpleasant might scuttle across the floor. He inserts the key, turns it carefully, opens the door—and here is a fine, untroubled room, large and light, its ceiling high, its window large.

Bolsover crosses to the window, throws it open, and discovers a view across the harbor toward a sandy bay. In the far distance is a rocky spur and a tall lighthouse: indeed, that's Handsome Point. *That little spark shines through and shows us the way home.* Handsome Point!

Yes, I could live here, says Bolsover to himself, hurrying here and there, trying the bed, opening cupboards, discovering the en suite facilities, white tiles, perfectly clean. This place has everything necessary for comfortable existence. It is a commodious room with a splendid view. It has a desk, a telephone, a swivel chair, and a folder filled with the headed notepaper of the Alpha Hotel.

He sits in the chair, rotating slowly. *Instructions for occupants in the event of fire*. I could live here with my books, turning whenever I'm bored to the window and that lovely view of Handsome Light. Certainly I could. Every evening I'll stroll on the promenade, chatting to people I've gotten to know. I'll make friends with the fishmonger and the newsagent. There will be an *Island Clarion* or some such, the sort of paper that covers the activities of the bridge club, the residents' association, and the society for the preservation of whatever, which I might one day join for the sake of civic duty. In due course I'll meet the canon and the councillor, the doctor and the plumber, and after six months or a year I will have become rooted, my roots spreading down into this curiously reddish earth until I can say—dare I say such a thing? Why not? Well, then: until I can say I'm quite at home. This is my room!

Bolsover gets up and stands again at the window. A woman is pushing a wheelchair across the lawn below. After a moment she glances up at him, then turns away and goes on pushing. Can one person feel the gaze of another, as that little courser might feel the stare of all those long lenses? Surely it's impossible, but she looked up, and straight at my window. The wheels of the chair have left parallel lines in the damp grass, her footmarks between them like notes on a stave, a woman with short gray hair, a strong-looking woman, pushing a man who lolls in his chair. Is she a nurse? No, she's his wife, certainly. No uniform, and there's something about the way she moves, her carefulness—yes, it's the way a woman pushes a baby. The man is wrapped in a heavy coat, scarf, gloves, and a woolly hat, his head nodding with the movement of the chair.

The woman stops and says something to her husband, bending her head close to his. He makes no visible response, and she thrusts the chair ahead.

"Brought your other case, mate." Ronnie again.

"Thank you, Ronnie," says Bolsover. "You're so kind. I'll be down for breakfast in a minute."

"No bother."

Bolsover turns back to the window. The woman has gone but the grass has retained her track. Beyond the garden the ground falls away toward the sea, now gleaming innocently in the sunlight. He takes off his jacket and shoes. I'll lie down for a moment. The bed is really very comfortable.

Some hours later he wakes, finding the room in shadow, Handsome Light a slim black pencil standing against the lowering sun, and knows that this room can become his home.

7

From their earliest meetings Kitty had shown even more interest in the garden than she had in the house, speaking with great excitement about the possibilities for its redesign and the introduction of new species. On their marriage, of course, she immediately assumed ownership. Bolsover had not the slightest objection, thinking that the garden might do her a great deal of good; she seemed to find it easier to relate to flowers, shrubs, and trees than to people, with the possible exception of himself and her two old friends. In time her principal interest wove itself naturally into their life, finding an expansive context in the story of Ravensdale (a valley soon populated with rare and intriguing species) and another in Bolsover's meandering inquiry into his "big questions." His wife's fierce sexual passion must surely have been related to the urgency that the crocuses and snowdrops displayed as they thrust through the hard earth into the chilling airs of March; and her beauty—well, wasn't she made of the same stuff as a delicate, wind-tossed flower, and didn't all beauty have the same fundamental purpose, to attract the bee?

Bolsover's own duties in the garden were merely to labor and admire. He carried out the heavier and more routine tasks and in time acquired some competence with spade, lawn mower, and shears. Only during the final stages of Kitty's illness did he assume full responsibility for the creation and maintenance of what was to be her last garden; its design, of course, remained her own.

Every summer Kitty took up her sketchbook and began a new garden design for the following spring, starting with pen-and-ink sketches of individual plants that had caught her attention. These she tinted with watercolor and eventually incorporated into a set of four panoramas, each showing the garden at a particular season of the year. She then drew up a planting program, each stage being carefully recorded as it was completed. Once her vision had been established, she required the garden to conform, and spent many hours ensuring that it did so.

Kitty told Bolsover that she was concerned not only with color but with line and movement. "A garden must take your eye from one feature to another. It must never be static. It has a story to tell, and it must keep the story moving along through the seasons."

Winter she called "the neglected season," telling him that it was forgotten by most gardeners. "You see such horrid, bedraggled gardens in January, but there's not the slightest reason why a garden should lack interest just because it's raining. I really can't abide sunshine gardeners! Don't they know what can be done with foliage? Don't they know about contrast and shadow, and the effect of a well-trained branch against the gray of the sky?"

The garden became Kitty's natural place, in which she could achieve complete peace of mind. Bolsover, waiting beside his wheelbarrow, liked to study her as she pricked out a row of tiny plants, or paused, pruning shears in hand and concentration on her face, before making an adjustment whose effect was to him invisible.

"Darling," she would say, amused by his ignorance, "I'm seeing the effect in my mind's eye. I'm seeing the garden as it will be in April, and watching it change as the months go by. Do you understand? It's not like looking at a picture; it's like watching a film in your head."

Kitty taught him to look not only at the color and shape of a flower but the style and shape of the whole plant—the geometry of its leaves and stems, the forms and textures of its foliage, the various ways in which it responded to wind, weather, and light. She told him he mustn't be dazzled by the features that first caught his eye. "You must look beyond first impressions, darling. The flowers of the Japanese anemone, as you can see, are immediately attractive—either white or pink, with yellow anthers—but you must also consider the *architecture* of that plant, which is special to it, and influences both its placement and the choice of neighboring plants."

Designing a garden, Kitty explained to Bolsover, was not unlike designing a house. "The garden is one of the most important places in which people live. It must be responsive to the needs of its occupiers, but must also possess its own integrity. It must contain surprises and moments of special beauty, but it must also be unified—that's the biggest challenge, because a garden changes all the time. The dimensions, colors, and textures of each element must be considered separately and together, and in the light of the passing seasons."

From these lectures, and his work in her garden, Bolsover learned to appreciate the quality of his wife's art, and to follow the focus of her garden as it changed from month to month: whatever the time of year, there was always a feature to which Kitty's garden drew one's attention. He was impressed by her considered approach to her gardening, and enjoyed her instructional sessions despite being unable to remember their details for more than a few moments. She in turn, when instructing him, was both delighted by his close attention and amused by his astonishing blindness to the beauty of the natural world; all in all, Kitty's horticultural lessons were an aspect of their life from which they both obtained much enjoyment.

In the last few weeks of her life—by then Kitty was too ill to leave the house—they worked together on a design that included all the flowers and shrubs that she regarded as particular favorites. Sitting together at her bedroom window, they looked down into the garden, Kitty working at her sketches.

"These are the ones I really love," she said. "Darling, these are the plants I'd like to keep forever and ever," and Bolsover took her words as a command.

Among her preferences were several varieties of rose, including Madame Gregoire Staechelin and Wedding Day. She adored the hydrangea, she told him, and her last garden would contain all three varieties: mophead, lace cap, and climber. Other favorites were buddleia, mallow, hypericum, scabious, and mock orange, and at the top of her list was *Campsis grandiflora*.

Every summer she had encouraged this opulent climber to spread up the side of the house and across the garage roof, and forbade Bolsover to assault it with the pruning shears. Its speed of growth was remarkable, as was the strength of its tendrils, which regularly split the slates of the roof and levered sections of guttering from their brackets. Kitty pointed out with delight that *grandiflora* did not know when to stop and took not the slightest notice of the seasons. "It's got the outrageous cheek to keep flowering into September."

One August evening, in the middle of a thunderstorm, she called Bolsover into the garden to show him a marvelous trick: the brilliant orange trumpets of *grandiflora*, uplifted as if playing a grand march, were filling with rain. As she and Bolsover watched, each flower filled until its weight bowed it gently down, whereupon it emptied itself, returned to its former position, and began again to fill. They watched this delightful slow-motion ballet for some time, until at last Bolsover suggested that they go indoors, take off their soaked clothing, and go to bed—which Kitty did with eagerness, despite its being nowhere near the usual time.

No other acquaintance of Kitty's would have associated the flagrant trumpets of *grandiflora* with that reserved and delicate young woman, but Bolsover had discovered, through his intimate relations with his utterly adorable wife, her possession of a vital power that he now thought essential to all life.

H*ow did I get here? What caused me? Where did I come from? Where did I begin?* Those had been the first questions he had noted as a boy, and he had worked hard at them; but they had remained unanswered all these years. Now he saw that he might make a considerable leap toward answering them.

Bolsover's reading had informed him, of course, of the subtle ways in which some of the tiny, random changes that occur in DNA are advantaged by a particular environment, and others are not. He had learned that this mechanism, repeated an infinity of times over millions of years, had created the astonishing variety and abundance of the living world. However, for a long time he had thought natural selection a dry truth, too dry to be entirely convincing. Yes, it worked with the precision of a clock, but somehow it wasn't quite enough; life, after all, isn't just mechanical.

And then, out of the blue, Kitty had displayed for him the element that was missing from his model. He felt desire—of course he did—but he was, after all, an Englishman with an ingrained habit of self-control. For much of the time, Kitty was at least as reserved as he, but when they were making love, there was a point at which her passion burst out with something close to animal savagery. It was quite astonishing; he might even have called it miraculous, had he not mistrusted that word. His urgent wife displayed to him the raw power of the sexual imperative, which he now realized as the essential driver of all life. Without desire, he argued to himself, the elegant mechanism of natural selection could not begin; without desire there would be no coupling, no replication of genes, no refreshment of the genetic mix, none of the tiny changes that allow the continuous and automatic process of adaptation and improvement. There must be desire, or humanity would quietly die away.

Bolsover knew that his wife had granted him a privileged insight into a fundamental of life, and that insight changed the direction of his thinking, enabling him to generate a good many new questions. Wasn't it possible that sexual desire was in some subtle way the cause of most of the complexities of modern society? Wasn't our restlessness, our apparently compulsive need to keep on making and changing things, to struggle for and against power—wasn't all this driven by desire? Did desire drive not only sexual activity but work, politics, art, philosophy, even gardening? And how did love fit into all this? Ah, love—it wasn't quite the same thing as desire, was it? He wanted his wife, certainly, but he also cared for her, felt for her, adored her.

Bolsover's thinking, that had for so long been stalled by the impossibility of answering his large questions, sailed away into this new territory entirely as a result of the sexual urgency of his wife. In the eager flare of the flowers of *Campsis grandiflora*, Bolsover was now certain, Kitty instinctively recognized something of herself. We have named nature cleverly, dividing and subdividing it for good reasons, but all species are surely driven by the same powerful force—by need, by wanting, by desire. Bolsover now understood that fact, and recognized in Kitty and her garden the same urgent strands.

His new thinking, his books and notebooks, his work at Butler's, Kitty and their nighttime stories, their house, her garden—these were the dimensions of Bolsover's life for those sixteen years. He quite forgot about his parents, the old Vauxhall, the railway, all that; he had started afresh with Kitty, and those years of marriage to her were marvelous because unexpected, unsought, unearned. Year after year their happiness continued, and when Kitty began to complain of backache, they were not unduly concerned; such things come and go, after all, and everyone gets aches and pains. But the X-rays frightened them, and not only the grainy shadows on the film but the charming manners of the consultant, by which the bad news was smoothly confirmed to Kitty and her husband.

By that time Bolsover's consciousness of his own ignorance had become urgent, and he had begun to read science and philosophy. He knew now that "cause" is a tricky notion, some denying that such a concept can be identified at all. David Hume, a nice enough man by all accounts, had presented the awkward and seemingly undeniable assertion that a causal relation is not proven by the fact that one thing follows another. Go down this road, as Bolsover did, and you discover that almost everything becomes a question of probability. Such and such might be the case, or it might not; it all depends. He read Hodges on *Basic Concepts of Probability and Statistics,* Monod's *Chance and Necessity,* and Lewis's *Beyond Chance and Necessity,* comprehending them with some difficulty, but none of them gave him the slightest insight into the reasons for his wife's illness, or rather, the reasons why it was Kitty in particular who had been chosen for affliction.

Meanwhile, he and Kitty moved their bedroom downstairs and had another bathroom built on the ground floor. By then she could walk only three or four paces without resting, and these modifications made life easier. Didn't that prove the existence of cause and effect? They had moved the bed downstairs and things got easier for Kitty: point proven. But no, you couldn't quite see the vital connection—the rope or chain that surely must link one thing to another, if causality exists. *Everything must surely have a cause. If something has no cause, why should it happen?*

Watching the increasingly frail hands of his wife as she painted and drew, Bolsover became closely familiar with the fine detail of *grandiflora* and the rest of her favorites, and for the remainder of his life he was to seek them out in parks and gardens, recognizing them with joy and pain. In her last weeks Kitty's commitment to her garden allowed them to look beyond the coming winter. "Spring and summer will come again," Kitty told him, "although it may seem impossible now. Spring will come because it always does, because it's natural. One day, my darling, the mornings will begin to get lighter, the evenings longer, and you'll need the extra light, because there will be lots of work in the garden."

And indeed, when spring came, there was much to be done, just as she had said. Bolsover completed the garden that they had designed together, and for several years maintained it as best he could. He welcomed the work, since it enabled him to submerge himself entirely in his memories of her. In the garden he could speak to her as if she were still present, and seemed to hear her voice as they worked together among the flowers and shrubs. The furry gray leaves of *Stachys byzantina* she had called lamb's ears. She told him that fuchsia flowers "dangled like earrings." As for penstemon—"Oh, it's got such lovely little mouths, such soft little mouths—can't you see?" As he touched and tended the flowers in her garden, Bolsover felt his love for Kitty with such intensity that he had only to look up to see her walking across the lawn in that pretty dress of white cotton, the one with a pattern of tiny blue flowers around the hem—but he did not look up. He kept his head bent and continued with his tasks, for he knew that imagination must not be confused with reality.

8

The residents' sitting room at the Alpha Hotel is a place of plump furniture and gloomy, indistinct prints.

"Good evening, everyone," says Mrs. K in an official voice. "I'd like to introduce our new guest, Mr. James Bolsover."

Bolsover and Mrs. K begin to circulate, and he is first introduced to the woman with the wheelchair.

"Mr. and Mrs. Morgan," says Mrs. K. "Mr. Bolsover."

"I'm Arabella," Mrs. Morgan says. "This is my husband, Leonard. I'm afraid he can't speak."

She's a big, strong woman, Mrs. Arabella Morgan, a determined-looking woman.

"Hello," says Bolsover, shaking her hand. The man in the wheelchair is wrapped in a rug and appears to be asleep.

"This is Kevin Brand," says Mrs. K, introducing a youngish man, short and slim, in a gray suit.

"How do you do," says Bolsover.

"I'm well," says the young man, his gaze flickering briefly over Bolsover before seeking something more interesting.

"Mrs. Allcard and Mrs. Walters."

"Hello," says Bolsover. The two elderly women smile and shake his hand delicately. They have an air of absolute innocence.

"How nice to have some new blood," says Mrs. Allcard. "We're all fearfully bored with one another."

"Really, Margaret," says Mrs. Walters, wrinkling her brow at her friend.

"Colonel Tapp." A white mustache, gray eyes, a deeply lined and leathery skin that has seen a great deal of sun, a firm handshake, a curt nod of the head.

"Miss Matthews."

"Hello." She's a young woman with a nervous tic in her right eye.

"Mr. and Mrs. Harwich." A large dark-suited man who thinks well of himself and looks as if he's something in the city. He grasps Bolsover's hand too firmly, but his wife smiles charmingly.

"Last but not least, Mr. Firth."

"Call me Joe. Everyone does." He could be a builder, this man, with his strong frame, big hands, and capable air.

Having completed his circulation, Bolsover returns to Mrs. Morgan and her husband.

"This morning," says Mrs. Morgan, "I believe I saw you while we were taking our early stroll. Weren't you at your window?"

"Oh. I was admiring the view. I hope you didn't think—"

"It's a fine view, isn't it? And a fine place altogether, this island. If you like islands, of course."

Her husband stirs a little and murmurs something that sounds like "arkey, arkey."

"Poor Lennie," says Mrs. Morgan. "He's trying to say 'car keys.' His car is what he misses most. He sulked for months when his doctor told him he'd have to stop driving."

She bends over her husband and opens her empty hands before him. "Car keys all gone, Lennie. No more car keys."

"I see," says Bolsover. Mrs. Morgan stands straight-backed, one hand resting on her husband's shoulder. He must say something, although it's meaningless. "Your husband's illness is evidently serious."

"Yes. Such things happen. One carries on."

"One does," says Bolsover.

"Do people call you Jim? Or Jimmy? Actually, by the look of you, I think you'd prefer James."

"It depends," says Bolsover. "Do people call you Bella?"

She laughs. "Certainly they do. Who could object? Bella, bellissima! I was that beautiful person, a long time ago. But you're somehow not a Jim, nor a Jimmy. I can see that now I look at you. I'm not sure 'James' quite fits either."

"Nor am I," says Bolsover. "Most people just call me Bolsover."

"Do they now? How odd. Bolsover—well, I suppose it's not so bad." She considers him. "It rather suits you, in fact. Bolsover. It's a sensible-sounding name, and you look a sensible sort of man."

What a sudden lot of folk. Some of these people—certainly Colonel Tapp, Mrs. Allcard, Mrs. Walters, Joe Firth, and Arabella Morgan—have every appearance of virtue, but there is something unsettling about Kevin Brand, who slipped from the room directly after his introduction, and that awkward, nervous girl, Miss Matthews—what's wrong with her?

"Mr. Bolsover," says Mrs. Allcard, appearing at his elbow, "are you by any chance a bridge player?"

"I'm afraid not."

"Oh, dear. Perhaps you'd like to learn? We have a little school on a Wednesday afternoon."

"Or there's the gardening club," says Mrs. Walters. "We have an allotment."

"I don't know much about gardening either, I'm afraid," says Bolsover.

Leonard Morgan is opening and closing his lips in the slow, deliberate manner of a goldfish. Bolsover takes an unobtrusive grip on the back of a chair. As a boy, when thinking of some large and confusing problem, he occasionally experienced a sensation of falling, and in the last few months, from time to time, that unsteady feeling has returned.

I might begin a clandestine campaign against bric-a-brac, thinks Bolsover while eating a pork chop in the Alpha's restaurant. Dim brown prints; lace-edged napkins; lurid napkin rings, place mats, and coasters printed with galleons; dried flowers; baroque candlesticks; a coffeepot ringed with red roses, sauceboat ditto; a condiment set with bluebirds in the Chinese style; and beside the door an enormous umbrella stand made not just from an elephant's foot but a good part of the creature's leg. How many elephants have lost their legs for the drying of umbrellas? Each day, stealing about the Alpha, I might pocket just one item, beginning with the smaller objects, and, in the course of an evening stroll, drop each into the harbor; in a few days, the hotel would be a much better place.

Evidently Bolsover is overcoming his anxiety. He is cheered by his irritable fancy, and when he returns to his room, he makes straight for the window and opens the curtains eagerly on the lights of the town, the harbor, and of course the lighthouse, winking in its slow and regular way at the empty horizon. Standing guard, you might say, and never mind whether anyone's looking.

There is a soft knock at the door. It's Mrs. K, carrying a tray on which are two glasses of red wine.

"A quick call, Mr. B, just to make sure you're settled."

"That's extremely kind of you, Mrs. K. Do sit down."

They sit before the uncurtained window and Mrs. K lifts her glass. "Here's to you, Mr. B, and may you be happy here."

"Here's to you, too, Mrs. Konstantinopoulos."

She laughs gaily. "Mr. Bolsover! You might be Greek!"

"Whatever I am," says Bolsover, "I shall never be Greek."

"Never mind what you are. We're all sorts at the Alpha."

It's a zoo, Bolsover thinks. This place is a zoo. Very likely there are tigers here, and creatures that drop from the ceiling in the night.

"We have our special guests," says Mrs. K, "and in the season there are holidaymakers, of course. Oh, we're very popular—it's a very popular destination, the Alpha, one of the most popular on the island. It means 'first,' you know, 'alpha' does. I'm sure you know that already. It never occurred to me until one of my gentlemen pointed it out. Said he was a Greek scholar, though I had doubts myself, him being as English as you or me. Was his name Wrigley? I do believe it was."

Mrs. K looks suddenly sad. "But of course in winter the trade falls off, so we're glad of the arrangement we have with your people. It's nice to have regulars. When we took on the place, my husband was alive, of course. He was a nice man, Mr. K was. A nice *warm* man, an *affectionate* man, if you take my meaning, never mind the length of his name."

"I think I do take your meaning, Mrs. K."

"Here's to Mr. B, then."

"Here's to the pair of us. Mr. B and Mrs. K."

"Your health, Mr. B." She hesitates. "Have you spotted the alarm?"

"Alarm?"

From the bedside table Mrs. K lifts a small plastic box to which is attached an electrical cable. "Should anything happen—not that it will, of course—you only have to press this button. Any time of the day or night. Just press the button and somebody will come."

"I see."

"There are a number of security systems in the building—you needn't worry about them, except that we always test the alarm bells on a Saturday morning at ten o'clock."

"No sleeping late on a Saturday, then."

"You'll get a sharp awakening if you do, Mr. B."

After she's gone, he begins to remove his possessions from the trolley cases and allocate them to drawers and cupboards. All the Alpha's special guests, he supposes, have something in common: we're migrants, our histories are uncertain, we're someone else, we're beginning again. And how is that achieved? By fitting in, joining, belonging. A person must have a few friends, mustn't he? Some may be colleagues at work, of course. And how many people does one know well, in the course of a life? Less than a hundred, less than fifty, perhaps only half a dozen? How many good friends does one need, how many good companions? One, at least. One is sufficient, provided it's the right one. Will one of these residents become a good friend? I am not hopeful of that, thinks Bolsover, but you never know.

He sits on the edge of the bed for several minutes, gazing at the small pile of printed books he has brought, and the larger pile of his own notebooks. Long ago he and Kitty came to an agreement about his books, which were beginning to dominate the house. She suggested a maximum of five hundred, which was a good many fewer than he possessed at the time, but her limit usefully forced him to cull the dross from his collection. ("Cull the dross"—that was surely a bold colloquialism.) He began to keep a record of every book that he read—a short comment followed by a score between nought and ten: *Thoughtful, sombre work: 8.* At least a six was required if a book was to be considered for his permanent collection. *Greatly overrated: 2.* Of course he kept many of the major works of the great English and American novelists, the complete works of Shakespeare in a single convenient volume, much English poetry, and a number of novels in translation—Tolstoy, Dostoyevsky, Zola, Flaubert—all of which scored a straight ten. He wanted to keep the standard high, but a few works he preserved in a special category without grade. They might be oddities, but nevertheless he found them significant, and one must have a few irrational favorites. The amount of pleasure that Bolsover derived from his small and ever-changing library—and from his agonizing over selection and rejection—was very great. *The Quiet American—perhaps his best: 10.*

Since his possessions must fit into a pair of Sovereign Diamond Journeyman Trolley Cases, Bolsover has brought to the island only four items from his library, all highly technical. The four works are Durrett's *Brownian Motion and Martingales in Analysis,* Bohm's *Causality and Chance in Modern Physics,* D'Arcy's *Chance and Choice,* and an essay by Bernard Williams on the concept of "moral luck." Why has he chosen these particular titles, all of which he has already read at least once? No doubt there are reasons, if one can dig them out—unless, of course, his choice is *stochastic,* which is to say, randomly determined.

His knowledge of this relatively abstruse term pleases Bolsover. He stands before the mirror. Tomorrow this man has an appointment with a publisher of guidebooks who might employ him as an editor; he's a proper grown-up chap, gray-haired, respectable, and looks competent enough. I am a townie, a man past middle age, on a strange island; no doubt the place is inward-looking, and stands somewhat in the past. It would be pleasant to scythe corn, drive sheep, stride the hills, load and unload wagons, but I shall take what I can get. If I don't succeed in becoming an editor of guidebooks, no doubt I could put on a yellow vest, sweep the roads, and wheel one of those mobile bins, snapping up fagends with long-handled pincers—but I hope that I will find something better. It will not be an impossible life; it might, in time, be perfectly satisfactory. I have a space of my own, a room with a view. I'll soon get to know people, surely I will. Arabella Morgan, perhaps.

That night he lies awake for a long time, listening to the regular chimes of a church clock and watching the patterns thrown on the ceiling by the circling beams of the lighthouse at Handsome Point.

9

Bolsover's crisp new diary contains only a single entry: *Warren's. 9:30 A.M. Mr. Andrew Warren.* The address is at the far end of the town, only a mile away. It's a fine day and he'll walk. He turns to the mirror: here is a middle-aged man in a gray suit, well breakfasted, modest tie, hair brushed, shoes polished, holding a leather briefcase (empty except for his diary, but it looks the business). A responsible, capable-looking fellow? Certainly. He steps out into the fresh sea air and the calling gulls, down the twisting High Street, under the pretty arch with its clock, all the way down to the harbor. No sign of that fine little ship; no doubt it's too early for her. He looks out to sea. There's a smudge of smoke on the horizon—ah, that's her! *Make yourself known to the ship.* Oh, someday I will, I will!

He steps briskly along the promenade—what fine associations that word has—pretty girls and parasols, ice creams and fluttering kites! Why, the English seaside is such a jolly invention! The sea before us, a very decent beach, a dog barking at his young master, a light wind off the sea, small waves sliding quietly into the sand. There was that girl, the girl on wheels. He looks this way and that, since this wide pavement is just the place for her meditative twirls, her speeding circles—but there's no sign of her. Instead, there's someone hunched on a seat—no, in a wheelchair. Isn't it that man—what's his name—Lennie? Leonard Morgan. Yes, it's him. Bolsover stops beside the chair. "Good morning," he says, but the man seems asleep. Is he always asleep? No, because he asked for his car keys: *arkey, arkey*. Leonard Morgan is wearing a woolly hat pulled well down, a long scarf, gloves, a heavy coat, boots. No doubt Arabella dressed him, took him out and parked him here; and where is she? Bolsover looks this way and that, but there's nobody in sight save the boy with the dog.

"Odd," says Bolsover to the hunched man. "She surely can't be far away, your Arabella."

Leonard does not stir. Is he alive? Bolsover bends and listens: there is the lightest whimper of breath. How odd that the man is here alone. Bolsover hears a cry, looks up. Somebody is swimming toward the beach in a vigorous breaststroke. Oh, she's waving! It's Mrs. Morgan—my, how strongly she swims! She wades ashore, shakes a glittering arc of water from her hair, picks up a towel from the sand, strides up the beach—a big, strong woman, this Arabella.

"Good Lord! It's Jimmy Bolsover!" cries Mrs. Morgan.

"It's Bella," says Bolsover. "Stone the crows!" It's old-fashioned, that phrase, but I'm an old-fashioned man.

"Brrrr!" says Bella, toweling her hair. "It's fine exercise, swimming, and it doesn't do your knees like jogging does. You can go on for hours if you take it steady, if the water's not too rough, if it's not too cold. Autumn is when the water's warmest, you know."

"Yes," says Bolsover, who does know that.

"It's not warm now, mind you. Bloody freezing. I know it's a lazy kind of exercise, lolling in the sea like a bloody great porpoise, but it seems to work. I like it best in the late evening in summer, when the moon comes up. You can keep your course by the moon and the stars. Oh, they're constantly moving, I know, but not fast enough to matter. I swim out with Andromeda and come back by Vega."

"You just made that up," says Bolsover. "About Andromeda and whatnot."

She gives a big cheerful laugh. "Of course I did! I like to talk. So do you, if I'm not mistaken. A person can have too much silence."

She towels one leg, her foot on the step of Leonard's chair. "Yes," she says, "I like to swim westward down the track of the sun until it sets, and then turn. Following the sun out and back—it seems natural, somehow."

"I'm sure you're right," says Bolsover, amused. Then he remembers, looks at his watch. "Oh, I'm so sorry, I've got to go. I've got an interview for a job. Damn."

"A job! Well, best of luck, old Bolsover," she says, clasping his warm hand in her cold ones. "We'll pray for you, Lennie and I. Let us know how you get on. What sort of job is it?"

"Editing," says Bolsover. "Editing guidebooks to the English counties."

"Guidebooks!" She wraps her towel about her shoulders and strikes an attitude, pointing upward. "You see before you the Ashlar Tower, built in 1492 by Peter the Great. Note the grand arch and the convoluted arbuckles."

"That's the sort of thing, though I doubt the arbuckles, myself."

"It sounds good, though. Arbuckles!" She laughs again.

"You ought to go for the job, not me."

"Well, it's an idea. I might, if it wasn't for old Lennie." She turns and looks at the man in the chair.

"I really must be off."

"Off you go, then. We'll get back to the Alpha shortly, for a mid-morning snack—maybe some of their shortbread biscuits, specialty of the house, made no earlier than yesterday fortnight."

As Bolsover walks away, she's still talking. "Now, what's old Lennie been up to while I've been gone, you naughty man? Have you been good, or have you filled your wretched trousers again? That's it, tuck your scarf in and keep your hands to yourself."

Bolsover hurries along, humming the song about the man who broke the bank at Monte Carlo. He's no singer, but he can hear a song in his head as prettily as anyone: *And I've now such lots of money, I'm a gent! Yes, I've such lots of money, I'm a gent.* That woman Arabella—she's taking things head-on, and that's a good trick if you can work it. Keeping everything airborne with nothing but your own will, and the hell with doubt squatting in a corner, a little smile on its face—but never mind that. *You can hear the girls declare, he must be a millionaire.* And why should I feel so happy all of a sudden? Because it's good to be up and doing, to have a purpose, that's why.

Warren's Publications occupies a Victorian detached house in gray stone, its gravel drive bordered by rhododendrons. Bolsover presses a bell, hears it ringing deep within the house, waits for a minute or two, rings again. The door is partly opened and a woman looks out—blue cotton dress, glasses, a frown.

"Yes?"

"My name's Bolsover. To see Mr. Warren."

"Ah. Mr. Bolsover. Of course." She lets him in and offers him a seat in the hall. "Mr. Warren will see you shortly."

Bolsover places his briefcase on the floor and leans back. This might be an old-fashioned private school: red and white diamond floor tiles, a long rack of hooks bulging with coats, a portrait of the queen, many old photographs—men wearing striped caps, women on horseback, a sailing dinghy crewed by two girls. The house is cool and quiet.

Abruptly a tall, thin man emerges from the back of the hall, takes his coat from the rack, and heads for the front door. As he passes, he says, "Don't do it. That's my advice." A trace of an Irish accent.

"Don't do what?"

"Just don't." And the man's gone, the front door swinging shut behind him. All right, he's a joker, but what does he mean? Don't take the job? What?

"Mr. Bolsover?" The woman in the blue dress has appeared at the top of the stairs. "Would you come up?"

The room is small and crowded with stacks of files. In the center sits a man of sixty-five or more, his face fleshy and tanned, his glasses tinted orange. He leans across his desk to take Bolsover's hand. "Warren," he says.

"Bolsover," says Bolsover. Don't tinted glasses always give a man a shifty look? You'd think people would know that—but of course he might have a medical condition, a hypersensitivity of the rods and cones. Warren is wearing a suit of royal blue pinstripe, a tie of red and yellow; a colorful chap, certainly.

"Do sit down, my dear fellow. Excellent references, Mr. Bolsover!"

"Thank you." So they should be.

"Plenty of experience. Jolly good. Do the job standing on your head, I'm sure. You'll be starting on the west country. Do you know Somerset?"

"Porlock," Bolsover says. "A person from Porlock." Dear me, the things that leap into one's mind!

"Excellent!" says Mr. Warren. "The Bell in Porlock is one of our regulars—they take a full page, and another in the Christmas hotels supplement. Make sure Porlock gets a good write-up, yes? A steady customer is worth a few bob, and a county guide has to play to its advertisers, of course. The laws of commerce, Mr. Bolsover. Bottom line, eh? Bottom line!"

"Yes," says Bolsover. "Will there be much travel?"

"Travel?" Mr. Warren looks at Bolsover over his orange glasses.

"I mean, if I'm writing about Somerset—"

"Oh, *travel*! Good lord, you won't have to go anywhere! Books, Mr. Bolsover! The Internet! Don't forget, Andrew Warren isn't made of money. First lesson." He laughs, tapping his chest with one finger. "Warren's not made of money!"

"I see. And photographs—?"

"Hunt them out, Mr. Bolsover. Download them. Plenty about, if you care to look. Ask if you don't know. Don't pay for them—get a salesman to take one, if you like. Costs nothing, after all. Bottom line, remember. All photographers are scoundrels."

"Maps, too?"

"Oh, we do the maps in-house as well. Scan them in. Photocopier, scanner, download, whatever. Give them a bit of a tweak to get them into our house style—easy these days. Amazing what you can find on the Net. Anything you want to ask, feel free. You'll be busy. I'm looking to expand, and I need editors who can deliver the goods, deliver them on time. Professionals, Mr. Bolsover, people with brainpower. Did you know that the human brain is the most complex machine on earth?"

"Well—I suppose it might be."

"I'm moving into Europe. The market's wide open. France, Spain—" Mr. Warren waves his arms. "Warren's men reaching out toward the east. Think of it! Soon we'll be in Paris, Milan, Lisbon. One day, Mr. Bolsover, it'll be Moscow and Vladivostok. You'll see."

"I don't have any languages—apart from English, of course."

"Good Lord, we only publish in English! The world's language, Mr. Bolsover, the world's language!"

Mr. Warren adopts a serious look and leans forward in his chair. "Well, then. Any questions?"

"Where would I be working? May I have a look?"

"My dear fellow! Jill will take you down." He turns toward the door and shouts, "Jill! Jill!"

She shouts from somewhere distant, "I'm busy!"

"Wretched woman. Thinks she owns the place. Take you down myself. They call it the Warren, of course. They would, wouldn't they? Forget who's in charge, most of them. Who signs the checks? That's the question. Come this way, Mr. Bolsover."

The door at the back of the hall opens on stone steps down to a dark passage, thence to a cavernous room lit by yellowing bulbs. Boxes of guidebooks stand along the rear wall. The filing cabinets have overflowed onto the floor, and every corner is stacked with maps, books, papers, and magazines. Three people are seated before yellowing word processors: the tall Irishman that Bolsover saw earlier, a young woman in a bright red dress, and a plump round-faced man with glasses who looks ill.

"New recruit," Mr. Warren announces. "Mr. James Bolsover. He'll be doing Somerset for a start. On the left, Molly Moon. In the middle, Sam Kavanagh. On the right, Adrian Douglas."

"I thought I told you," says Sam the Irishman to Bolsover.

"What did you tell him?" asks Mr. Warren.

"Not to bother," says Sam.

Warren turns to Bolsover. "Take no notice of Sam. He's a would-be comedian."

"Tell you what," says Sam. "You get along out of it, Warren, and we'll look after Mr. Bolsover."

"One of these days, Sam," says Mr. Warren, straightening his tie with a fierce jerk. He turns to Bolsover. "If they cause you any trouble, just call me. Otherwise I'll see you Monday week, Mr. Bolsover. I sent you the terms. Sign the form. That's all, and give it to Jill. Anything you want, just let her know. As for you, Sam Kavanagh, don't you forget who signs the checks." And Mr. Warren departs.

"Have a seat, James," says Sam.

"Warren!" says Molly Moon. "There you have him in all his glory, the little twerp."

"A third-rate scoundrel, our Warren, and lacks the killer touch, so we bully him." This is Adrian Douglas, plump, a little pallid.

"What do you know about Warren, Mr. Bolsover?" Molly again.

"Very little. He's a publisher of guidebooks and wants an editor. That's all I know."

"True enough. The devil lies in the detail," she says. "He publishes *Warren's Guides* to Cornwall, Devon, Dorset, Somerset, Pembrokeshire—all the holiday counties and a few specials—the River Thames, the Norfolk Broads, that sort of thing. Sells advertising to hotels, holiday cottages, and whatnot. We put the things together. He calls us editors." She laughs. "It's a courtesy title, you might say. We do everything ourselves. Write the copy, scrounge the pics and maps, paste up the pages, organize the printing. We do everything except sell the advertising and post the guides out."

"And why is Warren a scoundrel?"

"Ah," says Adrian. "It's all in the numbers. He's got a dozen salesmen—"

"Poor sad creatures they are," says Sam. "Holes in their shoes."

"They go round the hotels touting for adverts. What they say is, our guides are on sale all over the place. Only five hundred quid for a whole page. Wonderful value. They'll quote you an impressive circulation figure—"

"Fifty thousand, they'll say," says Molly. "How many do you think we actually print?"

"I see," says Bolsover. "Not as many as that, I guess."

"Three thousand if you're lucky," says Adrian. "Enough to send three copies to every advertiser and a few more to local shops and TICs."

"Tourist Information Centers," says Molly.

"You're so helpful, Molly," says Sam. "You're just a naturally good person. Now the question is, Mr. James Bolsover, are you willing to work for a crook? Do you have a conscience? Are you a religious chap? Do you really believe prison works? How about the short, sharp shock? Good idea or not? Get beaten as a child, did you? If so, did you enjoy it?"

"Or are you," says Adrian, "an ordinary guy just like the rest of us, needs a bit of cash, job not too demanding, time off when you want it, muck in together, get the work done, take the money, and let someone else worry about the morals?"

"Well, there's a question," says Bolsover, who feels quite relaxed now.

"We wait with bated breath for your reply," says Molly.

"Bated breath?" Sam shakes his head. "Bit of a cliché, Molly."

Bolsover laughs. "I think it's worth a try," he says.

"Wait," says Adrian, waving a finger at Bolsover. "Does this mean you're a man without morals? Do you know what happens to scoundrels and sinners?"

"They get rich," says Bolsover.

"Yee-hah!" Sam waves his arms and calls for a round of applause. "It's Bolsover's first joke at the Warren!"

"Now that you're going to join us, we'll have to celebrate," says Sam. "Put the coffee on, Adrian. Later we'll nip over to the Horse for a long lunch."

After coffee Bolsover is taken on a tour. Upstairs is Jill's office. "Jill really runs the place," says Molly. "She's the one who fends off the advertisers when they come shouting. She's fierce, she is."

"Some bastard has to be fierce round here," says Jill. "Otherwise it'd be bloody chaos."

A shed in the backyard contains more boxes of guidebooks, a packing table, and a young man sitting in a canvas chair reading a magazine, which he hides when he sees his visitors.

"Busy again, I see," says Molly. "This is the new guy, Jimmy Bolsover. Meet Wayne, Jimmy."

Wayne gets up. He is a tall, lugubrious young man with a wine stain down the side of his face. His large hands hang low.

"Hello, Wayne," says Bolsover.

"We send for Wayne when we want something lifted," says Molly Moon. "Don't we, Wayne?"

Wayne nods.

"Not a great talker, Wayne, but the strongest man for miles around. Aren't you, Wayne? The strongest man?"

Wayne nods again.

"This is Jimmy B," says Sam. "He's the new guy."

Wayne nods. "I heard you."

"We're all going round to the White Horse in a minute, to celebrate Jimmy's arrival. Are you coming, Wayne?"

"Yep," says Wayne.

After the celebration at the White Horse, Bolsover strolls back to the Alpha. My goodness, what a curious lot! But likable. Their jokes might pale in time, of course. Warren's a scoundrel, perhaps, but not a ferocious one, and that Molly Moon—she's a bright young woman, and in a burning bright dress, too. The others—Sam Kavanagh, another quick one. And that Adrian—something's wrong with him—he's ill, perhaps. But lively, all of them, except Wayne with his wine stain, the one they send for when they want something lifted. But he's all right, too. They're good folk, all of them—except Warren, perhaps. I'll tell Arabella about them. She'd like them. I'm sure she would.

Bolsover keeps an eye open for Arabella as he walks back along the promenade, but there is no sign of her, nor of the man in the wheelchair. I am become Jimmy B, thinks Bolsover, an editor of guides to the counties of England.

10

Bolsover steps out with an apple in his pocket and nothing but the drifting gulls for company. It's Saturday, his third day on the island. Earlier that morning the hotel's alarms were tested and their terrible clatter sent him hurrying from the building. He wants to place himself in the landscape, to discover the geography of this curious little place. Free and content, he turns away from the town along the empty, curving beach that leads to Handsome Point. He has selected the route carefully, for in his opinion a first-rate walk requires solitude, a prospect of water, and a decent gain of height.

It's a windless day, the sea innocuous, the sky pale gray. Yes, that's altostratus, a little wrinkled here and there, like an old dust sheet thrown across the heavens. And in the distance stands his first objective, the brooding bulk of the point and its light, that ever-fixèd mark. He stops and listens for a moment to what is surely a remarkable silence: ought there not to be birdsong of some kind—larks, perhaps? No larks in winter, Bolsover, but it seems that even the gulls are silent this morning. The tide is falling and he makes a steady pace along firm, damp sand, keeping his eyes open for anything curious in the way of flotsam— a message in a bottle, a mermaid carved from whalebone. What do they call it—"scrimshaw" is it? There is a sudden hiss of surf, and he looks up to see a dozen waves, much larger than the rest, running smoothly inshore, their crests beginning to break. He steps up the beach and watches them fall and crash, run forward and dissipate in froth. A minute passes and all is calm again, only a thin line of foam marking where the waves reached, high up the sand.

A passing ship made those waves, but the sea is empty to the horizon. What ship was she? When did she go by, and how far out? Perhaps it was hours ago that the ship passed, and the waves have been traveling all that time, silently and smoothly across the open sea. I'll have to tell Kitty—

But he won't tell Kitty, because she's dead. It's astonishing that he can forget that fact, but it happens from time to time, and on each occasion he feels not only shock but the shame of forgetting.

Oh, yes, Kitty would have liked the idea of the silent, invisible ship; certainly she would. In his mind he hears her laughing, not only at the notion of the ship but—as she often did—at the simple fancies of the man she had married. They had been so very different, he and Kitty! When he understood the depth of those differences, he attempted to construct parallels between them, to draw them together. He noted the careful way in which Kitty assembled a design, ruthlessly pruning her growing garden to get it just right. Well, wasn't that just like his way of writing? *If it isn't right, out with it!* Surely words were one language, gardens another. Both could be assembled in an enormous variety of ways and transmit all sorts of meanings; both were ways of communicating, both were subject to the conventions of particular times and places.

Bolsover's analysis began with optimistic notions, but when he placed the two languages, gardening and writing, side by side, there was an obvious difficulty. Compared with a book, a garden spoke to him with insufficient clarity. He did not deny that a garden might speak, and that its tone might be delicate, assertive, sensual, or whatever; but what exactly did it say? Could a garden ever have a *clear* message? That issue troubled Bolsover, seeming to doom his attempts to see Kitty and himself within the same purposive frame.

Bolsover stops walking and draws with the toe of his boot a large circle in the sand. In the great confusion of life he desperately wants things to be clear, but it has to be admitted that his *nosing about*—that's how he thinks of his habit of indiscriminate inquiry—generally tends to increase his sense of his own ignorance. Why does he keep looking when all he discovers is more confusion? Bolsover can think of no answer to that question, hence his *O* in the sand.

In only one particular area of activity does he feel he has made definite progress: *words are my business.* He wouldn't make that claim in public, but Bolsover says it quietly to himself, and isn't he fully entitled to, since he's made a living out of words for forty years? He knows how to be accurate, brief, and clear. He believes that the writers who really matter are the ordinary sort, whose words form the bulk of written discourse: writers of letters, e-mails, blogs, texts, or scribbled notes to their lovers—journalists, copywriters. In other words, people like himself. A work of literature, Bolsover says to himself, is no sacred repository, but merely a record of particular words at the instant of their printing. A novel is like a photograph: it freezes a chunk of language, locking it between covers so that it may no longer change and adapt. Words in books are dead, like butterflies pinned to a frame.

"Let's have no grand notions," Bolsover says aloud, waving his arms as he walks on toward Handsome Point. Isn't it the case that a novel is unable to convey more than a superficial, simpleminded version of reality, one that is obviously contrived, far too orderly? For goodness' sake—a novel can't portray what happens to a single person in a single day! It's a sketch, and must have form or its readers will complain; form means things omitted, reordered, tidied, pruned, and artfully completed. Consider my life so far, Bolsover thinks. Has it discernible form? Is it tidy? Does it possess grace? Reason? Logic? No, it does not. In life, things happen one after another and then you die, whereupon the world, forgetting your existence in a moment, goes on its merry way. A novel is a comfort, that's what it is. It makes us think we might understand ourselves and our lives, and it lets us worry in a nice safe way. It sanitizes trauma—"trauma," of course, being one of those words whose meaning is hazy but is likely to cause the abandonment of rational thought and a lot of wise nodding. Indeed, continues Bolsover, his mind beginning to race, it's an interesting category, the emotive, which includes words like "bereaved," a term that confers saintliness on any old ruffian of a widower. Or that old problem "tragedy"—he's unstoppable now—which doesn't require heroic failure or a vast number of deaths. Nor does it require fault or failure on anyone's part, as the churches and many another pontificating moralizer would have us believe. Tragedy has nothing to do with morals. Millions of perfectly good men and women, honest and serviceable, suffer in some awful and lingering way for no reason other than chance, as do an equivalent number of villains who deserve all they get. Just as, one summer's day, I was sitting in a waiting room while my wife died, not a sound emerging from behind the sunlit, flowery curtains surrounding the bed in that hot and scruffy hospital—oh, Kitty—

But was it chance? Or was it not? If everything's down to chance, can there be such a thing as fault, such a thing as blame? Surely blame is true, because I feel it my fault, and feel it strongly even now, so many years later. Here Bolsover sits down on a convenient rock and takes a few long, slow breaths.

Much about the man is explained by his training as a practical engineer. Engineering is the application of a set of well-proven laws of cause and effect, and its success makes some people believe it's the only way to think. Engineering materials may be held in the hand, their properties easily perceived: feel the weight of that. Such properties can be manipulated and things made to meet all sorts of needs; engineering is a world of certainty, an addictive place. You want to fly? *Come on up.* Your heart's failing? *Hey, I just made you a new one.* What's your problem? *Wait—we'll fix it.*

But not everything can be fixed—or even understood, which is the first stage of fixing. Take beauty: engineers can't quite get hold of that notion. True, they own to something called *elegance,* which has to do with using the least material to best effect, but it's not the same; beauty is something an engineer doesn't want, because it costs money and reduces functionality. *Functionality:* that's one of those engineering words, as heavy as a lump hammer but kind of useful, as hammers are. That's why Bolsover isn't good with flowers and can't read the language of a garden: he's an engineer. He read the gardening books and did what they told him, but the damn flowers didn't do it right. Despite his care, they wrecked the roof of the garage and drooped and died for no reason, just like his wife did— And here she is again, Kitty, coming out of nowhere and bringing tears to his eyes for no good reason. Sorrow—that's another one that's hard to fix.

This is Bolsover's difficulty: he keeps stumbling over things he just can't fix, and blames himself for not fixing them. When he asks himself why Kitty died, and why, later in his life, things went so wrong, he can come up with no answer but *himself.* The cause must lie with his own character—what other term is there in the equation? He wanted that frail young girl Kitty, and married her for reasons of lust that he hid from her. By an elaborate strategy he eventually had his way with her, and then he tried to pay her back by loving her truly; but he did not love her enough. How does he know that? Because she died: it's obvious. Kitty died in a slow and painful manner while he was waiting, as he had been told to do by an assertive doctor, in a room apart from her, so that she died alone when he should have been at her side. Oh, yes, Bolsover knows that to be true. And the whole thing, when described in a certain way, has an air of inevitability, easily supporting the proposition that, had he somehow loved her more truly, she might not have died, and surely would not have died alone.

Bolsover is aware that human beings may construct guilt that is not deserved, and that in some perverse way we may prefer guilt to innocence. He does not see himself in that category. His sorrow has certainly faded—why, he can forget, for days at a time, that she has died—but from time to time, as when he is walking along a deserted beach on a quiet winter's afternoon, the wake of a far-distant, unseen ship breaks suddenly, and reminds him of a debate that has not gone away, a debate that will, it seems, never be resolved.

The chalk ridge ends in a vertical cliff. A line of seagirt rocks continues seaward, and at its far end is planted the Handsome Light. Bolsover stands and gazes at it. The designers of such structures must consider the relationship between height, taper ratio, and flare, and they have chosen, it seems, a sine curve as the formula for that perfection: it is as if some giant huntsman, resting from the chase, has placed his horn, bell down, in the rocky shallows, and absently ridden off without it. A horn of gray granite, a spire, a tower—was there ever such a simple thing, something so grand, so beautiful, so unequivocally a contribution to the general good, as a lighthouse? *I saw you in the dark, I saw you in the storm, and you brought us home.*

"Why, hello there!" Bolsover turns and discovers his birding acquaintance from the ferry, Jack Wilson. He's wearing sensible boots and carrying a tripod and telescope. "It's Bolsover, the man with no name!"

"That's me," says Bolsover, shaking his hand.

"And have you come to see the courser?"

Bolsover shakes his head. "I was just exploring. Surely this isn't the country for a cream-colored courser?" He waves his hand at the long beach and the line of rocks that stretches toward the elegant lighthouse.

"Ah," says Wilson, "you're quite right. But around the point you'll find a shallow bay, and that's a different matter."

"Is it far from here?" Not the sort of question that a keen birder will answer in the negative, thinks Bolsover, in the middle of asking it.

"My dear chap, only a few minutes! And I'm sure you'd like to bag such a fine rarity!"

"Oh, yes," says Bolsover politely. "Indeed I would."

It's a hard scramble across rocks and pools for some hundreds of yards, during which Bolsover decides to buy some sensible boots like Wilson's. But as they turn the end of the point, the going improves; the land is lower here, and the deep, narrow bay, sheltered by the high ground of Handsome Point, is occupied by marsh and saltings.

"Have to keep pretty quiet," whispers Wilson, who is now crouching slightly as he walks. "It's not so much upsetting the bird; it's the bloody birders."

Parked in the fields behind the shoreline, Bolsover suddenly notices, is a press of motor homes, tents, caravans, off-road vehicles, hot dog stalls, and ice cream vendors; every thicket is alive with camouflaged figures and glinting lenses.

"It's a regular birder's town," Bolsover whispers.

"Good Lord, yes. Well, it's a rare chance, isn't it? A once-in-a-lifetime chance—what we call a lifer."

"A lifer. I see."

"And we're all keen listers, of course."

"So you told me."

"Did I? Oh, on the boat. Yes. And I'm afraid they'd call you a dude."

"A dude?"

"A beginner."

Lister, lifer, dude. Something about birders, thinks Bolsover, is deeply irritating. *Deeply.* Is it that they're so harmless, so good, so well-intentioned? Or is it that they are so simpleminded? For sure they haven't studied the biology, physics, ecology, physiology, distribution, migratory patterns, navigational methods, or aerodynamics of birds; all they want to do is *chase them down.* They just want to *name* the birds as they flutter past on business that remains, as far as the birder is concerned, absolutely mysterious. Why birds, particularly? Why not insects? Flies? Beetles? Small mammals? Kinds of cow, horse, dog, cat—put those in your notebook, matey. What is it about *naming things*? What is it about *making lists* and *ticking things off*? Why does merely *knowing a name* matter so much? What sad and simple things we all are! Birding's a hobby, which is to say a harmless activity pursued on a superficial level, other kinds being the making of ships from matchsticks, decorating eggs, and collecting curiously shaped potatoes—mankind reduced to small and apparently pointless tasks. Those fanatical birders, those twitchers, do they ever feel a sudden urge to take a shotgun from one of their long green bags and blow the birds into feathery heaven? If not, why not?

And the answer to all my questions, thinks Bolsover, is simple: *birds can fly.* They are free, they goeth where they listeth and are next of kin to angels, to whom we have loaned their wings. When I see a common gull, I may know flight: that bird takes me up, carries me into the air, until I can look down upon the earth. I leave earthly things, I rise, I soar among the clouds! They can fly and yet they are vulnerable; they are merely a few fragments of hollow bone and feather, as light as a puff of smoke on the wind. They are enchanting, they are fragile, and they are free, and that is why we long to know them.

"Tell me, Jack," says Bolsover, still feeling irritable, "why do birds migrate? Or rather, having got somewhere warm, why don't they stay there? Where's the sense in it?"

"Not so loud, old chap," Wilson whispers. "We'll stop here and set up the scope."

In the wavering circle of light Bolsover at first sees only cloud, then only sea. "Left, left," says Wilson, "much farther to the left."

A patch of muddy gray and green smears across Bolsover's vision.

"I can't find it."

"Farther left—near that tufty bit."

Which tufty bit? There are tufty bits all over—but wait—there's something—a little patch of brown, that might be a bird. He inches the scope to the left, turns the focus—and there it is, the cream-colored courser! That great rarity, that intrepid traveler! It has a perky look, this little bird, glancing this way and that, its pose, wings slightly open, suggesting a man in an old-fashioned frock coat, always supposing that light brown frock coats once existed. And as Bolsover watches, the bird takes a precise step directly toward him, its legs indeed very long, and having a silvery look—are they truly silver, or is it just an effect of light? The courser takes another step and then another, causing Bolsover to lose it and then find it again. It's moving now with urgent delicacy, suddenly on its way somewhere, as if stepping out to catch a bus, and on the back of its head there's a curious oval pattern, as if it were wearing one of those wartime caps—a forage cap, is it? And the bird isn't brown, nor cream, surely, but has a little touch of pink—oh, it's a little peach of a bird!

"What do you think?" Wilson is whispering.

"It's a sweetie," says Bolsover. "It's an absolute sweetie."

"And think of it, she's come all the way from North Africa."

"She?"

"It's a female."

"Oh."

It makes a difference. All these men with their scopes, their bins, and their long-lensed cameras, hundreds of them, eyeing up the slim, elegant little courser as she steps this way and that. She's concentrating on her own concerns, unknowing—and as Bolsover watches, she turns her head and runs her bill sideways down the fold of her left wing, turns her head, and does the same to the right. Preening, that's what she's doing.

"She's a long way from home," Bolsover says.

11

In the late 1970s the decline of the F. R. Butler company became sharply steeper, and its employees began to drift away. The typists went, and their typewriters with them, all save the last, which was presented to Bolsover: an upright Imperial, a very grand machine that was already a relic, and was soon put away in a cupboard, having been replaced by a word processor.

Kitty was seriously ill by then, so his attention was distracted, but Bolsover saw that Butler's was on the slide. What should he do? He began to sketch a curriculum vitae. When it came to the properties of steel tubes, he knew a lot about wall thicknesses, inside and outside diameters, transverse metal area, inside cross-sectional area, moment of inertia, section modulus, radius of gyration, and so forth. And the manner in which fluids and gases moved in tubes—he knew something about that, too: that was fluid dynamics, a large and complex topic. This knowledge was particular to pipes and valves, but one can't be any sort of engineer without picking up a lot more. On his desk at Butler's was an old copy of *Newnes Engineer's Reference Book*—never called by its proper title, but simply "Camm," after its editor, F. J. Camm, one of engineering's household gods. He was the editor of *Practical Engineering* and the author of numerous technical works—*Gears and Gear-Cutting, Practical Mechanics Handbook, A Refresher Course in Mathematics,* and so forth. In those days, in discussing an engineering problem, somebody was sure to ask, "But what does Camm say?"

Bolsover's copy of Camm had been inherited from his predecessor. "You can keep him," said old Arnott. "I don't want him near my deck chair."

The book possessed in its heft, its binding, and the fine translucency of its pages a strong suggestion of the Bible; its authority, in Bolsover's view, was considerably greater. Within Camm's 1,376 pages was a definitive statement of the theory and practice of mechanical engineering. Abbreviations and units, thermodynamics, the laws of fluids, stress formulae for beams, heat treatment, British standard specifications, cutting speeds for twist drills, moments of inertia, and more than three hundred other topics. Riffling through these pages reassured Bolsover that, despite his spending sixteen years in the same room, he knew about engineering.

In part, Bolsover's broad knowledge of engineering theory and practice was due to his work as a technical writer, since he might find himself writing about any aspect of Butler's work, but his browsing in Camm's pages had certainly helped. He was in the habit of opening the great tome at random during his tea break and testing himself, say, on the best cutting speeds for plane and shaper tools. Camm's attraction was not just his extensive knowledge but his certainty; in his foreword, Camm had written: "It is confidently expected that the work will be accepted as a standard in an industry where standards are the order of the day."

His knowledge of Camm convinced Bolsover that he was capable of writing about any aspect of mechanical engineering; when it came to his future employment, he need not restrict himself to flanges, pipes, cocks, and Reynolds numbers. The question became urgent when Bolsover returned to work four days after Kitty's death. The bicycle ride down the Fernley Road, the walk through the noisy works, the door marked TECH/W—suddenly he knew he could do no more of this.

Bolsover sat in his chair for an hour and stared at the wall, then wrote a note of resignation with immediate effect. He collected his copy of Camm, the cushion that Kitty had made, the little clock in its wooden case, and his old slide rule, which he no longer used but had been inscribed with his name at the start of his apprenticeship, twenty years before, and carried them away in a plastic bag.

A day later, while he was searching the trade papers and the local press, an attractively short, crisp advertisement caught his eye: *Freelance copywriter required for technical subjects. Call Turner & Turner.*

Freelance copywriting! He had never thought of such a thing, but the words had a thrilling ring. Bolsover obtained an interview and within a week was out on his own, a new recruit, so he was frequently told, to the growing army of the self-employed.

One would not expect Bolsover to make a good copywriter. For a start, he did not accept the convention that his principal duty was to bolster his clients' self-regard. Instead, he aimed to provide prospective purchasers with an accurate and useful account of the product. Why on earth not? Before he began work on a particular commission, he wanted to know that the product was worth promoting, refusing to concede that this isn't a central plank of marketing practice. He didn't believe that the association of a product with some striking image or witty phrase, regardless of its relevance, is essential to sales success; that might be all right when selling worthless products to stupid people, but he didn't have to do that sort of thing, since he was a freelance and might choose—within limits—what he wrote, and for whom.

Even in the case of ordinary products, useful things that worked well, he found the idea that the perfect advertisement might be created—something quite magical that would make everyone's fortunes—to be irritatingly persistent, and the bane of the copywriter's life. Clients had no awareness of the difficulty of applying creative wit to the sale of a numerically controlled drilling machine. In that particular case, Bolsover came under severe pressure to use the slogan "Your number's up!" until it was discovered to be already in use by two competitors. Didn't that just prove his point?

Many clients, in thrall to the myth of advertising and aware of the tens of thousands they were paying Turner & Turner, expected what they called "world-class copy." An accurate, brief, and clear expression of the benefits of their product, they often felt, was insufficient. They hankered after words like "new" and "unique," and looked gloomy when he explained that such words were utterly exhausted, and would pass before the reader's eye without transmitting any meaning whatsoever. But for Bolsover, copywriting, as with all practical writing, was simply a question of ABC, and it became his mission to promote that admirable notion to the agency's clients and to the agency itself.

Despite his apparent unsuitability for the fast-moving world of creative advertising, Bolsover was successful. He knew the ways of engineering; knew its designers, makers, and buyers; knew what appealed to them and said what he thought to be true. Soon he found himself being paid large sums for a small number of words, a satisfactory reversal of his experience at Butler's. The agency, finding him accurate, brief, clear, and quick, if not as inspirational as they might have liked, offered him more and more work. As time went by, he was required to bone up on new technologies—things like shunt-wound electric motors, digital data transmission, global positioning systems, subsea cable-laying, surface-mount electronics, magnetic resonance imaging, in-flight refueling systems, and anti-collision radar. On the latter subject, he came up with "Nothing comes close," which he regarded, despite his dislike of superficial witticisms, as quite a decent tagline.

This, then, was the new Bolsover, soon respected by the young graphic designers and account managers of Turner & Turner and perceived by clients as a proper old-fashioned engineer, not just another of those arty types.

At the start Bolsover still wore a tweed sports jacket with leather elbow patches, and was skeptical of the flowery open-necked shirts of the graphic designers. However, he quickly adjusted, and even began to enjoy himself. The flowery types were good at what they did, and he found the role of a freelance copywriter to be delightfully varied and lacking in tedious regulation. On every one of his four thousand days at Butler's he had been required to clock in before seven-thirty A.M. and clock out after six P.M., or lose pay. Now his only constraint was the delivery of an agreed piece of copy by a specific time. He had no objection to working all night if required—in fact, he rather enjoyed the air of panic that is normal in advertising. It was a novel notion to earn money—charged at double time, indeed—at two o'clock in the morning, dictating his words down a telephone to the studio as if he were a foreign correspondent. He soon felt that he was necessary to Turner & Turner, and that feeling, in his new condition as a footloose freelance widower, was useful to his morale.

In a tactful conversation the agency's directors persuaded him to buy a new car, in order that the agency's name should not suffer by association with his old one. It was pleasant to find that the new car, plus a good percentage of the costs of running his house, could be set against tax. He was earning proper money now, and developing, he felt, an easier and more loose-wristed style of writing—still accurate, brief, and clear, of course, but a tad more colloquial. His sports jacket had been perfectly acceptable to the agency, but a dark blue suit with a subtle pinstripe gave him even greater authority. And this new Bolsover, it soon became clear, required an ox-leather briefcase and a silver Volkswagen—secondhand, but a car of the well-made, unobtrusive sort that engineers respect. It was funny how often people noticed his car and ran their fingertips across the thick, soft leather of his briefcase. Carrying the briefcase, he attended trade shows in London and Birmingham and talked of market penetration, key benefits, and sales strategy; it was a fine thing to drive about the country on business of importance, and to be well paid for doing so. By this time he had a firm grip on the garden and there was only one real difficulty about his manner of life, and that was the fact that Kitty was dead.

Returning home became more and more unsatisfactory. The house in which he had lived for four decades he now found to be small and shabby, the wrong house in the wrong part of the wrong town. How odd that he hadn't noticed before! It was not the kind of place to which he could invite business associates—and the ancient garage, its roof now thoroughly penetrated by *Campsis grandiflora,* was quite inadequate for his new car.

I shall move, thought the new Bolsover, stepping through the front door of his old, small, shabby house. As he hung up his coat, he thought of buying a Sussex cottage on a leafy lane, convenient to the motorway, the airport, and the Channel Tunnel. He switched on the kettle, wondering whether Brighton might be preferable—a top flat with a view of the sea—or perhaps a town house in an up-and-coming part of Surrey—and then saw through the kitchen window the panorama of Kitty's garden.

Because of her garden, Bolsover remained for several more years in his shabby house, frequently being arrested by the memories that grew like cobwebs in unexpected corners. He would find Kitty's straw hat on top of a wardrobe, a faded paper rose in the hatband, and at once see it blowing from her head, turning over and over until it fell onto the sand. He picked it up and ran to catch her, to feel the touch of her arms, the long, narrow bones of her arms, so cool about his neck, her scent, the softness of her lips—and found nothing but silence and empty air.

At first such episodes occurred many times a day. His grief seemed deliberate, purposeful; he searched for memories of Kitty despite know-

ing that he would uncover pain. Time after time he deliberately constructed her, by careful and conscious efforts of memory and imagination, only that he might grieve again.

And yet, after a year or two, Kitty no longer came into his mind with
quite the same brilliance. After three years, she seldom returned in daylight, but only in the late evening and the early morning, the hours least
well guarded. He could still be shocked unexpectedly—by finding, perhaps, in the cupboard under the stairs, a pair of her sandals that bore the
impression, dented and polished into the leather, of her several and distinct toes—but such shocks now came more rarely, and their effects
were less severe.

After four years Bolsover knew that his attention to the garden was
not as close as it ought to be. He had failed to prune *grandiflora* with the
necessary authority: the garage must now be entirely replaced. At the
beginning the garden had served a purpose, but now he began to see that
his memory of Kitty did not require a monument, for she would exist in
his mind as long as he lived, and if he should move—why, she would
come with him, wouldn't she? How could he forget her?

At the end of his fifth freelance year Bolsover sold the house and
bought a flat on a new estate, a clean, modern flat with large windows
and a sizable balcony, a place that immediately conveyed an impression
of airy lightness and provided a view of the canal and the trees that lined
it. The old house and its garden had become too great a burden. *Yes.* A
term of grieving must be served, but it should not be the rest of one's life.
No. He walked out of his old house for the last time, pushing from habit
at the closed door to ensure that it was properly locked. He would never
forget her. *Of course not!* Before he turned the corner he looked back. A
young man had whirled his featherlight wife across that threshold: his
memory of her was changing, and it was now a mixture of pain and pleasure. *So it was.* She was lovely, his wife; he had made her garden, as she
had wished and he had promised, and now that chapter was concluded.
Yes. As for abandoning *Campsis grandiflora,* that rampant climber, he felt
only relief: one should not confuse the wedding ring with the finger that

once wore it. *Yes.* He loved her memory still, but there is a time when forgetting is necessary. *Yes.* The word was "closure," a word that gives permission to move on. *Yes.* That was something that people often said nowadays: *move on.*

Having reorganized his thoughts in this manner, Bolsover turned his mind to his new apartment—a much better word than the old-fashioned "flat." There were questions of decoration and furniture to decide. He must purchase one or two tasteful prints—modern colorful prints—to distinguish its fresh, blank walls. He had a balcony now, where he might sit and look at the sky; the balcony certainly required thought. *Yes, indeed.*

Living alone in his new apartment, with clients of his own as well as his work from Turner & Turner, Bolsover was busy and successful. The last years of the twentieth century began to tick by, and he enjoyed the wealth of that period. He traveled about the country, visiting clients and attending engineering exhibitions. He progressed to PR—writing company brochures, press releases, video scripts, and speeches for the top brass, and for several years he edited a company newspaper. Was there any kind of writing he could not do? He was always willing, always reliable, which were sufficiently unusual characteristics to get him noticed; and of course he aimed always to be accurate, brief, and clear. Many times he thought of his extraordinary good fortune in acquiring, on a sudden whim, such an entertaining and satisfactory life, there being no obvious reason why such as he, little more than a humble apprentice, should be in receipt of such gifts.

There was now only one difficulty: returning from Heathrow at midnight to his comfortable but silent flat, he would make himself a cup of coffee, thinking how pleasant it would be to be welcomed home—and even, he dared to think, how pleasant it would be to make love. He still used that ancient term, still assumed that love was essential to sexual intercourse. To make love, he believed, was to signify and affirm a unique relationship—though Bolsover shied at the word "relationship," which he believed to be empty, mechanical, and ultimately fatuous. A good many people used to think in Bolsover's way. It must be emphasized that it was once quite normal to associate sex only with love and marriage; they belonged together. Of course he heard people talking about *having sex*. He heard talk about *fucking*, men saying they had given some girl *a good seeing to*, a good *rogering*, and occasionally he even heard women talking in a similar way. When he heard talk like that, when he saw images of naked women on all the front pages, he knew that the world was on its way to a place he did not like. "Change and decay in all around I see"—quite so. Things fall apart—yes, yes, all that.

That Bolsover was a slow learner is clear. He had not made the discovery that the sexual act has no necessary connection with love, marriage, permanence, or trust. He had not learned that sex is a freestanding activity that one may do with anyone, that it's as easy as having lunch. He knew, in a dim kind of way, that his own ideas no longer fitted, but could not see how he might adapt to the new fashion. Surely, he kept asking himself, there must be—well, if not love, then *affection*, at least, or *respect*? Respect! It makes one wonder what planet the man thought he was living on.

But he had begun to think of women again; that's the important point. The thought of love was only a passing notion to begin with, but it grew, as desire does. He began to notice that there were women all over the place, not only at exhibitions but in the agency, at meetings, on trains, in the street—everywhere. So many women! Wasn't it possible that somewhere there existed a woman who might think him—think him what?—think him *compatible*, at least?

But it was one thing to notice women, another to do something about them. People now remained single—or, when by some oversight they made the error of commitment, they quickly became single again. Marriage, permanence, and loyalty, which place such inconvenient constraints upon individuals, were no longer well regarded, but what had replaced them? Was it possible that love might exist without bonds, between individuals who were single and free?

It was most confusing. There had been a vast increase in singles groups, dating agencies, and personal advertising; evidently people wanted to be free, yet they did not want to be alone. They wanted not a wife nor a husband but a *partner,* and the words "relationship" and "partner," which had replaced "marriage" and "spouse," implied no eternal bond. Is a partner, he grumbled vulgarly to himself, any more than a *fuckable friend*? Is not permanence the essence of marriage? And where is the permanence in a mere partnership, that may be dissolved in a moment? Have people changed so much that they no longer require, for their own happiness and the continuation of civilization, the notion of a *wife,* the sort that is loved and cherished, and a *husband,* who loves and cherishes?

Of course this confusion wasn't a problem only for Bolsover. The astonishing growth of personal advertising and dating agencies showed as much. *Bubbly blonde, likes dancing, seeks*—most of them were phrased in that manner, and such advertisements made him considerably uneasy. *Zany woman wants someone to make me laugh.* He shook his head. *Looking for someone to adore me.* Did that sound needy, or what? *Love music, seek emotionally intelligent man, over 6ft.* That's me out of it, then. *Seeking fun—no more gloomy men.* Was he a gloomy man? He supposed he must be, since fun wasn't the first thing that came to mind when considering his needs. *Want sorted gent. Need TLC. Petite curvy F WLTM nice man. Wistful maiden, loves cats, twilight, needs man to light her fire—*

Bolsover was not shocked by these advertisements, but he was surprised by their banality. Is it sufficient, he wondered, when seeking a person with whom to spend the rest of one's life, to specify oneself and her in such terms as these? What could it mean if someone said only that she was *spiritual*? Wasn't that more a failing than a virtue?

But one can't be certain; it was just possible that among all these women might be the one he was looking for. For several months Bolsover inspected the advertisements, marking most with a penciled "No" and a few with a tentative "Poss." The possibles he then considered again, until he had reduced them to a single one.

Her advertisement read, in part: *I'm looking for a man I can trust, and who will trust me.* That's plain enough. That's less woolly than the usual run. I'll phone her up. No, I won't. Yes, I will. No, I won't. Yes, I will.

They met for lunch. She was nothing like Kitty—not small, not delicate. She seemed nice enough, but wary, quiet. She talked about her former husband, who had run off with an estate agent, and as she spoke, she turned and turned her wedding ring—it wouldn't come off, she told him, and she didn't like to have it cut off. Oh, history, thought Bolsover, history! If he was to marry again, his history must match hers as a key fits a lock; but what shape is the key, and what shape the lock? Neither suggested another meeting, for there was no spark between them.

Bolsover did not look again at personal advertisements. No doubt that was a weak response to an early failure, but the whole process felt awkward and unnatural. It was as if he were choosing fruit at a counter: try that one, give it a squeeze—no, not soft enough. Here's another—too hard this time. I'll try you—I'll try you. That one. Third from the left. Yes, you. You're the one. Oh, no, you won't do at all. Sorry.

Briefly, he thought of advertising himself. I could do that: I'm a copywriter. He sketched a few ideas—*Man, 50s, medium height, widower, reliable, honest, solvent, reads a lot.* There was no doubt that such a description—accurate, brief, and clear though it was—gave no sense of himself. Or, rather, it gave the *wrong* sense of himself. He sounded, in this definition, amazingly dull. That might usefully deter wistful maidens who wanted their fires lit but would surely fail to interest a woman of character. Did he possess any unique selling points? In Bolsover's experience, truly unique selling points were rare, and if they existed, they were usually negative: *the Mk II fails less often than the Mk I.* What was unique about himself, Bolsover? Why, nothing, except that he was himself; but one can hardly write *I am myself* and expect an enthusiastic response.

Bolsover finally decided that *being himself* must be his only advertisement. Bolsover in person, Bolsover walking and talking, Bolsover reading his books, Bolsover writing in his notebooks, Bolsover in his square reality—only he himself could represent the man he was. As for the rest of his copywriter's checklist—*cost benefits, performance, reliability, accuracy, specification, customers' testimonials*—none of that was relevant. His only advertisement would be himself, and he would have to trust that, one day, he might encounter someone who would notice him.

The greatest of human concerns are liable to generate the greatest absurdity: Bolsover had often noticed that paradox. Now he had found himself unable to answer the simple questions *Who am I?* and *Whom might I love?* Was he so ordinary, so dull, so bland? Did he not fit naturally into the human race? Surely, that wasn't the case. I'm just an ordinary man, said Bolsover to himself, and what else can I say? There must be *someone* whom he might love, and who might love him; somewhere there's someone. It's unnatural to be alone, isn't it? One day he would surely encounter a girl—no, a woman—sheltering from a storm, reaching for the same book from a library shelf or spilling a drink down his jacket. Of course: that was how love happened—accidentally. Love wasn't something you could plan! That had been his error.

What might she be like, this accidental woman? He began to construct a future in which a delicate, dark-haired woman sat across the table from him, dusk coming on, a candle flickering between them, a late evening in summer. Her eyes gleamed at him in the candlelight—but if he reached out to grasp her hand, she'd somehow slip away, that slim, dark-haired woman, along with the table, the candle, and the warm summer night.

Obvious though it is, Bolsover didn't identify his imaginary woman with his dead wife; it was just that, when he imagined a woman, she was always small, light-boned, dark-haired, and very likely a keen gardener.

The idea of love did not go away. The thought of the woman, the flickering candle, the dusk, and the summer evening did not go away. He saw women who might almost be her—someone he glimpsed crossing the road, someone he saw in the studio, someone who caught his eye in a supermarket. Something about the turn of her head had deceived him, that's all—the way she moved, or her long dark hair.

12

Mrs. Arabella Morgan goes swimming at nine o'clock on Friday morning, thinks Bolsover. Does she do so every morning? He strolls down High Street, under the clock, along the promenade, and finds Leonard, that huddled figure, parked in the same spot, while out at sea—a good way out, in fact—there's a swimmer. She's a capable swimmer, Mrs. Morgan, an aquatic type, the watery sort, and a woman who likes laughter. Bolsover sits down on the end of a breakwater at a polite distance from Leonard.

"I saw you arrive," Arabella says, when she comes ashore, "but I have to do my lengths, and besides, I don't want to seem too eager. How are the guides to the English counties?"

"The firm's run by a man called Warren, a dubious character. Quite possibly a villain."

"Join the club," she says. "Lennie's a right old villain, that's for sure. Aren't you, old fellow? A proper evil villain, you used to be." She nudges the wheelchair with her foot but Leonard does not stir.

"Warren's publishing company isn't quite straight. He doesn't tell the truth all the time."

"Oh, is that all?" says Arabella. "That old truth thing. Such a nuisance."

"Quite so. He tells his advertisers that he sells a lot more copies than he actually does."

"Are there publishers who don't do that?"

"That's what I thought. However, he employs a nice bunch of people. Lively, amusing people. Quite young."

"It sounds as though you're tempted to join them."

"I have joined them," says Bolsover.

"Good. But you sound a little doubtful. What's wrong with Warren's?"

"Only that—this may sound silly—"

"Surely not."

"It's the sort of job I should have done twenty or more years ago. I'm a bit past that sort of thing now."

"What were you doing twenty or more years ago?"

"I was an engineer."

"Oh."

"I've often noticed," says Bolsover, "a lack of wild applause when engineering's mentioned."

"You're right. It's really quite unfair, when it's such a *worthy* occupation, so *clever*, so frightfully *useful*."

"Thank you."

"Not at all. So you'll give Warren a go, will you, despite being over-age for the job?"

"I will. Just for a while. After all, I may not be here forever."

"Ah."

There is a silence. The two of them gaze out to sea.

"Are you—" Bolsover hesitates.

"Am I staying here?"

"I was going to ask that, but I was warned by Mrs. K about being too nosy."

"Ask away. I don't have any secrets. Lennie's the one with the secrets, and I don't think he'll be bothered if anyone finds them out now. Ah, well." She massages her wet gray hair with her fingertips. "Whether we go or stay depends entirely on him. He's the reason we're here. Eight years ago I first noticed Leonard fumbling with his keys. He'd forgotten how to unlock his car. He had a very fine car, a Jaguar. I sold it without telling him. That was about four years ago. They were saying then that he'd go soon."

"He's been ill for eight years," says Bolsover. "Eight years?"

"Oh, yes. Is that right? It's such a long time. I think it's eight, but perhaps it's nine. You've got to give him credit for hanging in there. The car was the main thing. His main loss. I used to cry about that, but I've given up that nonsense. He kept asking why I wouldn't let him drive. But now he can't speak, so the problem's solved. He can't do much. I don't think he can hear anything. He sees things—I know that, but I can't guess what he makes of them. You think he's asleep; then you glance at him, and see he's looking at you. His eyelids, his eyes, and his mouth are the only bits he can still move. He follows things with his eyes. It's unnerving. You know, like—"

"The eyes in a picture," says Bolsover.

"Exactly," says Arabella. "They follow you about. I usually put him by a window, so he has something to watch if he wakes up. He was an awful man before he got ill. I realized that as soon as I married him. I thought I was pretty clever, but he'd taken me in. He wanted me because I was hard to get. We only had one bit of luck."

"You had no children."

"You're right. You're quick, aren't you, Mr. James Bolsover? I can see your mind working, the wheels whizzing round and round."

"Everybody thinks."

"Some more than others."

"I have to keep nosing about. It's a compulsion, I suppose. I can't help it. I've always been like that."

"I expect you read a lot of books. You reckon you know what's what."

"Yes," says Bolsover. "Books do have that unfortunate effect."

"Books do have that unfortunate effect," she repeats, laughing. She likes him: he amuses her. Then she puts both hands on her knees and looks at him straight. "But the real question is, are you one of the Alpha's wicked ones?"

There is a pause.

"I believe I'm not," says Bolsover.

"Humph. Not a speedy response."

"We've all got a history, or we wouldn't be here. I don't think you'd say that my history is wicked. It's possible to be unlucky, don't you think?"

"Unlucky, eh?" She laughs.

"Yes, I know what you mean. But if I told you the whole story—"

"Bolsover!" She seizes his hands. "We must exchange histories, because that's part of getting to know each other. It's quite normal, and nothing catastrophic will happen as a result. Today I'll tell you a bit about Lennie and me, and then we'll go and have breakfast at the charming Alpha Hotel. Tomorrow you will tell me about yourself."

Great things had been expected of Leonard Morgan. He was clever and handsome. He did well at school, and at university he made many friends, played a lot of cricket, and was expected to get a good degree. But he dropped out and bought a flat in London—somehow he already had sufficient money to do so. Soon he became rich, in the curiously effortless way that some people do. As time went by, scandal came close to him—drugs, a man found dying in an alley, a bribed politician—but he was never charged with anything. He was handsome, amusing, prosperous, and Arabella was flattered when he asked her to marry him.

"I was a lawyer, and ought to have seen him coming. But he hired a private plane to take me to Nice for my birthday. What do you say to that?"

Lennie had implied that he went to his London office every day, but she soon discovered that he had no office. Sometimes people came to the house late at night—Lennie said it was business, urgent business. What did he do all day? He made deals on the phone, talked, played cards, drank, went to the races, wanted no children, and frequently said that he loved his wife.

And then one day, as he set off for town in his Jaguar, she saw that he was fumbling with his keys as if he couldn't recall which key was which. That evening he didn't come home. Next morning Arabella had a phone call: he was in a police cell, making a statement in order to avoid prosecution for fraud.

Soon afterward Lennie and his wife were sent to see some people at the Home Office, who made arrangements for him to be guarded; a great deal of money had been involved, and it was possible that some of his former associates might attempt violence. The guards would also keep their eye on Arabella.

"They were talking about the possibility of kidnapping," she tells Bolsover. "I didn't like the thought of that much."

Lennie remained anxious and absentminded, and as the weeks went by, his symptoms became more obvious. Tests were made. It was not a matter of psychology but of neurology: he was suffering from a steady loss of brain function. The doctors said he might live for two or three years.

"Lennie was tougher than that," Arabella says. "At first I kept asking myself why two disastrous things happened at once. Did his being found out cause his brain to atrophy? You hear people saying that stress causes cancer—that sort of thing. But I soon saw it was a stupid question, and not worth asking."

"Those people at the Home Office—were they Miss Brown and Mr. Smithson?"

"They were."

"I know them."

"I dare say you do. It's time for breakfast. Come on, Lennie."

"This breakwater," says Bolsover, pointing. "You'll notice that it's made of rocks held together by boxes made of wire mesh. I discovered the other day that they're called 'gabions,' hence 'gabionage.' From the Italian *gabbione,* meaning 'cage,' originally from the Latin *cavea.*"

"I wonder why you told me that? It does seem rather—well—"

"Pointless."

"Exactly. But I'm grateful for the information. One never knows when one will need to speak of gabionage. Now, breakfast. I need breakfast, Bolsover! I must have my shower and I must have my breakfast. Come on, Lennie, old fellow, let's get rolling."

They walk back along the promenade, and then Bolsover drinks coffee while Arabella eats her breakfast. "You're very brisk," he says. "After so many years, I don't know how you manage so well."

"Anger," Arabella says. "Anger is the way. Take charge."

"You didn't have to do this. You decided you would look after him."

"I did. I left him when I discovered he was a crook, but I came back when he couldn't look after himself any longer. There wasn't anybody else."

"But he'd deceived you."

"We'd made promises to each other. He could break his own promises, but he couldn't break mine, could he?"

Bolsover nods; he understands and approves her logic, but the price is high. He looks at Lennie sleeping in his chair. "He has a distinguished face."

"He has. But a distinguished face is sometimes a warning of deviousness." Arabella turns to inspect Bolsover. "I wouldn't say that you have a distinguished face."

"I'm glad to hear it," says Bolsover.

"Were you ever married?"

"I was. She died."

"I'm sorry."

"It was more than twenty years ago."

"But you loved her, and you still miss her."

"Yes. Did you love Leonard?"

"I thought I did once. A handsome, rich man. Fast cars, fast talking, parties, a house in the country. I was a very silly girl."

"Do you read books?"

"Really, Mr. Bolsover!"

Bolsover is ashamed. "Oh! I'm so sorry. What a thing to ask! I was thinking about *Jane Eyre,* and I wondered if you—"

"I first read *Jane Eyre* when I was eight, I'll have you know."

"I'm truly sorry. Really, I am."

"Get on with it!"

"Well, then—you'll remember how quickly Jane shows intelligence and force of character. She's in command from the first sentence of her story. In a way, that authority transfers to the novel itself. You can't doubt its truth, though it's something of a melodrama."

"Well, there's an instant theory, Professor Bolsover. Nothing wrong with melodrama," says Arabella. "But what's your point?"

"I just thought—well, I was just thinking about—"

"Don't tell me I remind you of Jane Eyre."

"No, of course not, but I was just thinking—"

"Bolsover, stop thinking at once!"

"Oh, all right," says Bolsover.

"Mind you," says Arabella, "I doubt she'd be fun to live with."

"Jane Eyre?"

"Jane or Charlotte—either of them. I suppose writers always invent themselves, since that's the only person they really know. Do you have a car?"

"No," says Bolsover.

"A pity. I was just wondering. But you do drive?"

"I don't, in fact."

"Well, there's a thing. In this modern age, an engineer who can't drive."

"I *can* drive, but I don't."

"I thought all boys liked cars."

He says nothing.

"Oh, dear, I'm sorry."

"No, it doesn't matter. Really."

"I'm going to take Lennie away now. He has a wash and change at midday." She puts her head on one side and smiles a deliberately charming smile. "Thank you for an entertaining morning, Mr. Bolsover."

"And thank you, too, Mrs. Morgan."

13

A month passes, and Bolsover is gradually absorbed into the routines of
the island. The Alpha has become his home, Mrs. K his guardian. His
daily walks to and from Warren's are pleasurable, his new occupation intriguing, his fellow editors always entertaining. Exploring the island, he
frequently encounters his new friend Arabella, who spends much time
out of doors, swimming or wheeling her husband along the promenade
or the coastal paths. There is something rather special about this woman,
in Bolsover's opinion, and she apparently finds him likable and amusing.

From time to time Bolsover walks along the beach to Handsome
Point and checks that the courser has not yet flown. In part, he does this
at the request of his birding friend Wilson, who has now left the island.

He is happy to accede to Wilson's request because, despite his views on bird-watching, he has developed a close interest in this particular bird. He has even bought himself a pair of binoculars—not the enormous green sort, but a more modest kind, appropriate for a novice—and a pair of stout boots for the rocky stuff.

At Warren's, Bolsover knows that he is not required to make innovations, but sees that the Somerset guide could be much improved. He begins a careful study of the county, starting with Arthur Mee's old county guide, a substantial volume that provides a clear historical background. He discovers Warren's picture files—an ancient collection of boxes in urgent need of an archivist but containing many treasures. He makes notes on places in the county that catch his fancy: the pretty little villages of the Quantock Hills, the holiday town of Minehead, the charming harbor of Porlock Weir and the Somerset Levels—the flat, waterlogged country that stretches eastward from the Bristol Channel to the blue-and-brown mass of the Mendip Hills. There is something mystical about such places, he feels, something ancient and powerful that is worth exploring.

At the Alpha, Bolsover is increasingly persuaded into a round or two of whist—he's not yet skilled enough for bridge—by Mrs. Allcard and Mrs. Walters. The latter takes great joy in contriving jokes about Mrs. Allcard's name, which her friend suffers with remarkable patience; if these two are villains in hiding, it's difficult to imagine what their specialty might be—unless, of course, it's gambling. Miss Matthews and Kevin Brand remain unsettling and remote, but conversation with Colonel Tapp, when he gets started on Turkmenistan or the Empty Quarter, is difficult to stop. Many pleasant evenings may be spent in the residents' lounge with the colonel and Joe Firth. Joe's an uncomplicated fellow, with an air of sociable alertness like a well-trained dog. The colonel, it appears, has journeyed on camelback from the Aral Sea across the Kyzylkum Desert to Tashkent, and on to Namangan and Osh. He has slipped by night from Kyrgyzstan into China through the high Torugart Pass, and run a lorry-load of stolen rifles through Feyzabad and into the wilderness of the Hindu Kush; on that occasion he was fortunate to escape with his life and a bullet through his shoulder. He is absolutely convincing, this man; surely it is not possible that his stories are untrue, or that he is other than he seems?

Perhaps these early weeks at the Alpha are the most easily enjoyable of Bolsover's life; this may be more fun, he suddenly thinks, than those August fortnights that Kitty and I spent at Walton-on-the-Naze. Dear Kitty! It's something of a shock to think of her again, and of their holidays, their house, their garden, the story of Ravensdale—memories that are rapidly becoming, it seems to Bolsover, as distant as the Hindu Kush.

Every night he opens his bedroom curtains to allow the beams of Handsome Light to enter his room, and every morning he rises eagerly and goes immediately to the window to discover the mood of the sea. That interminable waterway might lead a man to the Indian Ocean, the mouth of the Indus, northward through Pakistan to high Kashmir and the peaks of the Karakorum—where, the colonel said, the traveler may stand and look eastward toward Tibet and the unmatched grandeur of the Himalayas!

On Bolsover's fifth Sunday at the Alpha, a little after four in the morning, Leonard Morgan's heart stops, Arabella presses her alarm, and the awful racket of the bells wakes the hotel. Seeing the ambulance's blue light flashing on his ceiling, Bolsover knows at once what has happened. He stands at his window and watches as Arabella emerges, walking beside the stretcher, and the ambulance drives away. For a while he sits restlessly on the edge of his bed, but when he hears the creak of footsteps in the corridor, he opens his door and discovers Joe Firth and the colonel.

"That racket woke me up," says the colonel. "Couldn't sleep. Going down for a pick-me-up."

"Good idea," says Bolsover.

The residents have gathered in the lounge. As Bolsover later writes in his notebook, *When something happens, people just have to talk*. Apparently Lennie is not dead; his heart has been restarted by the ambulance men, and there is some prospect that he will survive. The residents of the Alpha think little of that prospect, and agree that the most satisfactory outcome would be his immediate decease.

Bolsover, returning to his room, attempts to sleep but is unable to do so. Having tossed and turned for an hour, he dresses and sets off for the hospital. Lennie he finds to be in intensive care, and Arabella sleeping in a side room. He leaves her sleeping and waits in the canteen. An hour later she appears.

"Oh, it's you," she says. "That's good." She looks exhausted. He fetches coffee and doughnuts.

"I never eat doughnuts," she says, taking a large bite.

"There is a time for being picky," he says, "and there is a time for doughnuts."

"Oh, Bolsover," she says, laughing and yawning together.

Having drunk her coffee and eaten the doughnut, Arabella falls asleep at the table, her head on her arms. He wakes her, leads her back to the side room, and immediately she's asleep again.

"I'll be back this afternoon," Bolsover says to the nurse at the desk, and returns to the Alpha for an hour or two; he is in need of sleep himself, having spent much of the night with the colonel in Tashkent.

"The trouble is," says Arabella when he returns to the hospital, "Lennie's done this before. More than once. It's very difficult, the way he lingers and lingers. But this time he's had a stroke as well, so the doctors say, and he's likely to have another any minute. It may not be long, this time."

"A heart attack and a stroke, and he's still alive."

"It must be all that cricket when he was a lad."

"Would you prefer to be left on your own?"

"Oh, no. Well—if you want to go, of course—"

"It's Sunday," he says. "I have no engagements."

———

So begins a period of time in which it is not always possible for Bolsover to know whether he is awake or asleep, dreaming or simply remembering—remembering that other time, that other hospital. Lennie's bed is soon moved to a small room that is otherwise empty; evidently the full resources of intensive care are not to be employed again. He is connected to a machine that makes small sounds—a steady wheeze, a soft bleep—and surrounded by flowered curtains. Within this space, the vigil-keepers are provided with easy chairs, a table, and blankets, and a number of hours pass without regard for night or day.

Close beside the dying man, Arabella and Bolsover doze in their chairs. This is how it should always be done, he thinks. On that other occasion he had been shut away in another room in some faraway part of the hospital; no doubt it is better to wait within sight, listening for the slightest tremor in the sighing of the ventilator, startled from a doze by the brisk clack of the nurse's heels, straining to make out her whispers to the doctor. When at last he had been allowed to see Kitty, she had been *arranged* for him—yes, that was it—arranged symmetrically on her back, when in life she had always slept on her side, tightly curled; and now she lay on her back, arms at her sides, seeming to stare woodenly at the ceiling. He had kneeled beside her, taken her hand—it was so cold! He asked how long she had been dead; the doctor looked at his clipboard and said that she had died two hours earlier. Two hours before he even knew!

Tears roll down Bolsover's cheeks; he brushes them away, sits up, and sees that Arabella is awake and watching him. She makes no comment on his tears, no doubt because she has worked out their cause; she doesn't need telling, this woman.

"I'd go out for a while," Arabella says, "but he'll die if I leave him—I know he will. It's just the sort of thing he would do. I want to be here when he goes. I dare say it's silly, after all this time, but there it is."

"I understand."

"You could talk to me," says Arabella. "Talk to me about anything you like." She curls herself into her chair and closes her eyes.

Anything? Into his mind comes the girl on wheels, the birders, the storm, the captain and his little ship, *Providence.*

"I came here on a ferry," Bolsover says. "I mistook the departure time, and had to wait for hours on the quayside. There was a girl there, perhaps ten or eleven years old, dressed all in pink and wearing roller-boots. She was incredibly good on those boots. She should have been in a circus—perhaps she was. When it got dark, she put lights on her hands and feet—torches of some kind, I suppose. She looked like Tinker Bell flying in the dark, her lights whirling."

"How lovely," says Arabella, without opening her eyes.

"She must have been practicing for months. She was so good she might have been born with roller-boots on."

"Girls do that. They practice things endlessly. I did the same. It must be in our genes. But what are we practicing for? And why do women need such skills? Is skipping an essential skill for motherhood?" Arabella yawns largely.

Bolsover talks about the birders, the storm, the barman's invitation, the view from the bridge. Once or twice he assumes Arabella to have fallen asleep, but each time she opens an eye, wanting him to continue. At his conversation with the captain, she opens her eyes fully and tells him that men have a very peculiar way of talking to one another.

"I knew it was a bit of a game. The captain did, too."

"Chaps together, playing chaps' games."

"We all play games sometimes, don't we? Don't women play that sort of game?"

"Of course we do," she says, shutting her eyes. "Though not in the same way."

Bolsover describes the fishing boat, the great waves, the rushing moon, and the Handsome Light that showed them the way home, in response to which Arabella begins to snore, quite delicately, and is certainly fast asleep.

———

Waiting. Every life has its share of that, but poor old Lennie, however wicked he may have been, has been waiting too long. Eight years! Let him be released this night, thinks Bolsover. Let him go, let him fly away now, for he has surely reached his journey's end.

The only lamp is that beside Lennie's bed. It might be that they are waiting outside a nomad's tent, pitched at the foot of the great Karakorum, whose snowy peaks rear in the darkness behind. The curtained tent, Bolsover suddenly notices, is exactly the same as the one that surrounded Kitty, all those years ago. He looks at Arabella, curled in her chair and wrapped in a blanket, and at that moment she opens her eyes.

"You've stopped again."

"I got to the end. Besides, you fell asleep."

"I did not."

"Yes, you did. You were snoring."

"Was I? How embarrassing." She is not in the least embarrassed.

"It was a gentle snore, a ladylike snore."

"I doubt any kind of snore can be ladylike, but we'll let that one go. You can start talking again, Bolsover. I could be here for days, you know."

He doesn't reply, and after a moment she says, "No, it won't be days, of course. Not this time." She shuts her eyes and wriggles deeper into the chair.

He intends to tell her about his becoming an apprentice and learning to be an engineer, but finds himself talking about Kitty and her garden. In the middle of it he looks up and sees that Arabella is watching him again, her head propped on one hand. He describes Kitty's affection for *Campsis grandiflora,* and how the story ended in a ward like this one, with a lighted tent that was almost the same, even to the flowery curtains. At times he discovers some difficulty in the telling; when he pauses, Arabella says nothing, but only nods, and goes on listening, curled up in her chair. When he has finished, Arabella nods her head once more, and says nothing.

"I didn't mean to tell you all that," he says. "I'm sorry. I drifted off the point."

"You became entangled, I think," she says. "You got entangled in all those flowers."

"You mean, that's why I went off the point?"

"No—I mean you and Kitty. You got entangled with each other and wrapped up with all the flowers, so you couldn't see that anything else was possible."

"Did we?" He is puzzled. What else was possible?

"I think that's what happened. I may be wrong. It has been known."

He still doesn't understand. He sits there, staring at the yellow tent until a vision of the high mountains of the Karakorum comes to him, somehow triggering a grand adjustment. The familiar landscape of Bolsover's mind, which had been secure and permanent, begins to move, and slips away, and he seems to be falling.

"Oh," he says. "Oh."

It is midnight in the ward, and silent, apart from the steady tick and wheeze of the machines. Bolsover grips the arms of his chair as the tiny figures of himself and Kitty, hand in hand, appear to fall away down a long tunnel, turning as they fall—such an experience cannot be grasped entire, but only sketched, and falling is part of it, falling, yes, and a memory of a film run backward, an exploding house, its bricks and tiles, beams and doors, drawn spinning out of the air to create, from fragments and blackness, a fresh new house, solid and intact.

To Bolsover is revealed, in that swift moment, the true nature of his years with Kitty. His room at Butler's, their little house, her garden— how distorted their life had been, how ridiculously narrow, how entirely closed! Such possibilities in the world, yet we thought nothing of them, and never looked over the garden wall! Oh, now I know! Now I see! I'll take Kitty's hand and go to the door, set out with her, out into the light, out into the open. We'll begin again—oh, yes, we'll go to such places, see such things. Why, even the fantastic Karakorum is not beyond reach—at which he remembers everything, and sees things in their true light. He sits very still, waiting for the dust to settle, the air to clear.

"I think," says Arabella, gazing steadily at Bolsover, "that the great thing is to fight regret. One should try to know the truth, of course, and once it's known, there may be lessons to be learned, but regret must be avoided at all costs. Regret sneaks up on a person, and works its way under the skin without you noticing. In my case, I regretted meeting Lennie, I regretted marrying him, I regretted leaving him, I regretted going back to him. Finally I regretted that I hadn't pushed him over the cliff. Not far from the lighthouse there's a very fine cliff, with a high path, well suited to murder—you may have seen the place. I wheeled Lennie to the edge and then stopped. He wouldn't have known it was happening. It would have been a happy release. But it isn't so easy, when you get to the moment. If I'd done it for him, I could have lived with it, but I knew I was doing it for myself, and that's quite different. I didn't push him off, and now I've decided to give up regret. I'll stay to the end, and after that—well, I'll get on with my life."

She has filled a little time until he has recovered. "Thank you," says Bolsover.

She laughs. "We have here," she says, "a prime case of the blind leading the blind. I only know that too much thinking can be a mistake. Sometimes one just has to get on with it, and to hell with thinking."

"But I can't help thinking," says Bolsover, hearing in his own voice a plaintive tone.

"I know," she says. "We'll have to work on that."

Leonard Morgan died, according to his death certificate, at three o'clock in the afternoon of the second day, in full daylight, the Bedou tent folded away, the doctor and nurse in attendance. It was not a single dramatic event, as one expects death to be, but several small events, and mostly a matter of conversation. At ten minutes past three a woman doctor came to inspect the machine and the patient; she made some notes and walked briskly from the ward, shortly returned with a colleague and a nurse. Together they inspected the patient and the equipment, murmuring in low voices, and then the doctor approached Arabella.

Although the ventilator was wheezing in its usual way and Lennie still appeared, by the slight rise and fall of his chest, to be breathing, it was only the machine: the monitor now showed nothing, and the tiny spark of Lennie's life, which had been perceptible an hour earlier, had stolen away.

"I'm sorry, Mrs. Morgan," said the doctor in a formal tone. "In view of the lack of vital signs, our advice is that the equipment should now be turned off, your husband being beyond help."

At which, Arabella went to kneel beside the bed, the tubes and wires were disconnected, the equipment wheeled away, and the yellow curtains drawn while she said goodbye to the man whom, whatever he had been, she had once loved.

Bolsover, waiting again, wonders at the imperceptible manner in which so great an event has happened. Before the moment, last words are commonly reported; there is a final gasp, a shudder, a sudden tilt of the head, a horrid stilling of the staring eyes, a dropping open of the mouth. But not in this case: nobody could know exactly when this man ceased to be. Likely enough Lennie had been well on his way before the ambulance came. He'd been declining for years, his brain slowly darkening, the shadow spreading. As a test of life, brain stem activity was measured, but in what sense does life exist if a man is not conscious of himself? *Hope* may exist, hope among the bystanders, but the true test of life must be a person's awareness of it. It was only because the darkness and silence of Lennie's mind could not be measured, but only guessed at, that he had been sustained for so long in that awful parody of life. The event itself, his death, had been constructed only by the curtains, medical priests, and mysterious machines that surrounded it. Whether or not he's a scoundrel, a vigil must be kept, and death witnessed; I am honored in that duty, thinks Bolsover. Yes, *honored*. That's exactly the right word. And the death of this man, whom I never knew, has changed my own life, which begins again here, at this moment. In future I shall hold firmly to whatever appears certain, he tells himself, and I shall go ahead steadily, and never mind storms and tempests.

So Bolsover thinks, and it is evident that he is recovering his normal condition, following the strange and unsettling dreams of the preceding night.

When Arabella emerges from the curtains, her eyes are red but she is her usual brisk self. They talk of practicalities, and there is an unspoken assumption that it's convenient to do the necessary things together. That evening they eat together in the Alpha's restaurant.

"You've told me a lot of things about yourself," Arabella says, "but you haven't told me why you're at the Alpha, which is a place where villains go to hide. When are you going to tell me why you're here?"

Bolsover does not answer for some time, and at last he says, "I will try. But it will be difficult."

"Lots of things are difficult," says Arabella, picking up her knife and fork. "Doesn't mean they can't be done."

"That is so," says Bolsover. "I told you I would try. Do you mind if I don't tell you this minute?"

"Not at all. In fact, there are things I need to think about first. About twenty years ago Lennie told me he wanted to be cremated and his ashes to be scattered at sea. I'll do as he wished."

A cremation is arranged and Mrs. K tells Arabella that she knows a fisherman who has a sideline in scattering; it's getting quite popular these days. He'll arrange the boat, no problem. The fisherman asks whether she wants any extras—the vicar is his cousin, he knows a man with a portable organ, his son is in the choir, and if she wants flowers, he has a cousin who owns a florist—

"None of that," Arabella tells him. "Just bring the boat. That's all. Ten-thirty tomorrow morning at the quay steps—can you do that?"

"Yes, ma'am," says the fisherman. "Fifty pound for cash."

"Good man," says Arabella.

On the day the sun is shining, the sea calm. Mrs. K and the residents of the Alpha have been invited as witnesses. Half a mile off the harbor the fisherman shuts off his engine and the boat drifts for a few moments. Then Arabella takes the lid from the pot and tips the ashes over the side. The remains of Leonard Morgan settle in a gray carpet on the surface of the water, a small cloud of the lighter stuff drifting gently away.

"Goodbye, Lennie," Arabella whispers. She's leaning far over the rail, her hands reaching down toward the dusty water. "Goodbye, Lennie."

"Dammit," she says, standing up and wiping her face. "Dammit, Lennie, I'm sorry it took you so long. Even a bastard doesn't deserve that." She turns and says, "All right, skipper, let's go home now."

"Straightaway, ma'am?"

"Straightaway," she says. "He's been nine years a-dying, and that's long enough for anyone. It's all done now. Let's go home. Let's go home and have a glass of something."

The fisherman puts his engine ahead, the boat gathers way, and the little troop of mourners progresses in a broad curve across the bay and into the protecting arms of the harbor.

At the Alpha, Mrs. K insists on a toast. "To Mrs. Morgan," she says, lifting her glass, "and her future happiness."

"To Mrs. Morgan," the residents repeat, "and her future happiness."

"Thank you," says Arabella. "I'll tell you what, it's a great relief that it's over, but I'll miss you all, I really will. Here's to all of you," she says, and the residents drink, rather more cautiously, to their own futures.

She'll go away soon. Of course she will; there's no longer the slightest reason for her to stay, except that she wants to hear my story, thinks Bolsover.

14

The events that resulted in Bolsover's presence at the Alpha Hotel are closely related to his memories of his wife. Long after she died, her image remained vivid, and whenever he wished—often in the small hours, unable to sleep—he was able to summon a specific moment and run it like a movie in his mind. The way in which she inclined her head, the particular tones of her voice, the rhythm of her footsteps, her attitudes and beliefs, her laughter and her anger—all these he knew in fine detail; but best of all he knew her face.

Everyone is good at recognizing faces, of course. It's a skill that is evident soon after birth; no doubt it usefully improves the child's chances of survival. Kitty's face—that narrow oval face framed in dark hair, the fine nose with a slight curve, those high cheekbones, her slightly hollow cheeks, her neat little ears and soft brown eyes—was undoubtedly distinctive, but Bolsover's ability to recall her is not at all unusual. Any man knows his wife in a crowd by the way she moves, even if she's fifty yards away. A woman knows her husband by the way he clears his throat, though it's pitch-dark. From a great crowd of shoppers in Oxford Street we'll easily pick out our family and our friends by the stream of tiny and particular signals that they transmit, signals that we read so quickly and so well.

Except that, just occasionally, while hurrying for a train, running late, anxious, a man will spot his dear wife, rush up, and give her a great hug—and the hugged woman will turn, and be a complete stranger.

In the first instant we try to reject the negative evidence. Certainly it's her, but somehow she looks different—perhaps she has been to the hairdresser—so secure is our memory that we try to force the reality into the remembered mold. Milliseconds later, as our error begins to become apparent, we may feel a flash of anger—*I have been tricked! Someone is impersonating my wife!*—followed sharply, of course, by the awful surging heat of embarrassment. Now we've got it: this is another person entirely.

This commonplace event contains the seeds of Bolsover's more considerable error. We recognize what he did, and at least one of the reasons why it occurred: when we want something desperately, we're inclined to invent it.

In his freelance days Bolsover was often required to attend social events at Angelique's, a bistro used by Turner & Turner's to entertain their clients. Here Bolsover was the professional engineer, talking with authority to the client on technical subjects. He'd have a glass or two of wine and make perceptive conversation about the product, its design, its purpose, and the needs of customers who might buy it. At eight-thirty Bolsover would drive home, stopping on the way for a takeaway. He always went home the same way; over the years he'd found a number of back roads that allowed him to dodge the worst of the traffic.

He'd get home and eat his takeaway while working up his copy for the following day.

On that particular evening—a Friday in early January—Bolsover drove across town to Angelique's through large snowflakes drifting down from a gray sky. Several times that day he had been required to display familiarity with air-to-air refueling, a technology about which he knew almost nothing; but an engineer with his wits about him can always think of something to say. He'd studied the client's drawings and photographs, nodded wisely, made a few telling points, and suggested changes in the artwork for the company's brochure, thereby risking the irritation of his creative colleagues. Bolsover was not afraid to deploy his engineering knowledge impartially, knowing that it gave clients added confidence in the agency, balancing the wilder imagination of their graphic designers.

A contract had been signed with the air-refueling company, and Bolsover had contributed to its acquisition. At Angelique's he drank two or three small glasses of white wine—exactly how many, he couldn't afterward recall. His blood count was well below the legal limit, so it's unlikely to have been more than two. He drove home automatically, hardly noticing the weather. His warm and quiet Volkswagen, a glass or two of wine, an interesting new contract to which he had contributed—these were fine things, and a bit of winter weather was of no account. He called at the Koh-I-Noor, hurrying through the deepening snow to collect a chicken tikka masala, and drove on. The traffic light at North Road was red. He stopped the car and glanced to his right. A girl was sheltering in an estate agent's doorway, a girl he'd seen many times before. She often stood in that same doorway. He'd seen her before. He knew she'd be there. He'd seen her before, many times, when he happened to stop at the lights on North Road and happened to glance in her direction. He has seen her before.

What does she look like? She's a girl with long dark hair, a black leather jacket and skirt, long thin legs, bright red high heels. A small girl, pretty in a fragile sort of way. We'd say she is—what would we call her, nowadays? A working girl, a sex worker. A call girl—that's what they used to be called. A prostitute, a tart, a whore—those are ugly words, and she's a pretty girl. He's seen her many times before, always in that doorway, twenty yards away, never close. That doorway is her office. She works from there. He's seen her many times before at the North Road traffic lights when he stops the car and happens to glance across the road toward the estate agent.

Stationary at the lights, the car steaming up, Bolsover lowers his window a little. The girl looks at him, pulls her jacket over her head, and makes a run for his car. She runs through the falling snow, across the road, round the back of the car, opens the passenger door, jumps in, slams the door. *There's a girl in my car.*

She's so quick that he hasn't time to move or speak. The door opens, the girl slips in, slams the door, there she is. He stares at her. A girl in his car. And she's not just any girl, either, but a girl with a narrow oval face, a fine nose with a slight downward curve, high cheekbones, neat little ears, and soft brown eyes. She's Kitty. She's Bolsover's girl. Except, of course, she isn't. She's a working girl who's shivering from the cold.

"Twenny in the car," says the girl. "Forry if you wanna come back."

Twenny in the car. Her voice—what's wrong with her voice? Her voice isn't right. What's she saying? He ought to say, Please get out of my car. He ought to say it, but he doesn't. *There's a girl in my car*—that's all he can think. Not any girl, but this particular girl. I know her.

He knows her and he doesn't know her. All right, let's go to your place. He doesn't say that, because he doesn't know her. That's stupid— of course he knows her. He's seen her before, many times. There's a girl in my car. I know her. Who is she? *She's exactly like Kitty.*

The light changes. He doesn't move. A car's horn sounds impatiently. I'll say, "Please get out of my car," she'll open the door, get out, and I'll drive off. Simple: but he says nothing. There's a girl in the car, a small, dark-haired girl with red shoes, a girl he's seen many times before, standing in that doorway. It's his imaginary girl, a girl who happens to be a dead ringer for his wife. The car horn sounds again, more urgently. Without his willing it, Bolsover's foot depresses the clutch, he selects first gear, releases the hand brake, and drives away. He's a careful driver.

The girl sits back and puts on her seat belt. Click. That's it. It's done now. She can't get out now. She says, "I've got a place. I'll tell you the way. Forry quid at my place. All ri'? My name's Tina."

Her name's Tina. *Forry quid.* Forty quid, she means. He's working it out. Now he knows what sort of girl she is, unless he's much mistaken. Forty pounds isn't much for—for whatever she does. Tina. Forty quid. How much does she earn in a year? Depends how many times a day, how many days.

Here's a roundabout. "First exit," says the girl. Tina. That's her name. He looks sideways at her. Pale skin, thin legs, clasping her hands between her knees. A girl in my car. A girl called Tina. He takes the first exit.

"Next left, then second left," says the girl in his car. Red hands. Cold hands. Goose bumps on her arms and thighs. She's cold. Forry quid. Is this happening? It's happening. The girl's still in my car. She's a lovely girl, except she's got the wrong voice. Tina. Is he dreaming? No, he's not dreaming. He turns left, then second left.

"By that tree," says the girl. "See that space?" Tina. That's her name. "You can park there." She turns to inspect him. "You're all ri', are you? You're not funny nor nuffink, are you? You going to say hello or somefink?"

Is he all right? He isn't all right. Is he funny nor nuffink? She means, will he harm her? Of course he won't harm her! She's lovely, this girl. How old is she?

"I'm all right," he says to the girl. It isn't much, but at least he's started talking.

"Over there," says the girl. "Park by that tree. There's a space." She points with a thin finger. A parking space under a tree, cars both sides of the road, old houses, plane trees, tall Victorian houses, shabby, steps up to them, dozens of doorbells. He backs into the space, gets it wrong, bumps the curb, comes out, backs in again, gets it right this time.

"Come on," says the girl. How old is she? Twenty? She gets out, slams the door. Tina is her name. He could drive off now. He ought to drive off. He will drive off. He doesn't drive off. He gets out, shuts the driver's door, locks the car. The girl stands under the tree, her coat over her head. "Come on," she says again. She's waiting for him. She thinks he might do a runner. Yes, he might do a runner. He doesn't do a runner. He takes a step, and one step leads to another, another. He's following her up half a dozen stone steps, through a front door, up a flight of stairs, the wallpaper yellow, turning a corner, up another flight, the banister under his fingers cold and sticky with damp, following the girl's thin legs as she clatters up the stairs in her red heels, through another door and into a hallway. She shuts the door, turns to face him. "Forry quid," she says. Forty quid. She takes off her jacket and hangs it on a hook. In the gap between her top and her skirt she's got a butterfly tattoo, a small butterfly, only twenty-five millimeters wide. Something like that. An inch, give or take a bit. Thin, cold hands and little red marks in the crook of her elbow. "You got the forry quid?" The butterfly has red wings with oval marks that look like eyes.

He takes out his wallet, holding the warm leather between his fingers. This mustn't be done, can't be done, won't be done. I won't do this. It mustn't be done and it's gone too far to stop: both conditions are true. He takes out two twenty-pound notes, gives them to her. She holds them up to the light one after the other, like a girl at the checkout. Tina, her name is.

"I think——" Bolsover says.

She looks at him. "What?"

"I've made a mistake," he says. He's getting over the shock. He knows it's all wrong. He's ashamed. He wants her and he doesn't want her. He has to give her up. He can't do it. He's failed. He still wants her, but now he's decided.

"What d'you mean? Don't you fancy me?"

"No, I mean——" He's despairing now. There's no happy way out, no way to avoid the shame. He wants her, he doesn't want her.

"I seen you looking before," she says. "I seen you looking lots of times. You always look at me, doncha. I seen you stop and look over. I know what you want, so I got in your car, din' I? I seen you looking."

He can't deny it. She's quick and she's right.

"I seen you looking lots of times. There's no such thing as just looking, is there? Looking means wanting, dunnit."

She knows that. He looks and he wants her. Does he want her? Yes. She's his girl, the one he's always dreaming of. She has such a lovely face. He's used to her voice now. Her voice doesn't bother him anymore. He's talking to her and she's getting real. She's real, this girl Tina. Does her mother know? No, of course she doesn't. Look, it's all right. People do this all the time. It's natural. It's her choice, isn't it? The oldest profession. A lady of the night. Is she twenty years younger than him? Thirty? There's a tikka masala in the car and it's snowing. As for her face—those eyes, her little ears—she's the girl—she's lovely— what can he do? A red butterfly—he can go or he can stay. Obvious. But which? *Looking means wanting.* That's enough: he's going to leave. He's decided.

Is this to his credit? Either he's a good man, a moral man who's seen the light just in time, or he's a feeble coward. He wants her and he dares not have her. He hasn't even got the guts to consummate a perfectly normal desire. It's one of those things: he's got himself into this and there's no way out. Something like this, you can't go back the way you came, back to where you were before, because time only runs one way, and everything's different now.

He takes out his wallet and gives her another twenty. "I'm sorry." Why did he do that? Guilt money. He knows that. Groveling now. Abasing himself. Horrible. He's a waste of time, but she isn't bothered. Maybe she gets a john like him from time to time. A john—that's what I am. A john. American slang. A punter, a mark, a john. Please let this end soon.

"I'm sorry," he says. "I'm sorry." It can't be said and must be said. "I made a mistake."

"Did you reelly," she says in a slow, blurry sort of way. "Did you reelly." She turns away from him, crosses her arms, reaches back, and pulls her top over her head. She's taken her top off, this girl. She turns back to him, unhooks her skirt, lets it fall to the floor. He feels suddenly weak—here's a chair—he sits down.

"You made a mistake, did you," she says in that blurry voice. She's stepping out of her knickers now. She's wearing red high heels and a butterfly tattoo. "Come on," she says, holding out her hand. "Come on, mister."

He takes her hand. Now his fall begins. "The force that through the green fuse"—he takes her cold hand, stands up, follows her into the bedroom. Bolsover, that square man of middle age, follows the girl into the bedroom. She's a girl he's known for years, a girl with a butterfly on her back whom he met ten minutes ago. He follows her in and shuts the door behind him. Now his fall begins.

It is a close-run thing. Which way will it go? Nobody would have put money on it, either way. Sometimes sex is easy, like in the films. Maybe it *is* easy, sometimes. But not always, it isn't.

After a while—not more than fifteen minutes—the girl comes out of the bedroom, collects her clothes from the floor, and goes back in. There's the sound of running water. She keeps herself clean, this girl. She's a sensible girl. The two of them appear again, clothed now. Bolsover's fiddling with his tie.

"Come on," says the girl. Time's getting on. She wants to get back to her pitch.

"You gotta take me back now," she says. She wants to go back to her doorway, find another punter. Of course she does. "You brung me here. I wanna go back now, don't I? Come on."

He must drive her back. It's not the driving, it's not the time it takes. It's what you say in the car, or what you don't say, the silence in the car.

"All right," he says. What else would he say? It's snowing. She's got no clothes to speak of, just that little top and a skimpy skirt that doesn't join up.

This isn't love. This is business. He's given her sixty pounds. That's the measure of his guilt: sixty pounds. Not a lot of money, not enough to pay off the guilt. Money's no good when it comes to guilt. Whatever you pay, money can't get you out of it. It doesn't work like that: it's a different currency. Once something happens, you're stuck with it forever.

She's lost interest in him now. She's got the money and she isn't bothered about him. You get all sorts, and he's not the nasty sort but he's slow. He doesn't know what he wants, that's all. *Get real, sunshine.* There's a mirror on the wall. She gets out a lipstick and does her lips, then checks her watch. Nine-thirty—coming up to her busy time. "Okay, let's go," she says. This is the same girl as before, the one with the oval face, the neat little ears, and the wrong voice. He likes her voice now. It's got an edge to it. She knows who she is, but Bolsover doesn't. Sometimes he seems to know her, then again he doesn't. She takes no notice of him. She looks again in the mirror and decides to change her leather jacket for a proper coat. It's snowing. This is a girl who gets into cars with men she doesn't know, trusting only to her own judgment, a thin, small girl who feels the cold. She's more worried about the cold than the men. She can handle men. She's brave and she's stupid. But she isn't stupid—that's the funny thing. She isn't stupid, yet she gets into a car with a man who could be anybody.

Now he doesn't want to go. He's dragging his feet because he's one of those who muddle sex with love. He's made love to her and now he wants to talk, but she doesn't. She's done her bit and she's busy. She's got a lot more work to do. She goes to the door and holds it open. He goes out. She shuts the door and follows him down the stairs to the car. It's snowing hard now. She gets into the car. He gets a scraper and cleans the windscreen. He wants her to stay with him. Before, he wanted her to go; now he wants her to stay. What kind of stuff is that? Answer: ordinary human stuff, contradiction and muddle, despite the fact we're so clever. Clever! Better stupid than clever: clever sees the snags, calculates the odds, says it ain't worth it, so you don't do it; and then you do it after all. *Why couldn't I just say no?*

"Come on," says the girl. "It's getting late." Bolsover starts the car, drives away with the girl in his car, the snow coming at the windscreen and swerving away at the last minute, as if he's driving into an explosion. *Why couldn't I just say yes?* The swirl of the snow—Bernoulli. Vortex theory. Turbulence. *I could have said no.* He changes gear roughly, jerking at the lever. He never does that. He's a careful driver. *I could have said yes straightaway.* The girl says something. What's she saying? "Go slower," she says sharply. "There's a bad corner." A bad corner. "For fuck's sake," says the girl, putting her hands out in front of her. There's something in the swirling snow—it's only a parked car. He swerves round it. *What if I'd said to her—* There's a little bump—he's touched the curb—he straightens the car. "You stupid fucker," she's saying. She's yelling at him. Why? What does she mean? "Stop the fucking car," she's shouting. Here's another bend. He slows the car, looks at her. "Stop the fucking car," she yells. "You fucking hit someone." He hit the curb, that's all. "I touched the curb," he says. "I just touched the curb." She's banging on the dashboard with both hands. *"Stop the fucking car."* Here's a turning. He turns off the main road and stops the car. She throws off the seat belt, tears at the door handle, struggles out, slams the door, and is away into the falling snow. Tina. She's gone now.

For some time Bolsover sits shaking in his Volkswagen, the engine running, wipers going, snow falling. Eventually he turns off the engine, gets out of the car, and walks round to the nearside. At first he thinks there's no damage, but then he sees a scratch along the bottom of the door—only a thin scratch in the silver paint, a scratch about three hundred millimeters long. Metric units. Engineers talk millimeters now. He was brought up imperial but he's gone metric. Three hundred millimeters, that's all. If he'd hit someone, there'd be more damage than that. I touched the curb, that's all. He crouches beside the car, the snow falling steadily on his head, feeling the scratch with the tip of his finger. Only a little scratch. He stands up and looks back the way he came. Parked cars, a bend in the road, a streetlamp, snow falling, nothing in sight. No cars. No pedestrians. Nobody. Silence. Where is he? He's not sure. He brushes the snow from his coat and hair and gets back into the car. I'll have to go back. He'll have to find out. Where did she go? She ran off. She wanted to get away. She was afraid. Tina. That's her name. *What did I hit?*

He starts the engine. I'll go back, and what will I find? Blue flashing lights, of course, an ambulance, a crowd gathering round a body in the road. Really, Bolsover! He touched the curb, that's all. Just a little scratch. Go home, or the tikka masala will be cold. It's cold already. She's lovely, that girl, but she ran away.

He drives slowly forward, finds a side turning, turns the car round, drives back the way he came. Nothing but falling snow. Reaches the junction. He turns right, drives on. Nearly there now. What's that up ahead? A flashing blue light. He slows the car, pulls in to the curb, switches off the engine. A hundred meters ahead is a flashing blue light, an ambulance, and a little crowd of people.

It's still snowing. This is how things happen. One thing causes another. There's no stopping it. Even when you know you're on the wrong track, you can't turn back. There ought to be a way to go back to the last corner and turn the other way. It could have been a dog. Never mind. Can't be helped. No point worrying. What's done is done. Ma used to say those things, mopping his face, dabbing at his knee, and wiping his tears away. *What if the traffic light hadn't been red?*

15

"I don't know that I can go on," says Bolsover.

"I don't know that you can't," says Arabella. "For one thing, I've told you my story, and we can't be friends unless we're in balance. A story is owed a story, a truth a truth. That's how the world wags."

"I don't think that's true at all," says Bolsover. "You just made that up. You're too clever by half."

Arabella laughs. "I'm not clever, but I admit I'm devious. I am learned in deviousness because I was once a lawyer and because I was married for many years to a man of cruel and misshapen nature. You're just afraid I'll think much less of you."

"Yes," says Bolsover. "That's right."

"You're what's commonly called a nice man. I know that because I've known a lot of men, and you're no more wicked than I am. As for how foolish you've been—well, yes, you've evidently been very foolish indeed, but being foolish is one of the ways we learn things."

"I just think—I just don't think I can tell you the next bit."

"My dear Bolsover! I'm losing patience! I shall hear the rest of your story or we shall part! So let's get on with it, shall we?" Arabella laughs, but she's not the sort for prevarication, that's for sure.

"She got out of the car," says Bolsover. "She ran away. I saw her look back once, then she was gone. I got out of the car and found a scratch on the door. I turned the car round and started to drive back."

He takes a deep breath.

"I went back to the main road. There was a flashing light, a blue flashing light. I knew it would be bad as soon as I saw the light. The police were directing the traffic, someone was setting up a flood lamp, another person was wearing an oversuit—one of those forensic people, I suppose. I parked the car. It was still snowing."

He's speaking quickly now, not looking at her, looking down at the floor.

"As I walked along, I met two people out on the pavement, watching. A man and a woman, smoking and watching. The woman had a coat over her head and was smoking a cigarette. I asked what had happened. The man said, 'Some bastard ran over a little girl and drove off.' The woman said, 'Fucking hit-and-run.' Smoke came out of her mouth as she spoke. I remember that."

At this point Arabella starts to reach a hand toward him, then thinks better of it. Bolsover doesn't notice.

"One of the policemen was giving orders. I went toward him and he held out a clipboard. 'Keep back, sir,' he said. 'We're busy here.' I went closer and said to him, 'Is the child all right?' He was impatient. 'I don't know that, sir,' he said. 'I think it was me,' I said. He said, 'What do you mean?' He looked at me and I could see he was wondering if I were crazy. I said, 'I think it was me that hit the girl. I drove by here just now. I hit something.' "

Bolsover nods vigorously to himself. It's as if he is drawing the memories out into the light by main force. "I drove by here just now"— these are the words he used; he hears himself saying them in the peculiar silence of the falling snow, the policeman staring at him.

" 'You'd better come this way, sir,' the policeman said. He asked me for my keys and said they'd deal with the car. He told me to follow him and walked away. I thought of making a run for it. Ridiculous, I know. He took me to a police car and said to the driver, 'You and Edwards take this fellow back to the shop. He says he's the one.' That's what the policeman said. 'He says he's the one.' "

Bolsover is sitting in a bent posture, his arms on his knees, fists clenched, his head bowed.

"They took me to the police station, took a blood sample, and took away my watch, my tie, my wallet, my shoes, and my belt. They put me in a cell. The policeman called Edwards said, 'It'll be a while, mate. We're busy.' He went out and locked the door. There was a chair, a table, and a bed. I sat on the chair and waited for someone to come. I guess it was three or four hours. A very long time. Sometimes I heard footsteps or voices. It was hot in there. Eventually I lay down on the bed. There was no pillow, so I rolled up my jacket and made a pillow out of it. I kept thinking about the child. Round and round, round and round. Had I really hit a child? What had happened to her? I must have gone to sleep, and the slamming of the cell door woke me up. There were two of them, a sergeant and a constable. They'd slammed the door against the wall to wake me up. I hadn't seen those two before. For a moment I thought they were going to do something to me."

"No," says Arabella.

"They took me into another room, gave me a cup of tea, and switched on a recording machine. 'Now, sir,' said the sergeant, 'we're just going to have a chat, the three of us, and sort out what happened last night. We're recording this. Do you understand?'

"I said yes, and the constable said, 'I'm afraid we have some bad news for you.'

"I said, 'Is it the little girl?' and the sergeant told me she'd died in the General at two-thirty that morning."

"Oh, God," says Arabella. "Oh, Bolsover."

"In the cell I couldn't think of anything but her. I was just hoping and hoping, but it was no good. She had died. They started asking me who I was, where I lived, what I did for a living, all that sort of thing. Then they began asking about the accident. I decided I wouldn't tell them about the girl. Tina, she told me her name was. I didn't tell them about her being in the car."

"No," says Arabella again.

"Yes," says Bolsover. "I decided to leave her out of it."

"That wasn't a good idea," says Arabella.

"I know that," says Bolsover. "I'm telling you what I did. There was no need for her to be involved—that's what I thought. It didn't make any difference to the facts. I wasn't going to deny it was my fault. I was driving the car and she was there, but that didn't make any difference. It would have happened anyway. That's what I decided."

Bolsover looks up at Arabella, and she looks steadily back at him.

"Yes, I know," says Bolsover. "But I'm telling you what I thought at the time. I wasn't thinking straight. I know that. I just told them I was on my way home. I told them I'd stopped for a takeaway, which was true. The takeaway was still in the car. I couldn't tell whether they believed me or not. They just went on asking questions and making notes. I told them the whole story twice and they took me back to the cell. They said they were going to check the story. I sat there for another long time. When they came back, the sergeant told me to tell it all over again. He said, 'This time, tell us about the woman you had in the car.' "

"So then you told them the truth."

"Someone had seen us. I told them her name was Tina. The sergeant asked me her surname. I didn't know it. They asked for her address. I didn't know that, either. 'Here we go again,' the sergeant said. But the constable said, 'I know who she is. You picked her up in town, didn't you? She's a tart, isn't she?' I said yes. They fetched some photographs and after a while I found her. Her name wasn't Tina, it was Mary. Her real name was Mary Fielding."

"Well," says Arabella. "Mary Fielding. What a difference a name makes."

"She had been warned on nine previous occasions for soliciting in a public place. Twice she had been placed in the care of the local authority. Each time she'd absconded within a week."

"Placed in care? Do you mean that she—"

"She'd been a prostitute since she was fourteen. When I met her, she was seventeen. I thought she was twenty or more, but she was seventeen. That's not very old, is it?"

"No, it's not."

Bolsover waits to discover whether he is about to lose his new friend, whose limit of tolerance must have been exceeded. She doesn't move, and eventually he goes on digging.

"I know it makes things much worse," he says. "I know that sex is fine and natural when the participants are the same age. I know it's worse when one is virtually a child and the other is many years older. I know the blame lies with the man. It's wrong and there's something obscene about it, and it makes me feel—"

"Get on with the story, Bolsover. I just want to hear the facts."

The facts were that Bolsover, having been drinking and having sex with a prostitute, was driving at speed in poor visibility with the young woman in his car, which he initially denied. His actions resulted in the death of a three-year-old girl called Chanel Parsons. His vehicle mounted the curb; a man called Barry Parsons had been waiting to cross the road with his only daughter, Chanel. He was a single parent, his wife having left him a year before, and he had just collected his daughter from a child-minder. The child had been in a buggy. The car caught the front wheels of the buggy and flung it into the air; the child fell on her head, which caused a brain hemorrhage. She died in the General Hospital five hours later.

"When I'd finished talking to the policemen," says Bolsover, "they charged me with causing death by dangerous driving."

"Maybe we should stop now," says Arabella, looking at him.

"There's more you have to know. After I'd told them the truth, the policemen went away again. Later I heard her crying in the corridor. The girl."

"The girl? You mean Mary Fielding."

"Yes. They'd got her. They took her past my door. She was sobbing and shouting. 'You fucking pigs, it wasn't nothing to do with me. I wasn't driving the fucking car. That fucking creep was driving, that fucking weirdo. It's all his fucking fault, you bastards.' "

"You're going in very deep, Bolsover. Do you really want to do all that?"

Bolsover looks up. "I killed a child. I have to keep it all sharp. It mustn't be forgotten."

She looks straight back at him, and eventually she says, "You're wrong, Bolsover. That's nonsense. Don't you see that? It was an accident. Okay, it's natural to feel guilty, but it isn't natural to feel guilty forever. You have to let things go. You have to let time pass, and muddle through, and get over it as best you can." Suddenly she bursts out laughing.

"What's the matter?"

"Just me and my talent for lecturing. I know what's right for everyone."

He stares at her, getting only a dim sense of what she's saying.

"Oh, well," Arabella says. "Let he who is innocent cast the first stone and all that. Tell me the rest."

Slowly he begins talking again. "The name Barry Parsons didn't mean anything to me. The tall policeman said, 'He's not a nice man, Mr. Parsons. He'll want your number. Do you get my meaning?' I just looked at him. I couldn't think what he meant. They had to explain."

"Explain what?"

"Barry Parsons is a professional criminal and a very dangerous man. He's involved with drugs, fraud, and extortion. They said he'd come after me."

Arabella becomes very still.

"I'm sorry," says Bolsover.

"Let's agree not to say sorry," Arabella says, absently. "Do you know, it's strange, the feeling I had when you said that."

"Have you heard of Parsons?"

"Oh, no. I just thought—for a moment I thought maybe we hadn't scattered Lennie this morning. As if he'd—well, you know what I mean. Silly, I suppose, to think you can banish evil forever. This Barry Parsons is the reason you're here, is he? He's the reason you ended up hiding at the Alpha Hotel?"

"Yes, he's the reason."

16

How bad am I? Bolsover is walking toward Handsome Point to check again on the cream-colored courser. Don't we all feel a pressure, a draw, toward the dangerous edge? Even a man standing clear in the sunlight feels that draw; sin, like gravity, is an ever-present force. I'm not guilty, says the innocent man, but I might easily become so—and on that simple foundation is built the immense tower of morality and religion, God and the devil, heaven and hell, parables and miracles, doctrine, liturgy, law, judge, bishop, and priest, clergy and laymen—a tower of babble, all built on sinfulness! How strange, that the most innocent and thoughtful folk, driven by their fear of falling, are enticed into binding themselves with fantastical bonds, all because of the possibility of sin. Most of us are wonderfully harmless. We find a wallet, we give it back. All right, we give it back because we identify with the loser, or because it feels big to do so, or we want to be well thought of, or because keeping things makes us uneasy—some such reason—but we give it back. We don't want to sin, which means we don't want to commit a sinful act; wickedness only exists in action, and innocence can only be lost in action. I killed a baby girl, but did not intend it. I made love to another girl, and that I did intend. Which of these is the greater sin?

So Bolsover circles in confused fashion these ancient questions. Is sexual desire inherently sinful? Or do I just *feel* it to be sinful, because I am who I am? One night in Angelique's bistro he had been introduced to a man—one of the agency's clients—whose sexual behavior was not inhibited in the traditional English manner. He behaved like a happy, carefree dog—a highly sexed dog. When he encountered a woman— any woman, seemingly—this man employed a variety of tactics— charm, flattery, close attention, humor, generosity, impulsiveness, and pure cheek—with such conviction that he was almost impossible to resist. Watching him at work, it was quite evident that he had only one aim; he simply wanted (this is the new Bolsover, determinedly clear-minded) to fuck, and did not feel the slightest qualm about fucking. And many of his victims—if that is what they were—appeared willing to go along with him.

That man's freedom from sexual inhibition didn't make him a criminal, unless fucking a girl is a crime—and at this point Bolsover, who has been thinking energetically and freely, comes up against his own history like a blind man walking smack into a wall.

Mary Fielding, whose working name was Tina, was a witness at his trial. Prosecuting counsel reminded the jury that the accused had lied about her presence in the car.

"You might be tempted to think that the accused, by denying her presence, was attempting to defend the good name of Miss Fielding. You might be tempted to think that, or you might be of the view that Miss Fielding, when it comes to good names, lost hers a good while back."

Several members of the jury laughed at that. The man in the dock sat motionless and the girl in the witness box, thin and plain under the lights, clenched her hands on the rail before her.

"Members of the jury," continued counsel, "the good name that the accused was trying to defend was his own, of course. This outwardly respectable man, a widower, had been drinking and consorting with a very young prostitute. The facts are simple: driving recklessly, this man took the life of a child, and then lied about the circumstances in an attempt to disguise the depths of depravity to which he had fallen." Someone in the court giggled at that, and the judge looked up sharply.

Arguing that the accused had had no intention to harm the child, but had been severely disturbed by the close resemblance between Miss Fielding and his deceased wife, Bolsover's counsel submitted several photographs in evidence.

"There may be a resemblance," said the judge, speaking with the ponderous certainty of his kind, "but I invite defense counsel to persuade me that a passing similarity between Miss Fielding and the accused's deceased wife constitutes a defense against a charge of causing death by dangerous driving."

Remorse is just like grief. It's just the same. I have to go back and live it again and again. I can't help it. I have to see the girl standing in her doorway, feel the damp banister under my hand, watch her skirt fall, hear the jurors coughing, the shouting outside the court, the silence of the snow, the slam of the cell door, the voice of Tina in the witness box—

"What happened in your flat, Miss Fielding?" asked counsel for the prosecution.

"Nuffing out of the usual, if I'm honest."

"Indeed, I very much hope you *are* honest, Miss Fielding." That was the judge.

"He come into the hall and then he got cold feet. I starts taking off me stuff. Me cloves, I mean."

"What did he do while you did that?" Prosecuting counsel again.

"He didn't do nothing."

"What, he just stood there, did he?"

"Sat. He sat down. Just looking, he was."

"Watching you removing your clothes, I take it?"

"Looking like he didn't want to be there, if I'm honest. He sits down on a chair. I goes and takes me cloves off and does a little twirl, like. You gets a few like him. They gets nervous when it comes to it. You have to work them round to it, them sort."

"That's all part of the job, is it, Miss Fielding?"

"Some of them, it is." She held on to the front of the witness box with both hands: she might look twenty-five under a streetlight, but here she was no more than seventeen, this little girl.

"Didn't he say anything?"

"Not then, he didn't. Later, he says, 'You're lovely.' He touches me hair. You know—stroking it."

"That's a bit creepy, isn't it?"

"Creepy! Him? He ain't creepy! Look at him!"

The court laughed again, turning to look at Bolsover.

"So you didn't feel in any danger, Miss Fielding," asked defense counsel.

"Danger? He's a softie! Can't you see? Oh, I can tell you about the dodgy ones, all right."

"You never felt he might become violent or lose control of himself?"

"Nah."

"I doubt Miss Fielding's opinion of the accused's character will carry much weight with the court," said the judge. "Let's stick to the facts, if we may."

Prosecuting counsel resumed. "Well, Miss Fielding, was that all the accused did? Stroked your hair?"

"I took his cloves off, din' I."

"He didn't undress himself? You took his clothes off?"

"I told you."

"All of them?"

Bolsover sat in the dock, his head in his hands.

"We goes over to the bed, innit, then I takes his cloves off. Not his shoes and socks. He done them hisself."

Laughter, and the judge tapped his gavel.

"So you got him in the mood?"

"Yes," said Miss Fielding.

"You're the proverbial tart with a heart, are you?"

"Mr. Baldwin," said the judge.

"M'lud," said prosecuting counsel. "You then had sex with the accused, did you, Miss Fielding?"

"I din' know he was accused, did I?"

Laughter.

"And he managed to make love successfully? Despite his—coyness?"

"It's not clear where this is going, Mr. Baldwin," said the judge.

"M'lud," said the lawyer.

"He done it all right in the end," said the girl, and the court chuckled.

"I think that's enough of that, Miss Fielding," said the judge.

"All right, sir," said Miss Fielding.

Barry Parsons, the dead child's father, was a small, compact man with delicate hands. During the inquest and trial he wore gray or black suits, elegantly cut, with a white shirt, black tie, gold cuff links, and a gold watch. He reflected the action of the courtroom in constant small, intense movements—shaking his head, nodding, lifting an arm, tapping his fingers, shuffling in his seat, crossing and uncrossing his legs, writing notes, yawning, sighing. His lips moved in a continuous silent commentary that became audible at moments of particular stress: "Impossible." "That's a lie." "That's right." "Stupid bastard." He sent a stream of notes to his counsel and to the judge, who several times was forced to subdue him; on each occasion Parsons was surprised and angered, his body language becoming still more urgent. During Bolsover's examination Parsons stood up and told the defendant that he was a bloody liar, at which the judge warned him that any further interruption would result in his exclusion from the court. Parsons made no more interventions but his restlessness and murmuring continued, and it was often possible for Bolsover to lip-read his commentary—*Not true. Got to be joking. You asked that before, you stupid fucker. Didn't you hear what he said? Bloody nonsense. What bollocks.*

Being a criminal, Bolsover discovered, was not unlike being a patient in the hospital, with the difference that justice feels no duty of sympathy to those whom it treats. The script of his trial, like that of a nightmare, was mysterious to him, and drew him relentlessly downward.

When defense counsel implied, during cross-examination, that the child's father might have contributed to the accident, Barry Parsons again cried out that counsel was a bloody liar, and was again reprimanded by the judge, who also warned counsel to avoid provocative suggestions without supporting evidence. The defense had found a witness, a child-minder, willing to speak of Parsons's erratic and sometimes violent behavior toward his daughter, but her nerve failed when she was faced, just across the courtroom, with the pent-up urgency of Parsons himself. Prosecuting counsel had no difficulty in showing that the witness was unreliable, and very likely nursing a grievance.

"I'm not at all clear," said the judge, "that the character of the child's father has any bearing on this case. The central fact—that the accused's vehicle hit the child—is not contested. There is no witness of Mr. Parsons's behavior at the moment of the collision, and I have seen no evidence that he would not be capable of managing a child's buggy, even at night and in a snowstorm. The defense is not suggesting, surely, that the child's father had a deliberate intent to cause harm to his own daughter, even to cause her death?"

Defense counsel shuffled his papers and said nothing for several seconds.

"You fucker," said Barry Parsons, standing up.

"Quiet please, Mr. Parsons. Please sit down. I take it counsel will confirm to the court that he did not intend to implicate Mr. Parsons in any way, since he has not produced any evidence whatsoever on that point."

"Certainly I will confirm that," said defense counsel in a level tone.

"Very well," said the judge. "I see no reason to proceed with this line of examination."

"M'lud," said counsel.

"You are not a wicked man," said the judge to Bolsover, "but you are foolish and dangerously irresponsible, and I am conscious that the public expects justice to be done in a case of this sort, when an innocent child has lost her life. It is incumbent upon me to ensure that the sentence matches the seriousness of your offense. Every driver must know that his car may become a deadly weapon, and that it is his responsibility to use it safely. You have been found guilty of causing the death of a child by dangerous driving, of failing to stop after an accident and failing to disclose material evidence. I have taken into account your previous good record, your evident remorse, and your admission of guilt. You will serve nine months' imprisonment and be banned from driving for five years."

As Bolsover was about to be taken down, Barry Parsons stood up, pointed both index fingers at him like a pair of guns, and said, "I'll find you, you bastard"—and then he put his hands to his face and began to sob, at which point two ushers in dark suits led him away, leaving behind in the courtroom, for several long moments, a resounding silence.

Barry Parsons's remark was widely quoted in press coverage of the case. "I'll find you, you bastard" was an excellent headline; the press coverage attracted a small crowd of revengeful moralizers to scream at the accused as he was led out of the court and into the prison van, his head covered by a prison blanket.

Bolsover, walking in the open air toward Handsome Light, is stopped in his tracks by sexual guilt, but the steadfastness of the great lighthouse helps him to recover. Certainly he takes delight in that lighthouse. He welcomes its gleam into his room as if it were a dear friend, and if he should wake at night, perhaps trembling from a dream, he is steadied by its unwavering regularity, entranced by its uncomplicated goodness, its elegance, by the way in which, come wind, come weather, it stands to its work. Handsome Light, he decides, is an enduring example of a universal good. It has no complications, no hidden facets, is available to all and is incapable of betrayal; as such, it stands in contrast to the recent events of Bolsover's life, and proves to him that virtue exists.

This man is still in confusion, for he married a girl he thought simply lovely, and indeed she *was* lovely, but she was far from simple, and she died. Yes, Kitty died. Afterward he tried insufficiently hard to make a new life and leave the old one behind, until things at last came to a head. *Yes.* But he did not intend a death. *No.* What sort of criminal is he? Not the worst sort: surely that must be the truth.

Out in the open, as he walks along the beach toward Handsome Point, it seems to Bolsover that he now sees exactly what happened. There is no reason to nurture a guilt that he does not possess: that is what he tells himself as he walks toward the great light, but he is not quite certain that he yet believes it. Besides, there is the quite unexpected matter of Arabella, a woman who contrasts in every regard with his late wife. He should not be ashamed of his interest in Arabella, for he loved Kitty to his utmost ability. There is no doubt of that. One cannot mourn forever. One is allowed a friend. *Oh, she's just a friend, is she?*

After his conviction, Bolsover was imprisoned and remained so for eighteen weeks. The prison librarian took him aside. He would do well to avoid being alone, particularly in empty corridors or storerooms; someone had overheard a conversation—it might be nothing, but it would be just as well to be careful, wouldn't it?

No doubt Parsons had connections among the prisoners. Bolsover's own cell mates, he was sure, wouldn't know of any plot—they were merely would-be fraudsters who had been caught. After the librarian's warning he was careful to stay in the company of one or both of these men, and never to be alone. He was anxious, he was watchful, but nothing untoward occurred and he had no difficulty in obtaining parole at the earliest opportunity. On the day of his release he was taken into the prison office and advised to keep a low profile and not return to his flat. He went home despite the warning. That evening he saw a smallish man standing in the shadows under the trees on the far side of the road; whether it was Parsons he could not tell, but he was sufficiently afraid to pack some things and hurry down the back stairs and away through the gardens. He stayed in a hotel that night, and the following day, when he returned to arrange for the flat to be put on the market, he found that his lock-up garage, and the silver Volkswagen that it had contained, had been soaked with kerosene, set alight, and utterly destroyed.

The cream-colored courser is still there. She's still probing in the sand and the mudflats, still striding quickly about on her long and delicate legs. Bolsover, delighted with his new binoculars, studies the bird for some time in order to give a thorough report to his friend Jack Wilson. The birders' camp has thinned. Once they've eyed her, once they've put her in their books and captured her in the camera, there's no more to keep them: they're off home.

A little farther along the shore is a small flock of oystercatchers, black-and-white birds that look like a troop of waiters in a smart restaurant. As they paddle among the small ripples at the water's edge, they talk to one another in a bubbling murmur that is quite charming. Bolsover settles in a comfortable position on a sand dune and is about to take out the sandwiches that the hotel has supplied when a shadow falls across him.

"Mrs. K said you'd be here," Arabella says, sitting down beside him. "Let's borrow your glasses. Have you got a spare sandwich?"

"I have. It's ham and egg."

"Good. I like ham and egg."

She eats the sandwich and watches the courser for some minutes.

"What comes to mind," she says, "is that bird's solitariness. You wouldn't worry if there was a flock, but a single bird—I hope she can find her way home. Do you know where coursers come from?"

"Jack Wilson gave me a history. Their normal habitat is the desert. She probably came from the Sahara. They sometimes get blown off course by sandstorms."

"The purpose of a flock," Arabella says, "must be to defend the individual. You've got a better chance of spotting a predator. Besides, if a predator does come along, it's less likely to be you that cops it. And of course it's nicer to be among friends. You get all the gossip."

"Thanks for the explanation," Bolsover says. In his present mood, it's quite a cocky remark.

She laughs, still looking through the binoculars. "A bit of talk from your friend Jack Wilson doesn't make you much of an avian expert, old Bolsover."

She puts the glasses down and turns toward him. "In the area of human relations," she says in a formal tone, "it's difficult to know exactly what's what, isn't it? When you're young, you've plenty of time, and you can spend days chatting and finding out about somebody. Weeks or months, if you like. But when you're older, you don't have as much time left, not as much patience. When I think of the mistakes I've made in the past—you know, spending ages with someone, only to find out what a slob he is—well, I'm not sure I can go through all that again. I think I'd prefer to stay on my own."

She wants to stay on her own. That's what she's saying. She's giving him the brush-off. Is she?

"Indeed," says Bolsover carefully. "I don't disagree that there's a risk. But being single isn't the best condition to be in. It's worth taking a bit of a risk to avoid it, don't you think? In the end it depends on judgment, and you can't make that judgment without getting to know a person properly."

"You see," she says, not really listening to him, focused on her own process of thought, "I have an idea that you might be a grown-up man, the sort a person could talk to. The trouble with most men is that they don't talk enough. In fact, they don't talk at all, except about *things*. It's an important issue. Somebody ought to do something about the social incompetence of men."

"Some men can talk."

"Not very many, I can tell you. And another thing about you—you don't want to win all the time, do you? You really don't care at all about winning."

"Don't I?" Maybe she's right. "A lot of people—a lot of men—would say that striving is a good thing. If you asked me, I'd say that I don't want great success, but I like doing things properly—dear me, what a dull fellow I am!"

"It's a matter of balance. Balance between the halves of a couple, I mean. You want people to be a bit the same and a bit different, so things don't go stale. People who mesh together."

"The Arabella theory of love."

She laughs. "Absolutely. People have to think about these things a bit, and then go for it. Or not, as the case may be. Oh, I know you're a worrier, but you've got some useful qualities. Honesty is one of them."

"Honesty!" Such a thing has never occurred to him. Is he honest? "Do you know, this conversation is beginning to feel like an interview."

"There you are," she says. "Honesty. Of course it's an interview, Bolsover. It's a difficult decision."

"Oh. What decision is that?" He knows the answer perfectly well, but he wants to bring it out into the open.

"Whether I stay or whether I go. That's the issue before us."

"I sort of knew that's what you meant," he says, "but I wasn't allowing myself to think it."

"It'll be interesting to find out whether you're really as cautious as you appear, or whether it's just an effect of your recent history."

"Oh, history," says Bolsover. "That old thing."

Two weeks after Parsons had burned the Volkswagen, he attacked Bolsover in the street. Passersby dragged him off, and the following week he smashed the glass of Bolsover's front door and was pouring kerosene on the floor when the police arrived.

"They didn't know what to do about him," Bolsover said. "Were they going to lock him up because someone had killed his daughter? And maybe, in the end, give him ten years for manslaughter?"

"I see what you mean," said Arabella.

"The last time, he drove his car at me and broke my leg. After that, they told me they'd like to talk about options."

"They? Those Home Office people, you mean. Smithson and Miss Brown."

"Yes."

17

London, on a day of showers and a hunting wind. From the Home Office, Bolsover, his coat flapping about him, was directed round several corners to an unobtrusive door with an entry phone and told to ask for Miss Brown and Mr. Smithson.

"Do sit," said Miss Brown. "Mr. Smithson will take your coat. No doubt you know what we're about."

"Only that you may be able to give me some help."

"We provide a range of services for people in a particular kind of difficulty," Miss Brown said. "Our clients are usually experiencing some form of persecution. They need to be protected for a period of time. Sometimes it's a long period, though we don't think that will apply to you."

"We've got your details, of course," said Smithson. "We've assessed your case."

"Your situation is straightforward, and certainly falls within our remit." Miss Brown gave Bolsover a bright, official smile. "You'll realize that we're bound by certain regulations, and sometimes we may sound a little bureaucratic, but I can assure you that we have your best interests at heart."

"That's good," said Bolsover.

"We understand that your persecutor is a single person whose condition of mind is not entirely stable. We have a scale of risk, and in our judgment the risk is moderate. That means we can act to protect you, but there's no need for extravagant measures. You won't need to disappear completely, but we'll get you out of the way for a while. After that, we'll see how things develop."

"It must be hard for someone to disappear completely."

"Indeed it is." Miss Brown nodded several times. "It's a lot of work, and quite unnecessary in your case."

"A permanent identity requires no end of papers," Smithson said. "Records, bank accounts, financial transfers, mortgages, photographs, letters, school reports—"

"Not appropriate in this case," said Miss Brown.

"And of course a convincing departure scenario—clothing abandoned on a beach, perhaps a note—"

"Mr. Smithson," said Miss Brown. "I don't think we need go into details of that sort."

"Indeed not, Miss Brown," said Smithson, not at all abashed. "We're looking at something quite straightforward."

"We have a standard procedure for cases of moderate risk," said Miss Brown. "We believe it suits you perfectly well. We'll provide a temporary identity and a set of papers that's quite sufficient for normal purposes. We'll also provide a secure location for up to six months, after which your situation will be reassessed."

"A safe house," said Bolsover, afflicted not only with a strong sense of absurdity but also with a kind of delight.

"That sort of terminology is a little outdated," said Miss Brown. "Our service is perfectly straightforward."

"With your agreement, we'll make certain arrangements with your bank," said Smithson, "and inform other agencies as necessary. We'll keep an eye on your property, collect your post, and all that sort of thing. We'll keep your personal documents and records safe, and your original identity will remain on national records—the electoral roll, for example. Democratic rights must be preserved, of course."

"Of course," said Bolsover. "If you don't mind my saying so, it seems like an awful lot of trouble."

"Less trouble than a dead man, an inquest, a trial, and twenty years inside for the perpetrator," said Smithson.

Miss Brown tapped her pen on her desk. "In order to proceed, we need your signature on various documents, including a confidentiality agreement. You'll understand that our work mustn't be compromised, or many lives could be put at risk."

"We generally find," said Smithson, "that our medium-term arrangements are highly successful. It's the longer term that causes difficulties. People want to go back, want to go home. You'd think the past was over and done with, wouldn't you? But it's hard to live with the future if you haven't got a past."

"Thank you, Mr. Smithson," said Miss Brown. "We must explain the service we provide. We have a large database and maintain a selection of identities ready for immediate use. Each identity includes all the necessary documents, cards, and so on. Our system selects an identity of the right age, sex, and race, and suggests a secure location."

"Ready-made people," said Bolsover.

"Exactly. You'll realize that a new identity can't be created instantly. Some of our files go back a long way. We've built them up over the years and we work hard to keep them current. Of course it's all changing now.

We've had to take on extra staff to arrange Chinese identities, Indian, Russian—"

Miss Brown leaned back in her chair, a woman of authority.

"In your case," said Smithson, "the system has selected an identity called James Watson Bolsover. It's a slightly unusual name. We find that distracts people from the man himself. Nobody ever thinks a name like Bolsover could be false."

"Ah," said Bolsover, "unlike Smithson or Brown, you mean?"

"Precisely," said Smithson.

"Bolsover," said Bolsover, forming his lips around the name. "James Watson Bolsover. It's not such a bad name. It has a certain character. But of course I'm not from the north of England, and I can't see why your system chose that particular name."

"Because, my dear chap," said Smithson, "that sort of name broadcasts its own biography. One only needs to hear the name to know that James Bolsover is a sturdy fellow from the north of England, an honest but rather pedestrian type, the sort who's quite impossible to doubt. Think of it: how could James Bolsover be an invention? I dare say his friends call him Jimmy."

"But I'm not from the north—"

"Irrelevant," said Miss Brown. "Take my word for it, nobody will look past the name."

"But the accent—"

"You lost it during your years in the south."

"Did I?"

"Of course. You left home at nineteen to attend university in a southern town—Reading, in fact."

"Reading! I've never even been to Reading."

"You don't have to go to Reading to know all about it. Check the notes in the information pack. Just say it's redbrick—nobody's interested in redbrick universities. You got a third in English history."

"I don't know any history."

"You must know *something* about English history. Besides, nobody recalls their degree, thirty years on."

Bolsover knew by now that he would lose the argument.

"Might I not, at least, have done better than a third?"

"The certificate is already printed," Miss Brown said, "and a very nice job it is, too. A third-class degree explains your lack of historical knowledge. You're a graduate, but only just. Your qualifications aren't threatening. The point is to keep a low but respectable profile, and at all costs to avoid being interesting."

Bolsover's mind had begun to work, it seemed to him, in a slow and deliberate manner, as if he had indeed become a pedestrian northerner.

"What does he do for a living, this James Bolsover?"

"Oh, you're a writer," said Miss Brown. "We have to stick with that. It's hard to find anything else that a writer's good at."

"As for the location," said Smithson, "we're suggesting one of our most popular venues. It's a hotel on an island. A stranger is nothing out of the ordinary in such a place."

"An island!"

"We think of it as a kind of nursery. You'll meet other beginners, and you'll find the staff very helpful. You'll be perfectly safe."

"The point of such a place," said Miss Brown, "is that it takes the pressure off. It lets our clients relax, accustom themselves to their new identity, find out whether it suits them. In your case we've even found a part-time job that's ideal for someone with your skills."

Bolsover looked at Miss Brown, a neatly dressed civil servant wearing a restrained pearl necklace. In a moment she would come out of character and the whole thing would be revealed as a hoax, a bit of harmless fun. But no: she was speaking again, in a calm and sympathetic tone.

"Our clients are often startled at first, Mr. Bolsover. They take a bit of time to get used to our methods. But don't forget that the risk is real. At the very least, we'll give you a breathing space."

"Time to think," said Smithson.

"A chance to relax."

"To develop a new persona, if you will."

"To adjust—I think 'adjust' is such a good word—"

"In safety."

"In complete safety."

A small silence, then Smithson said, "And if anything should go wrong—"

"Terribly unlikely."

"Terribly unlikely, as Miss Brown says, but if it should turn out that your new identity isn't sustainable—"

"Such a thing has been known to happen, on very rare occasions—"

"We'll quietly remedy the matter."

"Remedy the matter," said Miss Brown. "That's a good phrase, a good calm phrase. In our business, calm and quiet are useful notions, Mr. Bolsover. That's how we like things to be."

A pause, and Bolsover said, "Of course it gives me a chance to settle myself down. I quite see that. And I suppose it's not irreversible, after all."

"Certainly not," said Miss Brown. "If you change your mind at any time, just get in touch. You'll find our emergency number in the pack, and there's always someone on duty." She paused and raised one finger. "You're a sensible man, Mr. Bolsover, but there are one or two things you ought to bear in mind. The first is to avoid confrontations."

"Arguments," said Smithson. "Just walk away."

"Disagreements, however right you believe yourself to be, can escalate into something quite disturbing. And in the early stages, while you're in the nursery—"

"The nursery," echoed Mr. Smithson with a smile.

"In the nursery you'll meet others in a similar situation. Obviously there's a need to respect their privacy, just as they must respect yours. It's possible that some will tell you their stories—their true stories, I mean. Some people find it necessary, despite our advice. If you hear anything, I'm sure you'll keep it to yourself, Mr. Bolsover."

"Of course," said James Watson Bolsover. A new name, a nursery on an island—the Lord bless my soul.

"And if you get an inkling of anyone's true identity—"

" 'Inkling's' a good word, Miss Brown—"

"You say nothing at all, Mr. Bolsover."

"Nothing to anyone."

"Nothing."

"Of course the island location greatly simplifies the security question. Visitors outnumber the native population. You're just another one."

"Another advantage," Smithson said, "is that we know who's coming and who's going."

Grossmith, said Bolsover to himself, George and Weedon Grossmith.

"Who's in and who's out," Miss Brown said. Wasn't that Lear?

"Their exits and their entrances," Smithson said, doodling on his notepad a map of an island.

"*As You Like It*," said Bolsover, unable to contain himself further. "One man in his time plays many parts."

"Mr. Bolsover!" Miss Brown was delighted. "So few people spot our little jokes!"

"I read a lot," said Bolsover. "I'm a snapper-up of unconsidered trifles."

"*Winter's Tale*," cried Smithson, and Miss Brown applauded. It was all very satisfactory.

"Now," said Smithson, "you'll find all sorts of useful material, including an excellent map of the island, in your information pack." He picked up a file box. "It contains everything you need."

It was an ordinary file box of the common mottled sort. *That's me. That's James Watson Bolsover in there.*

"You'll need to read it carefully. Start with the handbook—the survival handbook, we call it. Lots of hints and tips, and a set of frequently asked questions that I'm sure you'll find useful. Don't forget that the various agencies—your bank and so on—already know you. They've been dealing with you for years, and they won't be surprised to get a call. If by any chance there's something we've forgotten, you've got our number." Miss Brown gave Bolsover another of her bright smiles.

"You can be sure," said Mr. Smithson, "that if anything untoward happens we'll know about it."

"We'll have the matter in hand," said Miss Brown. "We'll be on the case."

"It's worth remembering," said Smithson, shaking Bolsover's hand, "if you have to invent something, remain close to the truth of your own life. You're much less likely to be caught out."

"The practice of a good liar," said Bolsover.

"Exactly," said Miss Brown. "We're not into morality, Mr. Bolsover. We're just trying to keep you alive. Oh—and would you mind leaving your wallet and diary with us? You'll find replacements in the pack, and a small cash float to get you started."

I am become another, thinks Bolsover as he steps down the Strand with his new identity under his arm. I am born again. I am squeaky-clean. He stops to examine himself in a shop window, finding that he looks just the same as before. Parsons might still find me. Suppose I were to fail to sustain my new and perfect life? Suppose he were to discover me despite these elaborate, not to say absurd, precautions? What would happen to my own possessions, my real records, my passport, my bank cards—all those things that are now, since I've signed them away, under the control of Smithson and Miss Brown? Why of course, I would be absorbed into the files. One day I'd be born again, and my identity transplanted to another. That person would take up where I left off, and I would live again in another body. Ah, Smithson and Miss Brown have it all ways: if they lose the new me, at least they've still got the old one. What a game! And with real people!

In his hotel room he leafs through the dos and don'ts in the survival handbook. *Talk naturally: avoiding people looks suspicious. In conversa-*

tion, ask sympathetic questions; people will talk about themselves and rarely ask about you. Don't invent things if you don't have to. Sexual relationships are an area of significant risk.

Obviously a modern state must maintain an agency charged with the protection of endangered citizens, and Smithson and Miss Brown appear to know what they're doing. To disappear is quite possible; people vanish all the time. Thousands of us—missing persons. And of course many appear, for we're always emigrating and immigrating, reinventing ourselves, learning a new language, a new trade, moving on, moving back . . . *Don't leave your contact details with strangers, shops, businesses, or Internet sites. Avoid committing any kind of offense. Beware of responding to your old name. Ensure that all supplied material is kept in a secure place and returned at the end of the agreed period; you will be charged the appropriate fee for any losses.*

He walked out of the door a new man, yet when he looked in the shop window, he saw the same face with the same parents; the same schools and employers; the same dear wife; the same anxieties; the same foolish, rambling, associative tendencies as the man he used to be. A man may be disguised, thinks Bolsover, but his essence is memory, which may not be altered.

18

Gradually things are getting clearer. Now we may consider, for the last time, Bolsover's big questions. Until now he has found no single method adequate to solve them; he has simply been feeling his way like a blind person, and by slow and erratic discovery has tried to assemble a picture that may, if he is fortunate, approximate the truth. But he has recently begun to explore a new methodology that looks promising. It was suggested by a dog-eared copy of a book about motorcycles and Zen Buddhism, a cult book from way back in the early seventies. Riding with the book's sorry hero and his even sorrier son across America, Bolsover discovered that the practice of engineering, which he had assumed to be a matter of *stuff*—material with physical properties, matter that you can handle and hammer and file into useful shapes—was nothing of the sort.

When you worked on a motorcycle, the book taught him, you weren't working on a lump of aluminum, steel, and plastic, but on a mental model of the motorcycle, a *virtual* motorcycle.

This is an idea, Bolsover feels, with the same explosive truth as Mr. Wootton's argument about words. A virtual motorcycle—of course! The logic of a motorcycle, the way it works—why, that logic doesn't exist in any real sense—it's inside your head. Oh, yes, you can represent reality in all sorts of ways, but engineering isn't done with your hands, however strong and square they may be; engineering is done with your head.

What an idiot he was, not to realize that long ago! Concepts, entities, must be framed, and the relations between them discovered, by means of mental models; a problem must be stated by means of words, images, numbers, maps, and only then can you get to work on it.

Sitting in his room and gazing out to sea, Bolsover practices his new technique by building a virtual island in his mind. He imagines himself stepping out for Handsome Point—he's often drawn that way by the lighthouse and the little courser, and by the sublime grandeur of the cliff where suddenly the land ends and the vastness of the ocean begins. It is a breezy day of clear air and small bustling clouds, and in his mind he takes the steep zigzag path from the beach to the cliff top and turns eastward along the limestone ridge. It's an old drover's road, a fine chalky path with an expansive view that amply justifies the expense of his new binoculars. On his left hand lies the open sea, ahead is the line of the path, and on the right are the valleys and woods of the island. Steaming away toward the horizon, perhaps, is a small ship of a workaday sort—maybe she's the same *Providence* that brought him here, the captain no doubt standing firm on his bridge. Full ahead. Aye, aye, sir, and all's well!

The tall light behind him now, the imagined Bolsover steps out at a brisk pace. The path runs parallel to the cliff edge, rising steadily, and a mile from the lighthouse is the spot that Arabella identified as a fine place for murder. This is the highest point of the ridge, and a limestone seat has been planted here. The seat—Bolsover walks round it, bending to inspect it closely—is a massive, rugged stone that has been hacked from the parent rock with no thought for refinement. Presented with such a grand seat, one must try it for size; seated here, he faces north, and before him is a patch of short-cropped grass and then the cliff edge. It is a sharp cessation, and if he listens, he can hear, six hundred feet below, the thump and flurry of the sea.

He holds his coat against the blustery wind and steps forward a pace or two to the very edge, until the white-capped waves lie beneath his feet. Why do we chance ourselves like this? Because we must test the limit of our nerve? He feels suddenly giddy, and steps quickly back. In *King Lear* there was one who gathered samphire, he remembers; that man was all in the mind, too, and none the less terrifying for that.

Now the chalk path begins to decline, turning southward toward the softer heart of the island. A string of villages occupies the valley here— comfortable, well-established places, each a proper mile or so from the next, each marked by a church with a square tower and a cloud of talka- tive rooks—and at its northeast corner the island has no harbor and no beach, but only a jumble of low black rocks against which the sea throws itself with thunderous force.

He turns southwest now, the path winding between woods of ash and oak, a muddy, uneven path that climbs to a modest height, slowly de- scending in the last mile until the roofs of the town are just below. A set of steps takes Bolsover quickly down to the harbor, and the rest is easy. He strides past the town hall, along the promenade—he comes this way on every working day—and so returns to the Alpha, up the stairs two at a time and into his room, which in truth he has never left.

It takes Bolsover a good five hours of walking, this journey, or about three minutes thinking, if he does it the virtual way. Either way it's good exercise, and although the mental model of the island is noth- ing like as complex as that required by his big questions, it's of the same kind. Considering his model, he can identify the island's components— its hills and paths and cliffs, the strata of its rocks, the patterns of its habitation—and can see the relation of each to the others. From a study of that model he might, if he wished, begin to understand the forces that have formed the island in time and space.

The mental model, Bolsover reckons, is a vital analytical tool, but it must be constructed on the right scale. As a boy he was taken to the great maze at Hampton Court, in which he immediately became lost; later he saw a plan of the maze and recognized its simplicity. How foolish to lose oneself in such a simple place! His confusion hadn't been caused by the *nature* of the maze, but by the *scale* on which he'd viewed it. He'd been too close; he'd needed a scale on which the regular pattern of the maze was easily perceived; in other words, a map. With a map—why, a boy easily finds his way about a maze.

Bolsover's questions were large and general; he could see that much. So far he had been poking about on a small scale and finding only more complexity. Now he began to wonder about broadening his view, assembling a high-level map that showed the broad sweep of the problem rather than masses of confusing detail; and the highest level, he decided, must be that of the universe. The universe was created by the Big Bang— or rather, from the behavior of the perceived universe, we infer that a Big Bang occurred, and since we cannot see behind it, we assume that everything we know began in that instant. "Everything," of course, includes the general laws that govern our universe, by whose discovery we may understand. Bolsover wants to make connections between levels, between the general and the particular; he wants to know why *our particular earth* is here, and why he, James Watson Bolsover, is present upon it.

The habitable earth looks as unlikely as I am, thinks Bolsover, since it has been placed in *exactly* the right position for life to emerge. A bit this way and we'd cook, a bit the other way and we'd freeze. Are we just lucky? Is the position of the earth just a bit of good fortune? What is luck, anyway? Mr. Wootton's strictures on the meaning of words comes to mind. "Luck": he must discover exactly what that word means. Suddenly excited, Bolsover goes after its meaning and finds that "luck" may mean a great many things: fortune, fate, destiny, providence, accident, coincidence, even God—but these words aren't *explanations,* he suddenly realizes. They're *synonyms*. They're just *more words for "luck."* He's struggling in the maze again; one word leads to another, and another, and another, and then he's back at "luck" again.

And then, in a moment of insight, he sees the answer. "He got lucky," people say with a shrug, and they mean that *they don't know why* he got lucky. Luck isn't an answer at all. It's a dead end, and doesn't explain a thing. "Luck" is just a word that people use when they don't know the answer to the question *Why did that happen?*

For a time Bolsover is discouraged by this result: luck had seemed such a promising avenue. However, in such a grand quest a few setbacks must be expected, and he continues his explorations on a different tack. On the island the nights are darker than he's ever known; one night he looks up at the sky and sees a big pattern, clear and bright, a map of the stars. Is the night sky on a useful scale? Is it like that drawing of the maze? Is the answer to his big question written for him in the brilliant scatter of the stars?

The air is clear tonight, and the sky filled with a thousand stars—no, not a thousand stars—far more than that. How many stars are there in our galaxy, how many in the universe? He looks it up, and discovers that there are thought to be a hundred trillion galaxies, containing perhaps three thousand trillion stars. He writes the number 3 on a piece of the Alpha's notepaper, followed by fifteen noughts. *Three thousand trillion.* That is a gigantic number. What is the meaning of a number like that? Suddenly he feels excited; he senses his quarry, and seems to hear, somewhere close ahead, its racing hooves.

Suppose you have that many stars—there may be many more—and each collects its little cluster of planets and moons, some of them just like our solar system, some very different. Most planets won't be habitable, but *some* will. With so great a number, possibility becomes certainty: that's the key. Stabilized in nets of gravity, and given the passing of some billions of years—yes, it must be the case that other galaxies contain other earths, other forms of life, and our own earth is nothing out of the ordinary.

What governs this conclusion? Why, *probability,* a known and tested method that predicts things correctly. He begins to tremble. Surely he's there now. He's got it.

"I know," says Bolsover, talking aloud to himself, "why a star is in one place and not in another. I know why our planet has one moon and the solar system has eight planets, only one of which is in precisely the right place to allow life. I know why I was born, and why Kitty died. I know why the child died, why I came here to this island, and why I met Arabella. One principle governs all these things, a perfectly understandable principle, and the name of the principle is *chance.*"

The science of chance must not be confused with luck: Bolsover is quite clear about that. Luck means nothing, whereas chance is the organizing principle of the universe. You can put it this way: because of its enormous numbers, chance can try everything. Big numbers—that's what it's all about. At last Bolsover knows that he made a fundamental error, all those years ago, when he decided he was unlikely; he isn't in the least unlikely. For a start he lives on a planet containing some billions of people: he's so likely that he's a certainty. Big numbers again. As for the existence of a planet at just the right distance from a star—why, just consider three thousand trillion opportunities for such a thing to happen: it's another certainty!

Bolsover has worked it all out now. He has discovered that chance— the benevolence or otherwise of chance—is responsible for our presence in this life, for the globe on which we live, for the galaxy in which our planet rides, and the universe through which we whirl together. He now knows there to be no other credible explanation. He knows that chance determines the nature and circumstance of our lives. That it appears cruel he knows, and that it often seems to kill for sport; but there is no *intention* behind such events, for chance has no mind, no intelligence, but only numbers, only probability. He settles for that. Indeed, it's a relief to know for certain that there is no Satan behind the scenery, but only the marvelous and random mechanism of creation, which is blind to particular consequences. And as for evil and good—why, they have no origin in the stars, but are made by men for human purposes, as Bolsover now entirely understands.

An enormous question has now been answered, but we should not imagine that his curiosity is satisfied: solve one question, and up pops another. It's all very well to know *why* we exist, but *how* are we to exist? There is such a thing as guilt, for example, which may be felt for good reasons and bad, and may be true or invented. Yes: one may encounter an event which, in logic, is a matter of chance, and yet carries an implication of guilt; and once it perches on one's shoulder, guilt is not easily shrugged off. As for *why* he feels guilt, and what relation guilt has to shame—those questions are among the loudest that now clamor for his attention.

19

Bolsover is able to talk almost without inhibition to Arabella, a circumstance that is, for him, quite remarkable. He confessed his story to her without an impossible quantity of dissimulation and heart-searching, and their friendship has developed quickly, easily, and naturally, which is for him unprecedented. How many women has he known well? His mother, his sister, his wife: rather few, in a lifetime. Perhaps he has somehow forgotten that Arabella is a woman? No, but her rejection of girlishness may make a difference. She is not small or shy or delicate, and he can't pick her up and whirl her around.

"You're a marvelous swimmer," he tells her, after watching her splashing vigorously across the bay. "You must have an aquatic ancestry of some kind."

She laughs. "You make me sound like a seal—no, bigger than that. What are those things—a dugong? A whale, even."

"More like a basking shark," says Bolsover—a risky, slightly anxious comment.

"A basking shark," she says, "as you ought to know, is a vastly harmless creature, feeding entirely on plankton and no threat whatsoever. Unless one happens to be plankton, of course."

Vastly harmless: he has noticed before that she rarely picks up on negatives. She didn't suggest, as she might have done, that his comparison wasn't tactful. She isn't concerned with trivialities of that kind. She lets casual remarks wash over her, unless it's an issue on which she wants to make a stand—as she did when he displayed a willingness to remain guilty forever. She doesn't worry about things that she's chosen not to worry about, and Bolsover finds her clarity invigorating. He can say what he likes without risking her disapproval; he can be himself, and when he's being himself in that particular way, he's *better* than himself. It's complicated, that.

How am I to be myself? He's never been in circumstances so favorable to considered thought. He knows that there has always been a nugget of uncertainty at the heart of himself—doubt, guilt, something like that. He was born with that uncertainty, and it made him a worrier. Since the death of the child, the nugget has grown, and now has considerable substance. He's exploring it cautiously, as one might poke a suspicious object with a stick. He isn't trying to fix it. Some believe that by unwrapping one's past all difficulties can be resolved; Bolsover has no such grand ambition. He's simply trying to understand who he is. He wants to go forward, and must first secure his ground. He knows that his natural tendency to doubt makes him good at finding complication, and he wants to find out something simple and true, something that he can rely upon. One might say that Bolsover needs to learn to be happy, that's all; but he believes happiness to be a perverse condition, unlikely to be conquered by direct pursuit. It must be stalked.

In a search for happiness Arabella Morgan makes an excellent model.

"I've decided not to go back to the mainland straightaway," she says. "I can't go back to our old house and just carry on as before. Now that Lennie's gone, there's nothing left of that, and I don't quite know what to do. Before I met him, I was making my way in the law, but Lennie swept all that away."

"Do you want to go back to the law?"

"I might, but I'm too old to make a career now. I've been thinking about Lennie's money. It's quite a lot. I've been thinking I might give it away."

"Give your money away? What, all of it?"

"Yes. Everything. I don't want the house or the money. It all came from scams of one kind or another—drug money, gambling, or worse. Best to give it away, I reckon."

"Couldn't you do something with it?"

"What sort of thing?"

"Something useful. Maybe something to do with the law."

She considers, her head on one side. "Do you know, that's quite a useful suggestion."

"I'm glad to hear it," says Bolsover.

"If I sold the house, a quarter of the money would buy me a perfectly good cottage."

"A cottage with an office for your legal work. You might establish some sort of trust for a worthy purpose. Make Lennie's money pay back something of what it owes."

"You have a point, Bolsover. I see that I need to give this a bit more thought."

Bolsover's work upon his big questions, his walking about the island, his conversations with Arabella, his work at Warren's—all of these are delightful. He is full of ideas and energy, and has now begun a complete revision of the Somerset guide. It's a consequence of a conspiracy between himself and Molly, Sam, and Adrian. The four editors have decided to take Warren on and demand proper budgets.

"What we need, Warren," says Molly Moon, "is the money to do a decent job. I'm fed up with repeating the same old stuff. I want to do something that's got a bit of style. I want money for research, pictures, and a new cover design. I want to edit guidebooks that people will want to read."

Warren, after a good deal of bluster, is forced to give in. Bolsover now plans to interrupt the weary alphabetical structure of the Somerset guide—Ashcombe, Barrow Gurney, Cary Fitzpaine, Compton Paunce-foot, Duddlestone—with fresh new sections. One of them will be called "Favorite Places," another, "Somerset Through the Seasons." He also intends to feature, here and there, the poetry of Wordsworth and Cole-ridge, former residents of the county, under the heading of "Somerset's Writers." After another argument with Warren, he commissions new photography, some of which he proposes to use in two-page spreads—a waste of space, Warren says, but Bolsover ignores him. He has issued careful instructions to the photographer—he has worked with many a photographer, in his time—insisting on a picture of the watery Somer-set Levels at dawn, with mist on the water, and another of a midsummer sunrise over Glastonbury Tor. "That early in the morning," says the photographer, "that'll be double time."

"Fine," says Bolsover. "I'll find someone else."

"Oh, very well," the photographer says.

Bolsover now possesses, for the first time in his life, a number of close friends. They are distributed between the agreeable folk at Warren's and the curious gang at the Alpha. He's learning to play bridge: Arabella's teaching him. He's a very poor pupil, but the new pair transforms Wednesday evenings for Mrs. Allcard and Mrs. Walters. On one occa-sion Arabella joins the late-night conversation between Bolsover, Colonel Tapp, and Joe Firth. "Boys together," she says to Bolsover af-terward. "In future I think I'll leave you alone with your calabashes."

"Kalashnikovs," says Bolsover. "But I take your point."

And there is of course his own room, room thirty-one, the door of which he now opens with a delicious sense of coming home. His books have their customary places, his notebook lies open on the desk, his binoculars ready on the window ledge. Beyond the glass is the sea, the sweep of the coast, the cliff, the lighthouse, and the line of the far horizon. Before he sleeps he invariably draws open the curtains, allowing the beams of Handsome Light to enter, and should he wake in the night— sometimes he wakes with silly feelings of apprehension, and checks that the alarm button is within reach—he has only to watch the revolving beams as they process through his room, one, two, three, and a long pause of darkness, and the light soothes him back to sleep.

When he's woken, early one morning, by his telephone, Bolsover stares at it in puzzlement: it has never rung before, let alone so early. Who knows he's here? Who knows his number? He picks it up cautiously— but it's only his birding acquaintance, Jack Wilson.

"I say, old chap, how are you?"

"I'm very well," says Bolsover, "and so is the little courser. I saw her only the day before yesterday."

"Did you? Are you sure she's still there, old chap?"

"What do you mean?"

"I'm at home. I've just had a call from a fellow I know. Frightfully keen type. Wanted to go and see the courser, but he's got word she's gone."

"Gone?"

"So he told me. It's only a rumor. Word going round—you know the sort of thing. Terrible gossips, us birders. Always chattering. Three calls already this morning, and it's not yet eight o'clock."

"I see," says Bolsover. For some absurd reason the news is unsettling; it's only a bird, after all, and birds fly away. He becomes aware that Wilson is talking again.

"I wondered if you could go and have a look, old chap. Frightful cheek to ask, but you know, horse's mouth and all that. Best be certain before one spreads the word."

"Of course," says Bolsover. "I'll go at once." He looks at his watch and then out of the window. It's a fine day, gray sky, calm. "Eight o'clock now. Let's say I'll call you back in two hours."

"I say, that's frightfully good of you, old chap."

Coat, boots, binoculars, and down the stairs past Mrs. K at the reception desk, and she calls out, "Why, Mr. B! You're an early bird!"

"Sorry, Mrs. K, I'm in a hurry—"

Off and running now, down the empty High Street, under the clock, down to the shore, and along the beach, where he slows to a fast march.

Ridiculous to feel so agitated. Only a bird, a single bird. Birds come and go, that's what birds do. What's the point of wings if you don't use them? How far will she go? Will she go home? The Channel, Biscay, Spain—will she fly that way? Is it a thousand miles to Gibraltar? Maybe it's twelve hundred. And then Morocco, Algeria—is that right? Along the coast to Algiers, somewhere like that, and then south into the desert, maybe. Would she be looking for others? How do they live out there, under that ferocious sun? What do birds eat in the desert? Is there water?

He checks the time: eight-thirty now. Handsome Point is ahead, and the light is yellow in the daylight—you'd think they'd turn the lamp off in the day—but if a sudden fog came up—

He stops. This is absurd. There is no need to be hurrying so. Here's a fellow walking his dog along the edge of the water—he's waving. "Fine morning!" Indeed it's a fine morning, a fine morning for flying, cool and calm, and good for walking, too. Off again, and going more steadily now.

Suppose she flies at thirty miles an hour—how long to the Mediterranean? Two days or more. She'd have to stop somewhere, stop for a rest, sleep somewhere. Maybe she doesn't follow the coast. Over the Pyrenees to Barcelona and straight across the Mediterranean—five hundred miles over the sea—a day's flying across the water, the air getting warmer, dust in the air, sand in the air, the coast coming up, and nothing but sand as far as she can see. She likes it. It's her place. Sand is her thing. There'll be others there—other coursers out in the desert, pecking here and there, striding about. Hard to see them against the sand. A pinkish tint, that little bird. Pink to match the color of the sand.

He reaches Handsome Point, and that awkward scramble across the rocks and pools. On the north side of the point everything looks the same as usual. Mudflats, shallows, patches of rough grass—what's it called? *Sedge,* yes, that's the stuff—and the hill rising behind. Except— no birds to be seen along the water's edge, and no sign of the birders, either. He takes out his binoculars. They've gone. The birding hordes have gone. Trampled fields, yellow patches where their tents and vans were parked, plastic bags blowing in the wind, a trash barrel overflowing with rubbish—everyone's gone.

Bolsover climbs a few yards up the slope behind the beach to make a thorough scan of the bay. That little courser is hard to see. She's quick on her feet. She might have scurried behind one of those tufty bits. Ah—a few birds are visible, way over on the far side. What are they? Some sort of wader—sanderling, something like that. Need a bird book. Small birds, they are, gray, busy in the shallows. Not brown, not pink. He scans the bay again, and then once more, just to be certain. It's true. She's gone, she's flown away. She's entitled to go if she wants to. Isn't that what wings are for? Birds fly away all the time. Maybe she's gone along the coast a little way. Bolsover fits the lens caps onto his binoculars and returns them to their case. The birders are gone—that's proof beyond doubt. They wouldn't have gone if she were still here. That's definite. He stands up and starts to walk slowly back. You can't see the lighthouse from this angle—it's around the point. He stops and turns, just in case—no, that's foolish—she's gone. Certainly she's gone. He must get back now, and tell Wilson. You've got to say, there's no point in having wings if you don't use them.

"I'm so sorry about the bird going," says Arabella. They're sitting in the garden of the Alpha and she's twirling the stem of an empty glass between finger and thumb. "You've got quite interested in bird-watching, haven't you?"

"I don't know about that," says Bolsover. "That fellow I met—Jack Wilson—he got me interested in the courser. It's a rarity. It shouldn't be here at all. It's a very pretty little bird, the cream-colored courser."

"You told me that before."

"Did I? Oh, sorry."

"Not at all."

There is a silence.

"What are you grinning at?" asks Bolsover.

"Am I grinning?"

"You are. If you think I'm going to sit here being laughed at, you've got another think coming."

"You know perfectly well why I'm grinning, Bolsover. Besides, you often laugh at me."

"Who, me?"

Flirting, thinks Bolsover. What a delightful activity is that!

"It's odd," says Arabella. "You'd think I'd feel relieved it's all over. You'd think I'd be happy as a lark. But I'm not. I feel utterly flat."

"I don't think it's odd at all. Nine years and all that."

"I suppose so. I'm fortunate. I can go away and do more or less anything I like. I can stop playing this silly game of hide-and-seek, I can stop being Arabella Morgan, and go back to—"

"Oh, no," says Bolsover. "You mustn't stop being Arabella Morgan."

She looks at him. "And what about you? Are you going to give up being James Bolsover?"

He looks away from her, across the garden toward the sea. "This business of being someone else is quite strange, isn't it? I can't quite get my mind round it. Surely I'm still the same person? But somehow I'm not. Being Bolsover—I think I'm happier being him than I've been for a long time. I've been thinking about staying here, whatever happens. I like the island, Warren's, the Alpha, all of it. And I like you."

"That last bit may not be very sensible."

"That may be the case, or it may not."

"You've got a home to go back to, haven't you?"

Bolsover thinks about his flat, his tidy, modern flat with its modest library and its balcony of flowers. "I can't go back there now. Everything that's happened—I'd have to go somewhere else and start again. Find a job and somewhere to live. I don't like the thought of that. I enjoy being at Warren's."

"No doubt you like having those lively young people about you," says Arabella. "Stops you getting gloomy."

"I didn't say that."

"But that's what you meant. One of the things I like about you is that you're transparent."

"Transparent? I'm not sure that's much of a virtue. It makes me sound simpleminded."

"Well—in a sort of way, you *are* simpleminded. You're not devious. You think in a straightforward way, an innocent way."

"Oh, well, in that case, I'm happy to be as transparent as you like."

"You've no idea how good it is to see into a person, right through him and out the other side, and not the trace of a shadow."

"Everyone has shadows, surely."

"Yes, but some have secret shadows. Deep, dark shadows. Shadows hiding something nasty. They're the worrying sort of shadows, and you don't have that kind."

Bolsover looks at her. "You've no idea how good it is to sit here with you."

"I dare say it is."

Bolsover is silent for a while, and then says, "Maybe it doesn't matter whether we stay or go. Whatever happens, we've changed. We've taken a new direction. It doesn't matter what names we happen to give ourselves."

"Bolsover, you do have a dreadful compulsion to sum things up."

"I know. I can't help it."

"Of course we've changed," Arabella says. "We change all the time.

The years are going by. Look at my hands." She holds her hands toward him, her square, strong hands.

"You have very capable hands."

"Thank you, but the truth is that I once had rather *elegant* hands. I look at my hands now and think, My Lord, I'm so bloody *old,* all of a sudden! How did that come about? Answer: living a dissolute life, caring for my husband, the passing of years, I suppose. But the point I'm trying to make is that the older you are, the harder it is to begin again. My hands can't begin again."

She puts her hands side by side, turning them this way and that, making Bolsover think of a pair of geese rising from a lake into a blustery sky.

"Our difficulty," she says, "is that we've both become detached from the past. From our proper past, I mean. We're rootless. We can go any way we like, and absolute freedom turns out to be a difficulty. People want roots."

" 'It's hard to live with the future if you haven't got a past.' That's what Smithson said to me."

"He said that to us, too. No doubt he says it to everyone. The question is, shall we go or shall we stay?"

"And there's another factor," says Bolsover. "Whether we go or stay *together.*"

"I've been thinking," says Arabella.

"I'm not sure I like the sound of that."

"I've just finished a lot of years looking after someone. People sometimes say that's a noble thing to do. It doesn't feel noble, being a nurse, I can tell you."

"I know."

"Oh—of course you do." She touches his hand lightly. "Stupid of me."

"Your nursing was much more arduous than mine."

"It was just something that had to be done. In a sort of way I was glad to do it, but in another way I'm not glad at all. I've lost sight of myself. Sorry—I'm not making much sense. I just mean that—"

"I know exactly what you mean," says Bolsover. "You mean you've decided to leave. You're going back to the mainland. You want to go away and sort yourself out. You want to be alone."

She looks at him. "Yes. You're quite quick, Bolsover, aren't you?"

"That's exactly what I thought when I first met you."

"Well, there you go. A perfect match." She looks down at the table, spinning the glass in her fingers.

"Off you go, then. And stop fiddling with that glass. It's getting on my nerves."

"Oh, Bolsover." She reaches for his hand again. "Too much is going on, don't you think? Too many things might not work out. All this is so unnatural. It doesn't feel right to stay. Not at the moment. I can tell things are wrong, because I'm speaking in clichés."

"It's quite all right. You can do whatever you like."

"Now you're being bloody noble."

"I'm not being bloody noble at all. You're quite right. This is a crazy time, and nothing's settled. But—sometime or other, if everything works out, it might be a good idea to see whether—"

"One day, it would be a very good idea to see whether." She picks up the glass again. "Mind you, I'm not sure about anything. I'm not at all certain that my leaving is the right thing."

"Neither am I. But it's the sensible thing."

"Dreadful word, that. Makes a person want to do something violent." She throws her wineglass hard at the garden wall. "Oops— dropped a glass. Don't tell Mrs. K."

"I'll get you another."

"That's a good idea. Get yourself another, too."

"I was going to."

"Sometimes you're so *prim,* you know."

"If you like me anyway, I don't care if I *am* prim."

"Fair enough. Who am I to want you different?"

"When are you going?"

"Tomorrow. I'm booked on the ten o'clock ferry."

"Oh."

"I'm just taking my travel stuff. Mrs. K will send the rest on." She considers him. "To be honest, there's another thing, too—"

"Parsons might get his man."

"You must stop predicting what I'm going to say, Bolsover. I wasn't going to put it like that, but it's true there's a lot of stuff that isn't resolved. For example, I've been wondering if I've got into a habit of looking after people."

"I don't need looking after."

"Don't you?"

"No. I'm quite grown-up. You can forget that issue."

"Well! Unusual forcefulness from Bolsover!"

"But you're going anyway."

"Yes. I'm going."

"Tomorrow."

"Yes."

"And you're sure."

"Yes."

"Well, that's all right. That's what wings are for."

"What? Oh, you mean that bird, your pretty courser. Bolsover, you're a terrible romantic."

She must do what she wants to do. Nine years of nursing! And Lennie tapering away until he could not know her, the glimmer less and less bright until at last he guttered out. What does a person feel then? Loss, sorrow, mourning, rage—that's a tangle, that is. But it's amazing how much endurance human beings possess; there's a way of clenching one's mind, of reducing one's purpose to a tiny focus, living in small steps, until at last it ends and you look up and find the day is bright again.

The following morning the residents line up outside the Alpha.

"Morning, folks. Lovely morning for a cruise." It's the usual cheery taxi driver.

Arabella exchanges tears, hugs, and kisses with Mrs. K and the others.

"Be happy," says Mrs. K.

"Go well," says Mrs. Harwich.

"Take care," says Mrs. Walters.

"Goodbye, ma'am," says the colonel.

Bolsover and Arabella get into the taxi and are driven away, Arabella leaning from the car window and waving as long as the Alpha is visible.

On the quayside, sitting on a bollard, Bolsover watches as the last container is swung aboard and lashed down. "Just now," Arabella said, "I almost changed my mind again. Bolsover, I still don't know whether it's right, but I'm going."

She's up there now on the boat deck, leaning on the rail. On the wing of the bridge appears the unmistakable figure of the captain. He looks fore and aft, commands the stevedores with a wave of his arm, and disappears into the wheelhouse. The ship's whistle sounds three blasts, and Bolsover, like any schoolboy, knows the signal means "My engines are running astern." The ferry backs away from the quay. *Providence:* yes, that's a fine name for a ship, one of those old-fashioned names that you see on fishing boats—*Tenacity, Good Fortune, Happy Days, God's Grace*—names that stand on humanity's side against the forces of the deep.

Arabella's waving now, and calling something that he can't hear.

"Goodbye, Bella," he calls. "I'll see you soon. Let me know how you are. Write me a card—"

She's leaning over the rail now, still waving. He keeps pace with the ship until he reaches the end of the quay, blows her a kiss, and stands watching as the ferry heads out between the piers; the sea is calm, small waves lap the rocks, and a cloud of gulls drifts behind the departing ship.

20

It is a commonplace to suggest that a person makes his own luck. Luck—well, that term is best avoided. Let's say that a person can improve his life by acting in certain ways rather than others: that's not metaphysics, it's common sense. Determination, focus, hard work—those things, we believe, are likely to improve our condition in life, and make us happy. But in what direction should one strive? One needs an objective; it can't be "happiness" or anything woolly like that. Happiness is a consequence, not an objective. The courser's gone and Arabella's gone, but such setbacks are the ordinary problematics of life, to be tackled and overcome. One lifts one's eyes and sets off toward the next goal; provided, of course, one can identify it.

Homespun philosophy of that kind is clearly Bolsoverian. As usual he's trying to work things out. No doubt there are positives: the security and good company of the Alpha Hotel; his work at Warren's, where he's making remarkable progress on the Somerset guide; and his delightful new home, the island and its beaches, cliffs, and hills. These are fine things, and he knows all too well that longing—any kind of longing—is one of man's most futile activities, and a certain route to unhappiness.

However, it is a curious fact that when one receives one or two knocks, more are likely to follow. On the morning after Arabella's departure he receives another call from Jack Wilson. "Old chap, bad news to report, I'm afraid. You remember the little courser?"

"Certainly."

"I'm afraid they've picked her up on the south coast—down in Cornwall. Someone found her on a beach—thoroughly bedraggled, poor creature. They took her to a bird sanctuary, but it was no good. Always tricky, trying to save a wild bird. Such a pity."

"Are they sure it's the same one?"

"They can't be certain, of course. But it's a female, and another cream-colored courser hasn't been seen in this part of the world for many years."

No Pyrenees, no Barcelona, no pink sand.

"What happened to her?"

"She'd been injured. She may have been attacked by a gull. The great black-backed gulls are savage. It could have been one of those."

Yes, focus and determination is the way to overcome minor setbacks. Bolsover knows people who have adopted alternative tactics—meditation, psychotherapy, prayer, therapies, the wearing of copper bangles—and he fiercely rejects them all. Such tactics are irrational, self-indulgent, and very likely dangerous. Of course they are! Who is helped by staring at themselves in a mirror? Lift your eyes to the horizon, whence cometh the light!

Oh dear, yes, Bolsover comes from the old school, and he'll bloody well work the problem out in his own way. How many birds die every day? Countless numbers. Suppose she wasn't a pretty little courser but an ugly creature—a toad, say. Would he have cared? He might, says a little voice, had he known her, for even a toad must have her admirers— all right, but that's not the point. The point is, thinks Bolsover, that I am alive and happy, that I live in a beautiful place among stimulating company. I'm occupying myself in a useful and interesting fashion, and I have some small hopes for the future. What more could a man want? But it was not a good idea to leave such a question hanging in the air.

As a further reminder of the correct course that a person in adversity should steer, Bolsover discovers that Adrian Douglas, his fellow editor at Warren's, has been suffering from multiple sclerosis for many years. Adrian hasn't mentioned his illness; Molly Moon tells Bolsover. Individual suffering, silently borne, is a useful reminder of one's good fortune. *I am perfectly healthy.* Since he's thinking so positively, perhaps it's not so curious that this man has not thought of Barry Parsons for some time.

The page proofs of the new Somerset guide are passed around the office and generally admired.

"You're a little too keen on sunrise photos, James," says Sam Kavanagh.

"The poems are lovely," says Molly. "I'll certainly have poems in my next one."

"Are there any poets in Yorkshire?" Sam again.

"Of course there are poets in Yorkshire, you ignoramus. The place is stacked high with poets." Molly stands up, calls for silence, and reads aloud the extract from Coleridge's "Kubla Khan" that Bolsover has placed beside a piece about Cheddar Gorge and the Quantock Hills:

And from this chasm, with ceaseless turmoil seething,
As if this earth in fast thick pants were breathing,
A mighty fountain momently was forced:
Amid whose swift half-intermitted burst
Huge fragments vaulted like rebounding hail,
Or chaffy grain beneath the thresher's flail:

And 'mid these dancing rocks at once and ever
It flung up momently the sacred river.

The reading is greeted by general applause and Bolsover feels a modest warmth at being the agent of this delightful moment.

"Dear Molly," says Adrian, "wonderfully read, especially when one considers the suggestive nature of the material."

"Suggestive?"

"Fast thick pants, dearest Molly. A mighty fountain."

Molly looks again at the text and blushes. "Oh, goodness, I suppose it is."

There is laughter, and Sam says, "I suppose we'll all have to have poems now. You and your innovations, Bolsover."

In his room at the Alpha that evening, Bolsover takes a sheet of the hotel's letterhead and transcribes the lines from Coleridge's poem. He's writing a serial letter to Arabella: the idea has just come to him, and he thinks it a good one. It won't be a letter, exactly, more like a diary. He'll just jot down anything that occurs to him. Why not? Why not, indeed. It's only surprising that he didn't think of it sooner.

24th April

Dear Arabella,
I've included this extract from "Kubla Khan" in my new Somerset guide. Molly read it out most beautifully in the office today. Adrian pointed out the innuendos and caused Molly to blush. I seem to have started a trend—they're all hunting for poems now. I dare say Warren will think it a terrible waste of space.

At this point it occurs to Bolsover that he doesn't have an address for Arabella; but that's all right—he'll keep the letter until she comes back. Or, if she doesn't get in touch, then he'll send it via Smithson and Miss

Brown. They'll surely know where she is, since they invented us all, thinks Bolsover.

I thought I'd keep a sort of diary while you're away. I'm a terribly fussy writer. I like to make notes first, and draw up a plan. Then I write a first draft, followed by at least one more draft before the final version. I always try to be accurate, brief, and clear. I take out every unnecessary word. But when I began writing stories for Kitty, I found another way of writing—a less organized way, perhaps a more liberated way. In this diary I shall try to write that way, and just say what I think.

At dinner that night Mrs. K hands him a postcard. It's a photograph of a cart horse standing in a field. On the reverse is a scribbled message:

BOLSOVER!! Sorry about the blessed horse—all I could find in the local PO. Chaos here—selling everything—house, furniture, carpets, curtains, clothes, books—even the lawn mower—every damn thing. START AGAIN—that's the idea. Repulsive fellow from the valuer creeping about—has a way of looking sadly at my treasures—that sort of thing USED TO BE FASHIONABLE, MADAME, but NOWADAYS—wretched man!!! Grand auction in three weeks. Be in touch soon.

AM

PS. HEY! I saw that girl on the quay—the girl in pink! I saw her! I spoke to her! I said "Hello" for you! She remembered you! Man sleeping on a bench with two great wheelie bags!

Arabella has seen the girl in pink, the girl on wheels! Mrs. K, standing and watching him, says, "So Mrs. Morgan's all right, is she?"

"She is indeed. By the sound of it she's absolutely fine."

"I'm glad to hear it," says Mrs. K. "If anyone deserves to be happy, it's that woman."

No address on the card. Perhaps she just forgot. Bolsover turns the card over and inspects the photograph of the horse, but can draw no particular meaning from the image.

25th April

I was so pleased to get your card and hear you'd seen the girl in pink! Isn't she wonderfully skilled? But there's something else about her, isn't there? Did you feel that? Something lonely. Who'd allow a girl of that age to spend half the night Rollerblading around the harbor? What did she say to you? Fancy her remembering me!

Since you went it's been quiet. Only the usual round of conversation and cards at the Alpha. Did I tell you—no, of course, you couldn't know that the little courser was found—she was found dead on a beach on the mainland. She'd been attacked by something—they think it might have been a gull. They tried to save her, but it was no good. That's a bit sad, I think.

Despite the loss of the courser, Bolsover finds himself increasingly intrigued by bird-watching. From the cliff-top path he happens to catch sight of a pair of kittiwakes, a species new to him. He notices them to be compact, energetic flyers, projecting a sense of speed and purpose. How different is the flight of these birds from the sinister patrolling of those scavengers, the great black-backed gulls! At that moment he decides to dedicate a new notebook to recording his ornithological sightings.

Bird-watching had been, only a few weeks before, superficial and sentimental, even self-indulgent. It wasn't really about birds but about *birders:* so much was obvious. It was a kind of hunting, the aim being to build a big score for oneself. That was his early and superior opinion, but a more sophisticated philosophy of birding is now required to secure and illuminate his own practice. Aren't there, among human activities, a great many that have no practical function? They don't add to the sum total of human knowledge, or achieve a significantly new objective; but they do provide satisfaction, companionship, and—yes—perhaps they assist in preserving one's peace of mind. Making lists, ticking things off, knowing things for certain—having seen them with one's own eyes— such activities may have a stabilizing function. To watch birds is restful, surely harmless, and in some curious sense *worthy*. Perhaps, indeed, bird-watching can be considered a significant statement against the greed, coarseness, and self-indulgence of modern life? He is not yet entirely convinced by this notion, but it's a fine proposal, sure enough.

Such is Bolsover's thinking as he follows with his binoculars a pair of kittiwakes—plump, short-winged, and such precise formation-flyers!— as they fall in a racing curve from the cliff top toward the steadily marching waves. Genus, species, variety: isn't it the case that bird-watching helps to maintain a sense of the orderliness of things? Isn't it the case that, since birds are essentially innocent, some of their innocence rubs off on the observer? And their freedom, too. Birding is one of those strands of human activity whose purpose is to knit life together, calming the mind and subtly reinforcing the notion that life is coherent and eternal. Birding turns one's gaze outward from petty concerns and up toward the sky. Birding gets one out and about, striding the cliff paths and into the company of other enthusiasts. Birding is a confirmatory activity, since such and such a species is defined in a specific way, and you may mark it with your own eyes. Such is Bolsover's rapidly developing position on the practice of watching birds.

Clearly this man is working hard at acquiring stability and redeeming himself; yet a nugget of guilt remains. However extenuating the circumstances, he has done wrong; he knows that to be true, not simply because he has been found guilty by a court of law but because, every day, he feels guilt and shame, and those feelings, however much he probes them, will not go away.

It now seems to Bolsover, sitting on the cliff top with his binoculars, that the key may lie in the events that occurred after the bedroom door closed upon Tina and himself on that snowy evening. He has come to

that conclusion simply because it is those particular events, of all that occurred, that he is least keen to consider.

It is the case that, despite his reluctance to follow his desires, however ambiguous and tortured his feelings about her, he had made love to
the girl. "He done it all right, in the end." After she closed the door, she
turned to him and said, "Oh, you're lovely, you are." She put her arms
about his neck and whispered those words into his ear. "You're lovely."
No doubt she whispered them to all her—what does she call us?—
punters, johns, something like that. She says that kind of thing because
she knows we want to hear it: words of that kind make the act seem more
like love and less like theft, less like a purchase. "You're a sweetie."
Words like that make things easier even if you don't believe them. I
knew she was lying, but her words told me she didn't mind, that she
liked it, too. And I wanted her not to feel abased, because her abasement
was mine also. I saw her pretense but allowed her words their draw, since
they were my permission. "You're lovely, you are." Her voice was high
and thin, and she gave the words a slur that she believed to be sexy. I
knew who she was, this girl. I knew she wasn't Kitty, though she happened to look like her. Of course I knew who she was. It's no good arguing that I mistook her for Kitty. That's no defense. "Go on, touch me,
I knows you want to."

I knew who she was all the time. She was Tina, the girl who also had
another name, the name of Mary Fielding. Oh, Mary, Mary, I wish that
you did not possess a name that echoes so with ancient sorrow.

21

Bolsover's new and revised Somerset guide is immediately successful. In three weeks the first edition has sold out. Warren is reluctant to order a reprint, and his editors dispute his decision.

"You don't seem to realize," Molly tells him, "that the job of a publisher is to sell books."

"The job of a publisher," says Warren, "is to make money, so he can pay his employees and stay in business."

"Selling guidebooks makes money."

"My dear Miss Moon," says Warren, leaning back in his chair and placing his fingertips together, "as you should know by now, in our business it's *advertising* that makes the money. Selling guides merely covers the costs of production and distribution—and let me tell you, printing costs a fabulous amount of money."

"Don't you patronize me, Mr. Warren!" Molly stands before him with her hands on her hips. "You evidently don't realize that Mr. Bolsover's work on Somerset has raised our reputation to a different plane. For the very first time, there's a strong demand for one of Warren's guidebooks!"

For some time the argument goes back and forth, but eventually Warren's defenses are beaten down by this determined woman and her colleagues.

"Oh, very well, Miss Moon. We'll print another five thousand. Get on to it at once, Bolsover. If we miss the season, we're in deep trouble."

Now there is an air of cheerful expectancy in the editorial office, and much discussion of new features for the guides, and of poems suitable for the various counties. The forthcoming guide to Dorset causes fierce debate: its most celebrated poet, Thomas Hardy, is accused by Sam Kavanagh of self-indulgence and melancholy. "Did Hardy ever make a joke?" asks Sam. "Can you imagine that he ever experienced the slightest *joie de vivre*? And why could he love a woman only after she was dead?" This is regarded as a strong case against the great writer, who gets the thumbs-down. A second candidate is William Barnes, another poet born and bred in the county, but Adrian believes that his dialect poems, while intriguing, are a minority taste—and so the discussion continues.

Was there ever a more entertaining occupation, wonders Bolsover, a happier way to earn a crust, than to be one of Warren's editors? Such colleagues—their wit, their knowledge, their warmth—plus the opportunity to browse among the history and landscapes of his country. How remarkable that things have fallen out so well! And his own writing, under the influence of his lively companions, is beginning to take more chances; he remains wary of the colloquial, but ventures on occasion toward wit and humor.

One afternoon, sunlight slanting through the basement's high window, the editors busy at their desks, Bolsover says to Molly, "Do you know, it's funny how quiet things seem at the Alpha, now that Arabella's gone."

Molly looks up. "Oh, that's your swimming friend, isn't it? I saw you with her on the promenade."

"Yes. I've mentioned her before, I think."

"You have mentioned her more than once, Bolsover. You told me she was an expert swimmer. You said that her husband had died, and that she has returned to the mainland to sort out her estate."

"Her name is Arabella Morgan."

Molly is amused. "Arabella is a lovely name. Anyone of that name is certain to be delightful."

With a shock Bolsover remembers that "Arabella" is not, in fact, her real name, but only another alias. *Who is Arabella?* For a moment he is unsteady, but then it occurs to him that she must have chosen the name herself. *Whom shall I become? I do believe I shall call myself Arabella!* Surely Smithson and Miss Brown haven't the wit to choose so perfect a name? Ah, but wait: that's not how it's done. Our names are picked from a list of real people whose names, and all the evidence of their existence, have been appropriated by the Ministry. There had once been another Arabella, and she—why did she no longer need her own name? Either she was dead or she had chosen to disappear, like the rest of us; and the same is true of my own ghostly predecessor, the original James Watson Bolsover. Who was he, when he lived, and what was his fate?

Molly is looking at him with her head on one side. "Where did you go just then, Bolsover?"

"Oh. I was thinking about names. Arabella's name. It's such a perfect name for her. A happy name. She's a very happy person."

"Is she! Happy! That's rare indeed. When is she coming back to the island, your happy Arabella?"

"That's the question," says Bolsover. "She might not come back at all."

"But you hope she will."

"Yes. I do hope she will."

"Bolsover's bird," says Adrian, without lifting his head from his work.

"Not at all," says Bolsover. "Arabella is her own woman."

"Bolsover's lost love," says Sam Kavanagh, leaning back in his chair and putting his hands behind his head. "The light of his life. Will she return? Or will he simply pine away, poor fellow? Perhaps, unknown to poor Bolsover, she has run off with another, and he will pine in vain."

"Don't be horrid, Sam," says Molly Moon.

"Anyway," says Bolsover, "I do think the name Arabella has something rather attractive about it. It has a special kind of ring." At which, his fellow editors say nothing but look from one to another, their expressions carefully neutral.

That evening, at the Alpha, there is a tap at Bolsover's door. It's Mrs. K, looking unusually grave. "Have you a few moments for a little talk, Mr. B? We're gathering in the lounge. Mr. Smithson and Miss Brown want a word with everyone."

"What? Smithson and Miss Brown? Here?"

"Indeed, Mr. B. It's unusual, I must say. It's the first time they've been here. No doubt it's something urgent."

Smithson and Miss Brown at the Alpha!

The door of the lounge is guarded by Ronnie, awkward in a suit and tie. Commanding the room is Miss Brown, sitting upright on a dining chair, Mr. Smithson standing beside her. Miss Brown is immaculate in a black two-piece and a crisp white blouse; around her slim neck, in place of the pearls that Bolsover remembers, lies a fine gold chain.

"I will come straight to the point," she says. "It is unprecedented for us to meet together in this way, and the cause is a quite exceptional lapse in security. I must first say that this lapse has nothing to do with the excellent work of Mrs. Konstantinopoulos and the staff of the Alpha Hotel, who remain as efficient as ever." She turns to smile graciously at Mrs. K, who dips her head.

"The fault," continues Miss Brown, "is entirely the responsibility of our London office. It is a failure of procedure. We have reason to believe that one of our junior staff has been compromised by criminal elements, and has revealed certain information from our secret files."

The residents of the Alpha shift in their seats and glance at one another. Miss Matthews gives a little gasp, and Mrs. Allcard pats her hand, murmuring something in her ear.

"Yes," says Miss Brown, "this is a very unfortunate affair, for which Mr. Smithson and I take full responsibility. Unfortunately, we do not yet know how much information has been taken, nor which of our clients has been compromised, if any. The member of staff was concerned with general office duties. His security classification was not high, but it seems that he may have copied material from confidential files as they passed between departments." Miss Brown speaks slowly and with great care; it is clear that these events are highly embarrassing to her and Mr. Smithson.

"Why don't you ask him? You can surely get the truth out of him." This is the toneless voice of Kevin Brand.

"We would ask him, Mr. Brand, if we could. Unfortunately, the young man is in intensive care, having been the victim of a brutal attack. If he recovers, we shall certainly talk to him, but at present his survival is uncertain. At best he will be unable to answer questions for several days."

The audience murmurs uneasily and one or two look toward the door, as if a vengeful adversary might burst in at any moment.

"Have the files been taken?" asks the colonel.

"No files are missing, Colonel. We believe some have been copied."

The colonel laughs, a short bark of a laugh. "No doubt you'll be wanting someone to track this fellow down—the attacker, I mean. I'm your man for that sort of thing."

"Thank you, Colonel, but our contacts in the Secret Intelligence Service are already working on the case."

"Pah," says the colonel, dismissing the SIS with a wave of his hand.

Mr. Smithson leans forward and says, "We feel that this is an occasion for working together."

"A sort of neighborhood watch, do you mean?" It's the colonel again.

"Really, Colonel Tapp," says Miss Brown, "your remarks are unhelpful. We are speaking of a genuine risk to our collective security."

"No risk to *your* security," says Mr. Harwich. "We're the ones at risk."

"A fair point, Mr. Harwich." Miss Brown straightens the gold chain about her neck and continues in determined fashion. "I assure you that we take your security very seriously indeed. We have already posted extra staff at the harbor, and we will remain on the island to supervise these additional measures until the situation becomes clearer. We have also arranged to provide extra assistance for Mr. Whitebeam's video monitoring duties."

"Who?" asks the colonel.

"Ronnie," says Mrs. K. "Ronnie Whitebeam."

All turn to look at Ronnie, standing sentry by the door, who is much discomfited.

"Whitebeam!" cries the colonel. "Ronnie Whitebeam, by God! Security!"

"One of our most important security measures is the closed-circuit video system operated by Mr. Whitebeam," says Mr. Smithson in his dry voice.

On his way back to his room Bolsover meets the colonel and receives some hints on hand-to-hand fighting.

"Got a weapon?" the colonel asks. "I can provide one, you know. A small cosh is silent and easily concealed."

"Certainly not," says Bolsover. "I wouldn't have the nerve to use one."

"Easy enough—back of the neck is best. Or you might like a pistol."

He shows Bolsover the butt of what appears to be a revolver, tucked into his trousers. "That's a Webley. None of your fancy automatics. The old sort is best. Reliable."

"I dare say it is, Colonel, but a gun isn't for me. I'd just be a danger to bystanders."

Chaos is come again, thinks Bolsover as he lies in bed that night. A savage attack, Miss Brown called it. Suppose it was Barry Parsons who assaulted that clerk, and that he has discovered the existence of the Alpha Hotel. Would he be deterred by Ronnie's video surveillance? By a couple of men at the harbor? By the colonel and his revolver? Of course not. Parsons is a man of exceptional determination and ferocity, who means to be revenged. He will have no regard for his own safety, and will be extremely difficult to stop. He might step from behind my yellow curtains in the next moment, and he will certainly have a knife; that's his sort of weapon. Barry Parsons . . . It's the name of a man who might drive a lorry, sell secondhand cars, or live next door, a man of no great ambition who means no harm to anyone. But no; Barry Parsons is another kind of man, the animal kind, free of conscience and humanity, and if he appears, there will be nothing that I can do.

Bolsover turns over and closes his eyes, but the memory of Parsons in court—his constant murmuring to his counsel, his involuntary movements, his outbursts to the judge—is too vivid for sleep. For an hour or two Bolsover dozes intermittently, but at last he gets up and goes to the window. It's midnight, and the gardens of the hotel lie calm and silent under a waning moon.

My principal difficulty in all this, thinks Bolsover, is that I'm not convinced that I've paid for my crime. If that were the case, I would be released from guilt; but trial and punishment don't cancel a crime. It's a ceremony for a quite different purpose, little to do with the crime or the criminal. Barry Parsons, according to natural justice, still has a case for my pursuit, and will always have a case; had I a daughter whom someone had killed, would I not pursue him to the ends of the earth? Of course! My only daughter! Would not pursuit be my right? And when I found him—why, his death would close the account.

It is a very old argument, that, and a powerful one. Bolsover opens the window, leans on the sill, and listens to the distant rustle of waves on the beach. In this curious light the hotel's gardens look like the set of an old black-and-white film, and it's easy to imagine the shadow of a man flickering through the tennis courts, up the ornamental steps to the French windows, a brief struggle. Poor Ronnie left in a spreading pool of blood—the click of the window, a creak from the floorboards in the corridor. He's at the door, stepping inside—

Bolsover draws the curtains, switches on the light, gets dressed, and puts on his stout boots. He looks into the corridor and finds it empty. The stairs too are unguarded, but in the foyer is the colonel, asleep in a leather armchair, his revolver swelling his pocket. Bolsover steps quietly across the carpet, but as he does so, the colonel opens one eye.

"Good man, Bolsover. Going after him, eh? No point in having your throat slit while you're sleeping." He taps his revolver. "Don't forget—get in close and strike first."

"Colonel," says Bolsover, "I'm going to walk up to the ridgeway. I can't sleep and I need some air, that's all. For God's sake don't shoot me when I come back."

"Ah, the ridgeway—a fine spot! Handsome Point! Watch the dawn come up, eh? If my legs were younger, I'd join you. And don't you worry, my boy, I've never killed the wrong man yet." The colonel closes his eyes.

The hotel's front door is unlocked, the street empty. Bolsover steps out into the moonlight and walks briskly down the hill, his footsteps loud in the silent town.

22

Enough of waiting, enough of thinking. Everyone should take charge of himself, choose a direction—never mind what—and follow it to its end; otherwise, you're no more than a fallen branch drifting in the current. Isn't that right?

I have almost forgotten who I was. I don't mourn him. What was my name? No matter; that's gone, too. And as for my new self—why, isn't James Watson Bolsover more interesting, more various, more closely engaged with the world than his ancestor? Of course! I have been given a fine place to live, a stimulating occupation, and many new friends—some of them quite delightful—and I have encountered someone who might, if things work out, become more than a friend. Yes, yes, all that is true.

If things work out. For sure, one must not seduce oneself into waiting for something that won't occur. That's one issue; and now another and greater difficulty has returned: my life, that I had begun to hope was settled and harmonious, a life with prospects, has turned fantastical again, and in a few hours all my hopes have whirled away like dry leaves. It is melodramatic, that image, but the thought requires something of that kind.

On the quayside Bolsover stops for a moment to stare up at the moon, a thin slice lost from its edge but none the less brilliant. A small swell is running through the harbor entrance, moving the fishing boats uneasily against their warps and fenders, and in this odd light the water has an oily look. The ferry berth is empty. He checks his watch: yes, the little ship is well on her way from the mainland, and will be here at first light. And among the passengers, this time, perhaps—

He turns and strides down the ramp to the beach. The tide is falling, the sand clean and firm, and he sets off toward the slow flash of the lighthouse. It is not true that I have forgotten my old self; I wish it were possible, but I cannot forget that snowy night, the girl under the lamplight, her thin body under my hands, the dead child—

Suddenly fearful, he turns and looks back toward the town, but there's only the empty beach, only the track of his own sturdy boots in the sand. He walks on, this foolish man—he told Arabella that he thought himself foolish. "Who would be called Bolsover," he asked her, "except a fool?"

"It's a bit late to complain now," Arabella said. "You should have objected when they gave you the name."

"It's absurd, but I don't mind anymore. It makes things simpler. With a name like mine I don't have anything to live up to. I can just be myself, and nobody expects anything more."

"Bolsover, you're right: you are sometimes a very foolish man indeed."

It's true. I'm unlikely, just as I always thought. I'm absurd and I can't stop worrying. I must wrestle with the events of my life, picking them over, requiring to know what is true and what is right. Is everyone like that? I don't know. Surely it's unlikely, or nothing would ever get done.

He's off again, and brisk walking has its usual steadying effect. On his left hand is the sea, ahead is Handsome Light, and behind it rises the dark bulk of the hill, running away to the northwest; such things stand firm. And above—he glances upward and stops abruptly—oh, yes!— above him is the watching moon and all her gathered stars, so close in this transparent night! He searches for the constellations that he knows: Orion, Ursa Major, Castor and Pollux. Certainly he should know more of these lovely stars. And glimmering over there—isn't that Sirius, the star that dogs Orion? They glimmer brightly enough, the stars, and the moon makes her silver track on the sea, as she always has and always will!

On he goes, stepping out. As for the stars, he allows himself a distraction. I'm looking for a cause, and when it comes to causes, time and distance are significant. You might look back a long way, searching for a beginning, but perhaps that's an error; a true cause is never in the stars, but always near at hand. Perhaps it began when I saw the girl under the streetlamp; was that the instant when the switch fell across, and the future was decided?

Here's a test: suppose it happens again. Suppose I'm driving home and the light is red. I stop the car, and again I see the girl sheltering in that doorway. Suppose she runs to the car. Knowing what I do, shall I let her in, or shall I drive away and leave her standing? Can I imagine that? Shall I, wanting her again, take her to her room, give her money—and everything shall follow as it did before?

Bolsover stops again and stares out to sea. I would not leave her beside the road. Something prevents me. Desire prevents me. And yes, everything shall follow, just as it did before. I cannot deny my wanting. I am drawn to her, and all the rest follows: her clothes falling to the floor—

such tiny scraps of stuff—those thin arms around my neck, the lovely
hollows of her neck, her tiny ears, the scent of her—

Keep walking. The soft rush and fall of the waves, the smooth sand
under his feet, the wind on his face—these things make thought possible. We were surely born to live in the open, in the wind and under the
stars; and when we lived so, were we anxious then? Or did we live entirely by desire, and never think of what might follow?

He's close to the light now. Its beams pass over his head and flicker
across the face of the cliff, the light as tall and steady as a great clock whose
hands are made of light. Such fancies have no great purpose, except that
they are pleasing, and steady the mind, like the waves and the stars.

To admit that shameful scene entirely—yes, that is the greatest difficulty. It is made from desire, thoroughly entangled with shame, coarseness, and absurdity. Doesn't a person require dignity, even when sinning?
What is a life worth, if a man values himself at nothing? Too many questions, insufficient answers.

Here is the zigzag path to the top of the headland. He climbs slowly in
the shadowed cleft, holding the rail, placing his feet carefully in the
steps, and at the top he turns to look back at the long curve of the beach.
In the far distance are the red and green lights of the harbor entrance and
the scatter of yellow lights that mark the town. The great lighthouse
stands below him now, its beams wheeling across the beach, the harbor,
the town—glinting for an instant, so he imagines, through the window
of his empty room—before sweeping far out across the quiet sea.

Here the ridgeway begins, a straight path that climbs at a steady rate
toward the summit of the ridge and that curious stone seat. The path is
even and the slope gentle; he sets off at an urgent pace, wanting to feel
the toil of climbing.

He wanted her: of course he did, and in the end, despite his tormenting
doubts—there's an absurdity—he took her. Only by an extreme effort

can he recall the moment, but surely one must drag such things protest-
ing into the light, and make their truth known. There was no romance.
There was only the act itself, a moment under a plain bulb in a bare
room. She applied some sort of oil to herself—was it oil or cream?—
kneeling on the bed, telling him to wait, wiping herself quickly, then
taking him in her small cold hands, rolling on the sheath, and lying back,
thin and pale like a victim. Here Bolsover begins to sob as he walks. He
knows no other way of working, this foolish man, save to probe deeper
into the wound, to draw out the poison.

She oils herself, lies back, and awkwardly he enters her. She shuts
her eyes, and when he starts to move, she grips the bed rail with her fists,
for she is small and light, which he is not. He sees all this, but does not
pause in his urgent walking.

From a high point, if such existed, we might see the whole island lying
in the dark water; the town; the harbor; the beach; the lighthouse; the
long, slow rise of the hill; the white line of the ridgeway; and there, just
visible, the tiny figure of the man, now halfway to the summit. We might
perceive, coming lower and seeing him more closely, his exhaustion of
mind. He is the sort who prefers to be accurate, brief, and clear, but now
his thoughts are nothing sensible, so it seems to him, but only a great
whirlwind of dry leaves.

She is so thin, so light, this girl, her collarbone so fine that it might
belong to a bird, her shoulder blades as angular as wings. Isn't she exactly the height that fits my own frame? Doesn't her head tuck neatly
into my shoulder? I could pick her up and carry her; I could hold her
close and press my face into her hair. Her limbs are so finely drawn that
I can circle her arm with finger and thumb, and her skin is the thinnest of
coverings over her bones. From time to time, while I admire her, she
looks up, catches my eye, blushes, and looks away. It's strange that she
doesn't wish to be loved. She has the darting nerves of a wild creature—
perhaps those of the quick, inquiring robin that flickers about her when
she works in the garden.

———

The man on the path stops suddenly, lifts his head, and looks this way and that, bewildered. Who is the woman I see in my mind? Surely she is not Tina, also known as Mary; this woman is Kitty, my wife, who died many years ago. I had not meant to think of her, but now I remember. She was my wife, and she had a garden that I tended when she died. I wrote a story for her, and called it Ravensdale. But she was not there on that snowy night, for she was long dead; and besides, she was not Tina, nor Mary, but another woman altogether: she was my dear wife, Kitty.

Bolsover's self-examination has reached its crisis. All its strands are gathered now, and the man himself has reached his summit. The rough-hewn stone seat that stands here has the grandeur of a throne, but carries no explanation of who might have placed it here, or why; except, of course, that its position is marvelous. Seated here, Bolsover looks out over the sea from an altitude of more than six hundred feet. From this height the horizon, in clear visibility, is distant some thirty miles, which means, according to his rough calculation, that his all-round view encompasses not only the entire island but as much as two thousand square miles of ocean and a gigantic expanse of the night sky. He is suddenly exultant. What he did was stupid, mistaken, and cruel, but now he understands his confusion, sees it square and straight. He confused love and loss, love and desire. Certainly he wanted the girl, but the girl was not Tina or Mary, but Kitty: the girl he wanted so unbearably was his beloved wife.

At the height of his mental fever it occurred to Bolsover—as it would have occurred to anyone with an interest in this affair—that he might take advantage of the high cliff to end his difficulties and leap to oblivion. When first he reached this place, that was still a possibility, but that option has now been swept aside. Seated under such a night sky as this, ablaze with a million stars, overlooking the silvered sea, Bolsover abruptly finds his despair absurd. In order to take those three or four quick paces across the grass and make that leap, one must feel no joy, no hope; but now he feels relief, and something else—yes, joy, joy at the sky and the stars! And doesn't he also feel hope? Why, of course he does! Arabella might yet return. He is entitled to hope, however slight it might be, for he now knows he is not a wicked man, but only a foolish one.

Behind Bolsover's shoulder, as yet unnoticed by him, the dawn has been making its silent approach. Now, happening to turn his head a little, he catches in the corner of his eye the gleam of what he thinks must be a raging fire. He leaps to his feet, turns to the east, and discovers that the rising sun has laid a blazing road of orange and gold from the horizon to this very place, this high summit. As he watches, the burning sphere lifts from the horizon, seeming to drip fire as it does so, and the wide dome of the sky takes on a radiant glow, the finest shade of pink, as the new day begins. Oh, my word! He looks again, and suddenly spots a faraway scar on the surface of the sea, a line drawn across the sun's golden path—why, it's the wake of a ship. It's the wake of the inbound ferry! In this ecstatic state Bolsover turns to scan his vast domain and sees, as he looks down the slope of the chalk path toward the lighthouse, a dark figure coming up.

He steadies himself and looks again. The figure is too far off to be identified. It comes on steadily and projects, at this range at least, no significant sense of urgency or pursuit. It might be nobody but an early walker—a birder, perhaps. It might be one of his companions at the Alpha—the colonel, quite likely. Or it might be Barry Parsons. For a moment Bolsover hesitates; but one must take control of one's life or become nothing but a broken branch, drifting in the current. He steps away from the great stone seat and sets off, walking steadily westward down the long chalk line of the path.

ABOUT THE AUTHOR

MARTIN CORRICK, the author of *The Navigation Log,*
is a graduate of the creative writing MA program at the
University of East Anglia and was formerly a lecturer
at the University of Southampton. Corrick is now a
full-time writer and lives on the south coast of England.